Portrait of Emma

By *Lillian Cheatham*

PORTRAIT OF EMMA
THE MARRIAGE PACT

Portrait of Emma

LILLIAN CHEATHAM

PUBLISHED FOR THE CRIME CLUB BY

DOUBLEDAY & COMPANY, INC.

GARDEN CITY, NEW YORK

1975

All of the characters in this book
are fictitious, and any resemblance
to actual persons, living or dead,
is purely coincidental.

Library of Congress Cataloging in Publication Data

Cheatham, Lillian.
  Portrait of Emma.

  I. Title.
PZ4.C5138Po [PS3553.H348]   813'.5'4
ISBN 0-385-11241-6
Library of Congress Catalog Card Number 75–14812

To Bart

Portrait of Emma

8017

"One passage to Boston. The stage leaves at five sharp and there'll be no tarrying, even to accommodate the young lady." The coachman handed over the ticket in exchange for the sheaf of new Continental bills as he added the warning for my benefit.

Singled out thus by his words and conscious of the many curious looks already sent our way by the jostling crowd of rough men who filled the posting inn's taproom, I shrank back against Joanna for comfort that was not forthcoming. Not for the first time, she reminded me sternly that such would be my expected lot if I persisted in traveling such a lengthy distance unescorted. Once again, she renewed her plea that I give up my projected journey and continue to seek the hospitality of her home. It was an offer that had been made and rejected before, but she did not guess the wrench it cost me to refuse, although I had never wavered from my original decision. Now, within minutes of departure, with the emotion of our farewells rapidly dissipating from the tedium of waiting upon a dawdling coachman, I was aware of a spurt of impatience at her persistence, and knew a strong wish to finally cast off those coils of love and duty that had bound me to Joanna for most of my lifetime.

A fledgling seventeen-year-old, swaddled by her devotion, I was at last slipping my moorings and setting out upon my own voyage of discovery, my craft built of necessity but, nonetheless, sturdily forged from the stuff of independence. Breaking from a past spent in subservience to the wills of others had been difficult, but with each decision made and firmly expressed, I reasserted the right to guide my own destiny, while Joanna, alarmed by this mood in one whom she still claimed was a child, clung all the more desperately.

Thomas had left the bar now, and slid onto the wooden settle beside us. In the waning candlelight his face was pale, unlike his normally ruddy countenance.

"This ticket will see you all the way to Boston, Emma. The coachman here will be your driver to Providence, and when you cross the ferry you will have another driver, and be the stage line's responsibility," he added remotely.

Thomas was worried, but he had done his best for me and, unlike Joanna, did not belabor himself with the mingled feelings of guilt and reproach that moved his wife. I regarded them both with loving eyes. At thirty-eight, after a life devoted to my mother, and later to me, Joanna had taken unto herself a husband, Thomas Eaton. She had been a childless widow, with a small competence and a gentle, pretty manner, but her loyalty to me had not encouraged the suitors who might otherwise have been tempted to ask for her hand. It had taken the good Thomas to bring about her capitulation, and then only because she believed his need to be greater than mine. That her belief was a mistaken one, she now mourned with a quiet persistence. Was it any wonder that I could sense Thomas's eagerness to see the last of me, in spite of our affection for each other?

As though reading my thoughts, Thomas said quietly, "You know you have a home with us, Emma. It is still not too late to change your mind." But I was already shaking my head.

Outside, despite the early hour, the inn yard was bustling with activity. Dark shapes were becoming recognizable in the growing light. The Fife and Drum, one of the largest hostelries in the city, was on the road to Providence and catered to the stagecoaches running north and south. From where I sat near the window, I watched a southbound coach roll into the courtyard, its iron-rimmed wheels striking sparks on the cobblestones. The sleepy passengers stumbled out, rubbing their eyes, and surveyed with loathing the landlord standing in the doorway, breezily inviting them to try his breakfast.

We had already enjoyed his hospitality: the hearty breakfast I had just consumed would be the measure by which my meals for days to come would be found lacking. Not knowing this, however, I cheerfully readied myself for departure, while my driver fortified himself generously at the counter with cider, bread, and cheese.

To a query from a passenger, he pronounced the day past the hottest he had ever experienced in his twenty years on the New York–Providence run, and predicted that today's temperature would soar even higher.

Joanna had insisted that I dress as a lady should when preparing for a long, dusty coach ride—the heat was to be no consideration. Muffled in my corset and several petticoats, the topmost being of drugget flannel to protect me from mud splashes, all of which was overlaid by a woolen round gown of camlet with puffed sleeves to the elbows and a cross-cloth neckerchief, I also wore my heaviest stockings and my half-jean boots. A bonnet swathed in black veiling to indicate my mourning state, beneath which my face was masked to protect my skin from the tanning rays of the sun, as were my hands in their elbow-length gloves, completed my traveling costume. In addition, I carried my cloak of scarlet whittle over my arm, as well as a basket within which crouched my cat, William.

When Joanna had raised the tentative suggestion that my employer-to-be, Mrs. Southwick, might not care for cats, I had beaten down her objections with the confidence of the very young, pointing out that any woman with two daughters must be accustomed to cats and therefore would not notice the addition of another on her premises, particularly a well-bred mouser like William.

By now a ribbon of light was showing itself in the eastern sky, striking glittering sparks of pure gold from the metal chimney pots surmounting the crowded rooftops that made up the city's skyline. Our driver scraped back his chair and rose with deliberation, causing a concerted rush to the door, but Thomas, wise beforehand, had already installed me in the coach, next to a window.

The coach filled rapidly and the outside passengers lingered, waiting to leap aboard. It was then, at the last moment, while the ostlers clung to the reins of the leader, that Joanna hugged me to her yet again, and, slipping a bracelet off her arm, slid it onto mine. It had been hers since childhood, given to her by her parents in Salem, and was hammered out of iron with an odd, writhing design worked into it.

"I want you to have it," she stopped my protests. "You'll need it where you're going and I have used it up."

I gave way. The wardrobe of stout, serviceable clothes in my trunk had been a gift from Joanna and Thomas; apparently, she felt now that my prestige would be further enhanced by the bracelet.

Before I could thank her the whip cracked, the ostlers sprang away, and Joanna's anxious face passed beyond my vision, my last sight of what was familiar and dear. There were tears in my eyes when I settled back against the hard leather cushions and met the curious looks of my fellow passengers. All male, they were tolerant of my tears, but it took William, mournfully groaning within his wicker cage, to set them to talking.

When I explained that the cage contained my cat, understandably not a good traveler, I was informed by an irascible elderly gentleman that the stage-line rules forbade livestock.

One of the other passengers took issue with the term "livestock," and then and there began a discussion which came to involve all of us, with positions taken in a spirited argument. I was both embarrassed and apologetic until the realization dawned that I had unwittingly provided entertainment for what otherwise would have been a dull coach ride. Until then, I had known only three people well, and of those, my father had been austere, Joanna gentle, and Thomas restrained. Nothing had prepared me for the hurly-burly nature of the quarrel that raged over me and my cat, with everyone shouting his opinion in a loud, cheerful voice above the trundling of the stagecoach. It was my first introduction to a pastime dear to the hearts of my fellow Americans, a pastime so national as to be later ridiculed by Mrs. Trollope herself; that of argument, loud, violent, opinionated, but conducted so cheerfully and without malice as to be almost endearing.

Alarmed, I sought to bring it to a close, and it was reluctantly agreed to allow the driver to decide William's fate.

Now that a rapport had been established, I was taken up as the next topic, and with fully as much relish, I was subjected to a good-natured barrage of highly personal questions. I shrank from their intimate nature, but could do nothing to stop them, short of turning my face to the wall and refusing to speak. One of the gentlemen, who had earlier demanded my ejection merely on the grounds of my owning a cat, now led the way in asking my name, the names of my parents, why I was in mourning, my relationship to Thomas and Joanna, if my orphaned state had left me destitute, and then, finally, why I was traveling to Boston. All of these questions were asked in a disarming, ingenuous manner that I found impossible to repulse, and since I had never learned the art of gracefully lying, my fellow passengers soon learned all of my business.

However, to give them credit, once they had wrung me dry as a subject, they were just as curious, and as frank, with one another.

I can smile now when I think of myself upon that memorable journey, too young to know how to avoid the impertinent questions of strangers and too insecure to doubt their right to an answer. Just so did I suffer the stifling closeness of a veil and mask, merely because Joanna's sense of decorum dictated that they be worn, at whatever cost, to prevent my skin from tanning, although the resultant cost might include a heat stroke, and the skin so carefully protected was already marked beyond repair by the lingering scars of smallpox.

A portrait hangs in my drawing room. It is of a lady, and her beauty is found in large, haunting eyes and a tender mouth, which are illuminated by soft light from somewhere above while leaving the rest of the face in shadow. The portrait, though unsigned, is of museum quality, and people always notice it and wonder about its origin. The lady is, of course, myself, and I see the speculation in their eyes as they glance from me, the reality, to the painted likeness. Sometimes they question him about the artist, and he, eyes twinkling in my direction, invariably answers the same way: "I believe it is considered his best work."

I know it is.

My story could have begun with the painting of that portrait, or perhaps the prosaic fact of my birth, rather than the stagecoach ride to Boston, which in itself signaled such a change in my life. I could have even begun with my twelfth year, when my mother died of the smallpox which I had passed on to her, and I lived. By that act, an unconscious one on my part, my life, which had heretofore been uneventful, changed, and what had been pleasant became unpleasant, what had been safe became dangerous, and my normal, well-cushioned existence was ripped apart, and I was thrust into bitter, raw, daily encounters with my father, as I gradually came to understand that I had offended him grievously by living when my mother died.

At fifteen, in a passionate orgy of self-pity, I wrote a long, very bad poem entitled "Meditations of a Lady whose Beauty has been Destroyed by a Common Disaster": in this case, smallpox. I thoroughly enjoyed myself, shedding tears over my paper, smearing the ink, and filling the pages with copious exaggerations, while I drew heavily upon Greek and Latin references, and referred to myself sentimentally as Chlorinda. At fifteen, pitilessly facing myself in the mirror and surveying the puckered scars that seared my forehead like an ugly blot upon an otherwise flawless complexion, I could see no beauty in wistful dark eyes and a sweet face.

That year, also, I understood why my father had always hated me, and not just since my mother's death. It was Joanna who told me, of course. Dear Joanna, to whose arms I fled after a particularly acrimonious passage between my father and me in which he had flayed me with his usual biting sarcasm. There was nothing new in this: I had been enduring his jealousy in one form or another since I was old enough to recognize his frowning face as it came between my mother and myself. But, until her death, it had manifested itself in nothing more than putting me aside impatiently when I demanded too much of her attention, or quelling my dependence upon her with heavy restrictions. I had always sensed that invisibility was my best defense in his presence, although she shielded me as much as possible. That is, until she died.

He came to my bed that morning and looked at me coldly. In brutal fashion, he had just informed me of her death: I was still racked with grief, and momentarily stripped of the barriers I normally erected in his presence: also, I was clinging with fragile tenacity to a foothold acquired after weeks of a day-by-day struggle with illness and fever. He made no acknowledgment of the change in my thin, limp body, which he had not seen for a month: instead, his eyes filled with hatred as he told me grimly how I had killed my mother, how the smallpox which I had brought into the house had done no more than partially scar my face, but had taken her life, weakened as she was by nursing me. He told me how she lay downstairs, her beauty destroyed in death, and lastly, how glad he was to see that I had been punished by my pockmarks, by having my prettiness blemished forever, leaving me disgusting and repulsive.

He was careful that no one else heard him. And having delivered the words he had always wanted to say but had never dared while my mother lived, he felt a certain measure of relief. But a dangerous precedent had been established, for he had learned how to rid himself of his accumulated rancor when it grew too bitter to be contained. As for me, I was not surprised by what he said, either then or later, and I never forgot any of it.

But I still did not know why he hated me until Joanna told me.

As a demure, already established young matron, a distant relative of my mother's, she had filled her role as chaperon with enthusiasm and vicarious enjoyment in the success of her beautiful cousin. "I was with her when she met your father at a ball, and I saw his face when they were introduced. He was stunned, but she was accustomed to making such an effect on gentlemen, and hardly noticed her new beau, who was so much older and more worldly and assured than the others. From the beginning, he knew that he must have her, so he went straight to her parents. He was wealthy and was clever enough to appeal to their cupidity, so that in the end, the three of them between them wore her down.

"Perhaps it would have worked out all right if he had not been so greedy, but having won her, he must have it all, her past as well as her present and future, and I saw her daily grow more silent and unhappy. And then—you came. Babies are very effective when it comes to healing broken hearts—and mending sick marriages—but he was told by the doctor that she could not have another child or she would die. She had almost died bearing you, and he had had the fright of his life. So, there they were, and you a girl, and there would never be another. You see, women like us, Emma," Joanna added timidly, "—ladies—do not know how to prevent pregnancies. Even that, however, would not have made him hate you, if it hadn't been that he could see for himself that she was—relieved. So, when he looked about for someone to blame, he found you."

I was only fifteen but frank talk did not offend me. I had inherited an earthy wisdom from a lusty, brawling age which saw a world changed by revolutions and Indian wars and an upside-down society that accepted a pirate as a gentleman and a courtesan as a lady. We had left the first half of the creaking, archaic eighteenth century far behind us, and were almost through the second. From cursing King George in the marketplace, we had progressed to the Continental Congress with scarcely a pause to change the name. Washington had arrived in New York that spring and reluctantly taken up residence on Cherry Street to await his inauguration. There were blockades and counterblockades, but the Brussels lace and the Parisian silks continued to appear in the shop windows, and the daring sea captains who slipped in and out of the harbors, conducting business with both friend and enemy alike, had the unlikely blood of the Puritans in their veins, a heritage that could hardly be bettered when it came to playing pirate and striking bargains with the Devil.

No, frank talk was no stranger to me; it was in the air around me.

In the end, however, Father won the bitter duel he waged with me. Or did he? When he played his final jest, his last revenge, upon the daughter whom he hated, did he not realize that his hatred had made me strong? But it had. From some inner resource, I summoned the necessary courage when they told me of his suicide and, later, that there was no money left. It had all been a house of cards, his reputed wealth, which had come tumbling down the instant his suicide was known. His business, which had been so disastrously conducted since my mother's death, in the end had resulted in nothing, and more particularly, in no future for a blemished daughter who must depend upon a dowry to find a husband.

But at seventeen I was young and strong, and for the first time in my life no one hated me. My education had been allowed to lapse in favor of my role as housekeeper to my father, and with immigrants arriving on every boat to hire out for a pittance, clearly my inexperience was a dreg on the labor market. Someone would have to find me work. Relentlessly, I hammered at Joanna and Thomas.

"I'll go anywhere to seek work. Preferably out of this city. And I'll do anything—housekeeper, cook, nursemaid. . . ."

Joanna was distressed. "Emma, you have no idea what you are talking about. You'll be better off finding genteel employment among some of our friends—"

"People who know my story and are sorry for me? Never!" I replied firmly, clinging to my pride with the tenacity of one who could ill afford the luxury. "And I have no intention of battening on you and Thomas!" I added. Thomas, at least, could understand my point of view. No man with a frail, delicate wife wants her mothering a strapping seventeen-year-old girl, particularly when he hopes for children of his own.

In the end, they found what I wanted. A Madam Southwick, of Boston, needed a strong young woman to work in her home. The situation was ideal for a city-bred girl who would not be overawed by the teeming city of Boston, which was almost twice the size and consequence of New York. The work was varied, with both housework and shop work. The lady's first husband, a middle-aged gentleman of considerable wealth, had left her with a thriving pottery, which was located behind the house and employed three men. She offered some of the best pieces for sale in a small shop she had converted from the front room of her house. She was also a moneylender (a fact that I found slightly repellent in its lack of gentility) and this business she conducted from another room-turned-office, which was reached by an outside door opening onto an alley from the street.

From her description, she sounded formidable, but I was relieved to learn that she had been married the second time to a sea captain, a black-eyed charmer generally conceded to have been her true love. He had been dead now for a year, and she had borne each husband a daughter. She spent most of her time in a wheelchair, having fallen about the time of her second husband's death and injured her limbs, but she could walk when necessary with the aid of canes.

"But you will not be expected to take on her care yourself, for she has a housekeeper named Jane Piper, who is also her personal maid and who would be jealous of any intrusion upon her duties. She has lived with Mrs. Southwick since she was a girl, and is devoted to her."

I raised my eyebrows at such detailed knowledge. "How did you learn of her?"

Joanna looked confused. "I have always known Silence Southwick. She was originally from Salem, as I was, and Papa and Mama have always known the family. Papa has done some business with her. When I heard of this position, it seemed the best at hand, since you so want to leave the city. Now, through Papa, I will not lose touch with you, and perhaps we will even be able to see each other when I return for a visit."

This prospect was one of the additional attractions of my new post, and I wasted no time in replying to Madam Southwick's letter. Later, Joanna told me a little more about the daughters. "Honor is only eleven and I know nothing about the child. But I saw the oldest one, Patience, when she was a baby. She is about seventeen now, and my parents have written that she is quite beautiful, but not very bright. Not that that matters, for Mrs. Southwick has trebled her husband's pottery business over the years, and she is by way of being an heiress. And an heiress is never mentally deficient! She has many beaux, so perhaps one of them will look your way," she added gaily.

It was talk like this which Joanna persisted in and from which I flinched away. It was true that candlelight was kind to me, but one must conduct a romance occasionally by light of day, and then my pockmarks were cruelly apparent. Nevertheless, I felt my spirits rise. A girl near my own age would be a welcome addition, and even a haughty beauty who spurned my friendship would be a change. I could watch from afar and enjoy her successes, if nothing else. It could only be an improvement over my old life, and I would not lose touch with Joanna, so, excitedly, I made my plans to leave.

By the time the coach reached our noon dinner stop, the morning having been punctuated by halts at twelve-mile intervals to change the horses, I was faint with the effort to retain a few shreds of personal privacy. The coachman had silenced William's detractors by allowing him out of his basket, and now his plump body warmed my lap more effectively than a stove, so that the heat, which had increased with each passing mile, grew steadily more oppressive within the closely packed coach.

The Alexander Hamilton Inn, its signboard giving indication of having been recently relettered, was rough and ready, bearing less resemblance to its present dandified namesake than to its original Royalist one, George Hanover. It was a great favorite, apparently, of the driver, and he was in the habit of making a longish dinner stop there. The innkeeper was named Joe, and there was a great deal of loud, boisterous conversation between the two of them at the table.

We were served in the kitchen at one table, sitting with the innkeeper and his family on long, low, backless benches. Not being very knowledgeable in the matter of inn meals, in the stampede for places I had allowed myself to be squeezed in between the children, with our backs to the fire, which, although banked to a bed of glowing ashes, was uncomfortably, then unbearably, hot. I managed to sit very straight, so that only my shoulder blades touched my heated dress, but the children squirmed continuously on either side. They had inherited their spot because of their youth, I, because of my ignorance, and together we suffered the ordeal of being roasted slowly as we ate our dinners.

We ate from wooden trenchers with wooden spoons, in the old country way, and drank our cider from pewter mugs. The few pieces of pottery on the cupboard shelves were apparently considered too fine for everyday use. The landlord and his wife shared a trencher at the head of the table, and she served our stewed rabbit and boiled cabbage from polished applewood bowls. With it we ate a johnnycake made from coarsely ground yellow Indian meal.

No one seemed to find anything strange in this communal dinner, so I presumed it was common practice. I had to admire the innkeeper's good wife for her housekeeping. She must have had an everlasting tracking in of people on her floors, and strangers at her table, yet the tablecloth was spotless and the floors bleached as white as river sand could get them. I found myself watching her thoughtfully, her limp brown calico buttoned to the throat, her eyes cloudy from the heat, and I pitied the drudgery of her days. Small inns such as this one, manned by the keeper and his wife, dotted the roadside, and so often it was the wife behind the scenes who, between childbearing, performed the true labor, while the husband kept the board and dispensed the hospitality.

I seemed to be the only one at the table too miserable to enjoy my dinner, and since I was too timid to rise I pushed my food from one side of the trencher to the other, and hid beneath the johnnycake the stew my stomach revolted at eating. Finally a voider was passed around, everyone brushed their crumbs into it, and the dessert was ladled directly onto our cleaned trenchers. It was a hasty pudding, thick with rich, clotted cream, and my stomach rose at the sight of it. Hurriedly I made my escape, followed by most of the children.

Thirty minutes later, I was back in the swaying stagecoach, my dinner an indigestible lump in the region somewhere beneath my breastbone. Hours later, the unpleasant memory of that meal still lingered.

Our way was running through the forest now, where the trees met overhead, shading the road and giving an illusion of coolness. During the afternoon I had glimpsed deer through the sun-dappled branches, and once a bear, on his haunches, placidly munching berries, but no Indians. We had been assured by the stage line that the roads were safe, but with the memory still fresh of those days of King Philip's War, when the Indians had murdered and burned, no New Englander could feel completely secure. Like all children of my generation, I had been raised on stories of Indian massacres, and I shivered fearfully at the thought of menacing red bodies slipping through the trees, as we entered the first forest I had ever seen.

The afternoon had advanced to that hour when the heat was at its peak and the air was hazy and slumberous. The dust from our wheels rose in a choking cloud, coating the branches and weeds of the roadside with a thick chalky layer. Most of the passengers were dozing, stupefied by the motion of the coach, when with a loud, "Whoa!" the driver pulled the horses to a halt. Looking out,

I saw that we had stopped at a way station, the most primitive we had yet seen, for it was hardly more than a shed located in a clearing in the woods, with the horses penned within a lean-to railed enclosure. To my horror, I saw that my worst fears were to be realized, when an elderly Indian emerged from the shed to amble toward the horses' heads.

"I thought I'd let you folks cool off." The driver flung open our door. "It's another three hours before we stop for the night and there's a nice, cooling stream and a shady spot to rest, down through those trees. Walk down the river a ways, ma'am, and you'll have some privacy if you want to bathe your face and hands," he suggested delicately. "It's perfectly safe if you watch out for bears."

I had already learned that the driver, not the line, made the rules on the stagecoach run. He alone decided how fast he would push the horses, where to stop, and the length of the stay. If he was of a reckless disposition, and inclined to take chances, the passengers rode in fear of a spill and broken bones, while he claimed the envy of every small boy on his run for his daring driving. Already now he was lifting a small keg of cider from the footboard of the coach, and I saw the Indian watching him eagerly. Obviously he had no intention of shortening his rest stop.

But he was right about the coolness. When I parted the dusty bushes and cautiously descended the bank, with William on a string, I could see a running stream, bubbling over flat stepping stones. I took the driver's advice and followed the stream as it curved and widened. Here there was more sunlight and a flat, low meadow, yellow with wild flowers. The water sparkled and foamed over the rocks, sending a fine cooling mist into the air, which bathed my face as I bent over to drink. The earth was damp and smelled of rich, black soil, and I could see the flash of trout as they wriggled near, attracted by my dabbling fingers. William forgot his dislike of wet paws long enough to leap to a flat rock and dip first one, then the other, paw into the water.

I removed my mask, bonnet, and gloves, and stretched out full length beside the stream, my hands trailing in the cool water. It was as clear as a mirror, and I could see a vivid reflection of my face as I bent over a small, deep pool that had been trapped into stillness among the rushes at the edge of the bank. The heat had ringed my eyes with dark shadows. My fringe fell forward, revealing the puckered scars as well as the graceful, unflawed sweep from cheekbone to throat.

By wearing my mask and veil I had surrounded myself with mystery, and succeeded in whetting the curiosity of the other passengers. I was now one of the world's workers, I reminded myself firmly, and could no longer afford the luxury of anonymity, but must be prepared for insensitivity from probing strangers. At least, the unpleasantness need be faced only once today: tomorrow's would be a problem for tomorrow.

In the end, I bent and picked up my things, then, lifting my head proudly, sallied forth among my fellows, feeling like an aristocrat facing the hungry eyes of the mob in Paris. They stared, yes, but there was none of the repugnance I had been accustomed to receiving from Father, and their curiosity was short-lived. For the remainder of the trip, the casual kindliness I would receive from strangers gave me the courage I needed at my journey's end, when I was again made burningly aware of my deficiencies, both of face and fortune.

When I returned to the coach, the elderly passenger who had elected to remain behind and finish his nap awakened to welcome me back and offer me a seat beside him.

"Is the little missy back safe and sound?" The driver, the last to return, bobbed up at the window with a cheeky grin.

"The old nodcock has a skin full of cider. He and that Injun have been soakin' it up this past half hour, and if we're not in a ditch by nightfall it'll be a blessin'," grumbled one of the passengers.

We weren't in a ditch, but our descent down hills and around curves was sheer recklessness. However, we made our evening stop in less than the three hours predicted, to find our inn shaded by great, spreading oak trees which cooled the taproom where we were to eat our supper. I had time for a tepid sponge bath by candlelight while I peeled off layer after layer of clothing, and later enjoyed the privilege of having the narrow trundle bed to myself for half the night, until near one o'clock, when another woman was ushered in to share my bed. I slept fitfully after that.

The heat wave continued on into the second week of my journey, making each day a merciless test of endurance. Flashes of heat lightning pierced the sky as thunderheads built up in the north, and we in the coach prayed for the rain to hold off, in spite of our gasping need for relief. We had been warned that wheels mired to the hub in mud would slow our progress, perhaps delay it indefinitely, and no one wanted to prolong the ordeal by a stay in a country inn. The horses seemed particularly fractious: more than once, we heard the coachman attempting to soothe them. The atmosphere within the coach was only slightly less tense than that without, as the passengers bickered incessantly and eyed the darkening sky uneasily.

Slightly before noon on the eighth day, the coach rolled up into the yard of a small tavern located at a crossroads, and here, with the first raindrops spattering the dust, the coachman warned us to be prepared to stay.

"We'll not go on, folks, until this storm blows over. I won't drive a team that's ready to bolt the traces any minute."

The storm did not blow over, but descended, bringing hailstones, drenching rain, and high winds. It was the third day before the rain lulled slightly and late afternoon of that same day when the first traveler was sighted, a lone horseman from the south.

It was the mail carrier, astride a large, raw-boned cob, and his news was gloomy.

"All the bridges are out to the south and I am told the situation is worse north of here," he said, shaking the raindrops off his hat and flinging the mail down upon the table, to be pawed over by all comers. "The corduroy roads are washed out—nothing but a sea of mud and floating logs."

I looked around the taproom. By this time I was thoroughly sick of my fellow passengers, the innkeeper's blowsy wife, and the enforced intimacy of my circumstances. Therefore, when the stage driver approached me later, I was almost tearfully agreeable to making the trip northward the following day in the postman's company.

"The line's responsible for getting you through to Boston," he explained, harassed. "We'll pay for the change of horses and any expenses. The postman's taken on this task for us before—he knows what to do. At the earliest opportunity he'll shift you to one of the line's stages, and too, there'll be another passenger from here going all the way to Boston to keep you company."

When I saw the other passenger my heart sank. Carping and critical, it was he who had contributed to a large part of the strain of the past three days. He had been an outside passenger on the coach, and it had taken only a few hours in his company to appreciate what it was to be without it. He was a Puritan, his faith proclaimed by more than his clothing: the sober, homespun suit, the shovel hat, and the unmistakable squared linen collar. He also wore an unbending air of censure and meddlesome piety, which had cast a constraint over our small group, thrown so closely upon one another's resources and hungry for the leavening relief of good humor. So far, I had not found this gentleman to be possessed of any of the virtues of his fellow Massachusetts Bay Puritans, although of their intolerance he had plenty.

Now, with his spindle shanks astride a nag as lean as himself, he rode beside me. I had used the landlady's help to divide an old skirt, since there were no sidesaddles in the barn, and I had expected his reproof for riding astride. But there I wronged him. He came from a long line of adaptable ancestors, and his eyes approved the unhampering modesty of my skirt as I easily kept up with the two men. The postman's route was direct and hard-riding, and did not depend upon the roads, which were, as he prophesied, awash with mud and great branches of trees that would delay all wheeled traffic until they were cleared.

"At this rate, we may be in Sudbury by nightfall," my companion suggested, and I was cheered by the thought.

Later, while we leaned against the stone wall of a farm and ate our lunch, washed down by buttermilk provided by the farmer's wife, my companion indulged his curiosity by asking my business.

"Where might you be working in the city, my girl?"

I was tempted to avoid answering, but the habit of respect for age and position was too strong. "For a Madam Southwick, sir, a lady who owns a pottery and shop on Hanover Street."

For the first time, his censuring frown lifted. "A good place and a fine woman. A woman who is highly respected and one who has always put God first." His words made me wonder depressingly about my employer. "I am beginning to think there is some hope for your future, my girl, with the influence of a righteous woman like Silence Southwick as your guide. God has seen fit to bludgeon her with adversity and I am happy to say she has remained firm in her faith."

"I thought she was a wealthy woman?" I asked.

"I don't speak of adversity in that respect," he said repressively. "Your pertness ill becomes you and shows me just where your values lie. I speak of the loss of her two husbands, the last through dire circumstances, and her own crippling infirmities."

"Dire circumstances?"

"Would you not call murder dire?" he asked sternly. "Of course, God's punishment was reserved for the victim, for Mrs. Southwick was too godly a woman to merit it. Her husband, however, had a loose reputation; he was a sea captain, and I suppose that the years away from the influence of a good home, spent in heathen climes, worked their toll. Not that such is the usual case," he added hastily, for many a devout Puritan followed the sea, "but Captain Southwick was deficient in his duty toward his men, preferring to pamper them with privileges not ordinarily reserved for seamen, such as abandoning the use of the lash for discipline, which could only result in a general laxness of their moral fiber. In the end, one of them, of course, killed him."

"But why? If he pampered them—"

"It seems poor payment, indeed, but only to be expected from one of their kind. Who else could it have been? He was wearing his banyan and carpet slippers. Dressed in that way, who would have expected him to be carrying money? And as a matter of fact, he wasn't, although he was robbed of his pocket watch. But it had to be a grudge killing. He was followed down his own garden path, to the door of the pottery— Girl, what is it? You are pale!"

"You didn't tell me the murder was committed in his home, sir! I assumed it was done on board his ship."

"Mayhap it wasn't a seaman, after all, but an Indian," the postman, who had been following the conversation closely, remarked.

"Considering their cruel natures, one of them might kill for a pocket watch."

"And so would a seaman, who would have an equally cruel nature and would have been far less noticeable wandering the streets of Boston," snapped our righteous informant. "But thievery was done. There's no denying that. And the murderer was never found. The captain was not known to be wealthy, nor to wear rich jewelry on his person. His death did not enrich his widow at all, for her first husband, John Henry Pride, had left her the holdings that made her a wealthy woman. The captain had just returned from a sea voyage, and he had promised his wife it would be his last. Perhaps his plans did not suit some disgruntled seaman, or—"

"How was he killed, then?"

"He was struck down with one of the pieces of pottery. Apparently, there was a quarrel and the murder was committed in the heat of the moment. Afterward, the villain searched his pockets and found the pocket watch, which he pilfered. But you have nothing to fear, my girl, for that was a year ago, and the murderer is long gone by now. Just keep to the path your mistress lays down," he added benevolently. "List to her words, read your Bible, attend church, be of sober, downcast countenance, heed the counsel of wiser ones than yourself, and if you are industrious, hard-working, and, above all, do not lift your eyes lustfully to any man, you will prosper and perhaps someday acquire a husband. You are a comely girl, although there is a certain sauciness there that you must struggle to overcome."

Aware of the postman's covert amusement, I cast my eyes down and preserved the sober mien he had recommended, although the impulse to give way to my saucy spirit threatened to overwhelm me.

We reached Sudbury that night after all, to find the Red Horse Inn crowded with stranded passengers. Mud-spattered and weary in every bone from the unaccustomed horseback ride, I was glad to be allowed to share a bed with two other women, and I slept without turning over the entire night. It was after noon before I was able to obtain space on a coach, which rolled into Boston that night by the light of flaring side lamps. The rain had begun again, drumming on the roof and the cobblestones and drenching the outriders and the driver.

I spent my first night in Boston at the Lafayette, an inn of superior quality. I was offered a hearty supper, a hot bath, and a private room. Such unaccustomed luxury caused me to sleep late, and I came down to an empty taproom, filled with welcoming sunlight and a cheery greeting from the innkeeper's wife.

She too knew of Silence Southwick and informed me that her house was only a few blocks from the inn. She suggested that I hire their ostler and his cart for my trunk, and walk beside him.

"It will be cheaper, unless you're too proud to follow a cart?"

"I'm not proud, and I don't think I have to impress my employer by a grand entrance in a hired coach."

"From what I've heard of her, she's more approving of economy than style." I was depressed again by this reminder of the parsimonious disposition of my employer.

The innkeeper's good wife was eager to give me her version of the murder, a subject that came up early in our conversation. In fact, nothing could have prevented her from telling her story, and I dimly realized what an absorbing mystery it had been a year ago, and still was.

"The servants were in the kitchen, all of them, as well as the potters. The captain went out the kitchen door leading to the garden path, toward the pottery. He was looking for one of the potters, Obediah Watson, but did not know that Obediah had been sent on an errand by his mistress sometime before. The servants could not see the captain after he went around the side of the shed to its door, but they had a clear view of the garden gate, and no one came in that way. The gate squeaked, and they would have heard it if it had opened. Mrs. Southwick was in her office, and because it was a hot day her door was open, and she swore not a soul passed that way. The third door was through the shop, and Jane Piper was tending shop that day, and no one came through, she said. Later, they regretted making such positive statements, and Mrs. Southwick changed her story, and said she might have been mistaken, but by then the tongues were wagging and the old rumors flying."

"Well, I should think so!" I declared. "It seems impossible for anyone but one of them to kill him! What old rumors?"

By now she had my rapt attention and became coyly evasive. "Can a human fly? Or wriggle along the ground like a snake? Or become invisible? Well, you know the answer to that as well as I do!"

"No," I said doubtfully, "I don't believe that I do."

"It is not for me to tell you, then. Nor for you to ask. Nor for anyone to speak of, if they wish to avoid trouble." I listened to her strange words with astonishment. "I will warn you of one thing, lass, you're going to a house where a witch lived and died, and it is a cruel thing to thrust you into without a word of warning, for you are hardly more than a child yourself, and I'd not want one of my own to live in that house. Happily, however, you've taken precautions to protect yourself."

I blinked. I had no idea what her words meant, beyond a vague notion that they portended a warning of the supernatural, but this, in itself, seemed so unaccountable that I supposed I must have misunderstood some part of the conversation. I had heard of witches—who had not?—but I could not believe anyone would seriously believe in their existence.

"Do you mean—that is, ma'am, are you telling me, or do I mistake your meaning—are you speaking of a ghost?"

"Maria!" It was the innkeeper, standing in the doorway, frowning warningly at his wife. With a swift look at me that promised of revelations yet to be made and stories yet untold, she flounced out, and I heard him scolding her in the passageway. If she did have more to say, she was not granted the opportunity, for he took over the transference of my trunk to the cart outside, summoning the ostler and receipting my bill.

"No tarrying and no gossip," he growled at the boy as we left the inn yard, with William, a seasoned traveler now, riding like a royal punjab atop my shoulder.

The streets were crowded with people drawn outdoors by the crisp, fresh air and brilliant sunshine. I saw strange people, the like of which I have never seen before in my narrow, sheltered life in New York: oddly dressed, foreign-looking people; wicked, scowling seamen wearing earrings; a foppish, mincing gentleman with a long curled peruke and quizzing glass; and a lady dressed in silk and diamonds, seated in an open carriage opposite a small black boy wearing a turban. These and many other odd sights passed before me, and I stretched my eyes to their widest and bumped into the cart ahead as I tried to see them all.

The city and its people were a revelation to a girl who had never been allowed the freedom to walk down a street unaccompanied. Now, following the boy and his cart, we passed through Clarke Square, with its shop windows full of exotic goods not to be found elsewhere, for Boston was famous for thumbing its nose at the British blockade; through Woods Lane, from where I could see the imposing spire of a church; and into Middle Street, which inexplicably became Hanover Street near Mill Creek.

"This is it, mum." The boy had stopped before a locked shop door. "Looks like no one is minding the shop right now." He peered through a dusty, mullion window where a stack of pottery ware could be dimly seen.

I looked around uncertainly. The shop door was indeed barred, and since it seemed to be the front entrance to the house, how did one gain entry? I was faced with blank, curtained windows and a six-foot-high wooden wall reaching to the end of the block. I later learned that the holdings of Silence Southwick consisted of this half block of city property, separated from its neighbors on one side by a narrow alley, and on the other three by cobbled streets, with the whole enclosed by the wall. There were no stables within the walled enclosure, for she kept no horses, being convinced that the unnecessary beasts earned their keep in wicked idleness while filling their stomachs. Within the enclosure, however, were the pottery shed, the kitchen garden, the fruit trees, the beehives, and the residence, a three-story-, half-timbered rabbit warren of a house with offshooting gables which overhung the street, and mean little rooms made even darker and smaller by low ceilings and sloping floors and small fireplaces which only heated the immediate area around the hearth. All of this, and more, I learned later: that the kitchen, which was destined to become my bedroom, was the only comfortable room in the house, and that beyond the kitchen were the scullery, the buttery, the distilling room, and the dirt-floored preserving room, with a pit in the center for a fire. I learned too that the shop was usually cold and a lamp grudgingly allowed only when it became too dark to otherwise count money. The office occupied the other front room and was reached by a door opening onto the alley, which in turn led directly into the garden. Remembering the innkeeper's wife's words this morning, I looked for a gate cut into the wall near the pottery, and found it at once by its leather hinges and thong handle.

This house is like a fortress, I thought, a fortress that no one in his right mind would want to storm. This opinion, made on the spot, was never changed; the other, made in an equally hasty mood, that the rumor of Mrs. Southwick's wealth was exaggerated, was later discarded.

Since a decision must be made, and at once, I led the fidgeting boy toward the gate, behind which the thump of pottery wheels could be distinctly heard, and sent him inside to bring one of the potters out for my trunk. He returned with a young man of about my age, wearing a layer of fine clay dust on his leather apron, who brushed past me with a surly grunt.

Taking this to mean permission to enter, I pushed open the gate and found myself on a well-brushed path, with the long, low pottery shed on my right, and to the left a kitchen garden bordered by an aromatic boxwood hedge. As kitchen gardens go, this one was an achievement of restraint over prodigality. The vegetables grew in rigidly defined rows; the beans firmly bound to their poles, the hillocks of earth topped by the feathery tassels of carrots and tightly coiled cabbages, their outer leaves gently unfurling to sparkle with moisture under the morning sun. Espaliered against the outer wall were the fruit trees, heavily burdened, and the air was somnolent with the murmur of bees, an intrusion of sensuality upon what was otherwise a triumph of man's rigid control of nature. Squarely in the center of the garden was a scarecrow, plumply bursting with straw. A blackbird swung from a nearby limb, eyeing me alertly, as though testing my reaction to this strange apparition.

Looking toward the kitchen door, I saw a rain barrel beside the steps, set to catch the water from the rain spout, and handily nearby was the well, wearing a fresh coat of whitewash. An oaken bucket, mossy and damp, rested on the ledge.

I understood, now, a part of this morning's conversation. From the kitchen window there was nothing to hinder the sight of the gate, although the path beyond the corner of the garden was obscured by trees and flowering bushes. My way lay clear to the kitchen, where I might announce myself, but a flit of movement ahead decided my course, and I moved toward a small grove of trees where an attempt had been made to create an idyllic retreat. In the center was a shallow pool, floating with water lilies, and a willow drooped its branches into the water. Feverfew and gilly flowers clambered across the ground, encroaching upon the candy-tuft and sweet alyssum that bordered the stones lining the pool. From a nearby dovecote I heard a low, throaty murmur. The air was scented with flowers, dappled with shade, and altogether an island of serenity, with the workaday thump of the potters' wheels only a dimly heard intrusion.

As I approached, I was startled by an explosive "Damn!" There was a splash, and a child jumped into the pool. She stood knee deep, her skirt fanning out into a circle from her waist, black hair spiky and wet, and lifted startled eyes at my appearance. Honor.

"Did you hear me?" she demanded fiercely.

"Well, yes," I said apologetically, "I could hardly help it."

She whitened and I added quickly, "But I have a bad memory; I can't tell you precisely what you said."

She smiled then, her black eyes sparkling. "It was the frog," she explained. "Mama told the gardener to get rid of it, and I was trying to save its life, but it jumped. It's too stupid to save."

I nodded gravely. "If you can't catch it, perhaps the gardener can't either."

She brightened, then was gloomy again. "No, the gardener knows he *has* to catch it. Whose cat is that?"

"Mine. His name is William."

She clambered, dripping wet, from the pool. "My name is Honor Southwick, and if you're the new servant, Mama won't allow you to keep the cat."

I flinched. "My name is Emma Ashton. And I will try to persuade her. Don't you have pets?"

"No, and no one persuades Mama to do anything. I already know your name, thank you. I believe that I like you, but don't be cheered by that. I am the least important member of the family. You'd be much better off if Patience—my sister—liked you," she added gloomily. "That's unlikely, too, however, for unless my sister takes one of her fancies to you, she won't like you at all. She is my half sister, our fathers were not the same. Hers was a rich man, and mine a poor one. He was killed near that pottery shed a year ago."

"Yes, I know. I am sorry."

"So am I." She was vainly squeezing out the hem of her skirt. "He and Patience did not like each other."

"Then she did not take one of her fancies to him?"

"No. She wished him dead, and being a witch, her wish came true."

"Being a witch? Nonsense!"

"Of course she is a witch. She would tell you so herself. She is a natural, and all naturals are witches. Didn't you know that?"

"I certainly did not!" I said hastily, kneeling down. I thought it was time to change the subject. "Here, let me do that. I like your flower garden, Honor. Your mother must enjoy it very much."

"It is not a proper flower garden, and Mama does not like it. She allows it only because it was my father's, and he left it in my care. He built the pool and planted the willow tree and the flowers. Whenever he left me to go to sea, he would ask me to care for his garden."

I nodded slowly. "I see. Will you take me to see your mother, Honor? And keep my cat while I talk to her?"

She beamed. "I'll take you right to her office, for that's where she is now."

"When does the shop open, Honor?"

She answered me with an exasperated cluck. "You mean that it is not open? That's Patience's job, you see, to unlock the door and dust the shop every morning. When the bell tinkles, that means someone has come in, and Patience is not to tend the shop, but come and get one of us. She is not, on any account, to attempt to sell any of the pottery herself, for Patience is stupid, you see, and can't make change, nor tell a price right. Mama says people will cheat her. But Mama says she is bright enough to open the shop. Mama will be angry, but not with Patience, I am sure. Probably with me." She sounded resigned.

The little girl led me, by way of a sheltered path, to another door, one I had not previously noticed, since it and the path were hidden within a recessed gable of the house. It opened directly upon a narrow, dark passageway, smelling of dust and gloom, and ended in a small, dark hallway. Here she left me to wait while she went to tell her mother of my arrival.

I looked around curiously, surprised at the air of dirt and neglect. Beside me, a set of box stairs, carpeted in dirty drugget, led steeply to the gloom of the upper floor. Through an open door I saw a room, apparently the parlor, filled with stiffly arranged furniture and darkened by heavy draperies that only partly concealed its ill-kept, dusty appearance. Another door, half opened, led to the shop: I heard the slap of a duster and a tinkle of breaking pots. Honor, emerging from the third door, flinched at the sound as she told me to go in.

"Piper saw you from the window. She told her that you were here."

Piper. Joanna had promised me jealousy, and I recognized it, but she had not prepared me for the hostility that met me like a blow.

"Move aside, Piper, and let me see the gel."

Silence Southwick amply filled her wheelchair, her plumpness an apparent sign of good health until one noticed the lines of pain scoring her forehead and fanning out from the corners of her mouth. Her face was pallid, and her hair streaked with white, without the aid of powder. The beauty which she must have once possessed had fled, leaving only the brilliant eyes to attest to its existence.

She made no welcoming speech, but looked me over thoroughly before plunging immediately to the point, every word she spoke a whiplash to hope.

"I understand you have been used to think of yourself as a lady of quality, and as such, perhaps fancy your position in this household as a sort of companion, or even another daughter. If so, get that notion out of your head. Your friend, Joanna Eaton, suggested it in her letter to me. Silly, twittery female!" She snorted. "If she gave you the same impression, I wish to correct it right now. I have no need for another daughter: the two I have now neither toil nor spin. I have still less need for a companion. Piper fills that role admirably. Limit your companionship to a discussion of your work in this house, and you will please me. If you have been used to giving yourself airs, cast them off, or take yourself right away now. Is that understood?"

"Yes, ma'am." I tilted my head and matched her, look for look. I had not expected to use so soon the hard lesson learned from my father.

"Your work will be to eventually take over the housekeeper chores from Piper, leaving her free to attend to me and my daughter Patience, as our personal maid." I now understood the fierce little woman's hostility: her homely small face, mobile as a monkey's, mirrored her jealousy. She must fear a younger, stronger rival, who was capable of performing the overwhelming duties she was no longer able to undertake. "I also expect you to be responsible for keeping the shop, with occasional help from Honor and Piper, or even Obediah Watson, my chief potter, who will set the prices for the pottery. The shop is only a small outlet for our pottery: we don't make enough from it to justify a full-time employee, but for the few hours it remains open, I expect you to listen for the bell and tend shop when it rings. For all this, you will start with a salary of fifty dollars a year, and it will increase as your responsibility increases. Is that satisfactory?"

I blinked. I had no idea if it was satisfactory, but I had no choice, either, but to agree. I had a vague impression that the sum mentioned was a generous one, an impression strengthened by Piper's startled face. "Yes, ma'am."

"Good. You will share a bed in the kitchen with Mrs. Margate, the cook. She is a stout Irishwoman, and I advise you to get along with her, for she suits me admirably. You will, of course, help her when you have free time. Before you go, however, we'd better reach an understanding and start out as we wish to go on in the future. I am paying you twice what I would pay a girl just off a boat, merely because of your inflated value as a gentlewoman. But I am not prepared to put up with any pseudogenteel airs from you. A servant cannot afford pride. I will make all the decisions, and I expect you to remember that in the future. Is that understood?" She waited grimly, then added, "Turn around. Let me have a good look at you in the light."

I turned, flinching at the identical looks of gloating on hers and Piper's faces, and I realized that, rather than being put off by my appearance, they were obscurely pleased with it.

"You look a little peaked. I hope that doesn't mean you are sickly."

"No, ma'am. I haven't been eating well on this trip."

"I see. Well, I don't permit temperament here, certainly not from the servants. You'll get your orders directly from Piper for the time being, until you have learned your own routine. We seldom entertain, but when we do you'll be expected to sit at the table with us. One of the pleasant side effects of your gentlewoman status." Her smile was about as kindly as a wolf's. "If you're hungry, go out to the kitchen and get some food and meet Mrs. Margate."

"Come with me, Emma. I'll take you to her." It was Honor, a clean, dry child now, who was waiting at the door.

Her mother's eyes flickered at the sudden intrusion but she did not reprove her beyond, "You're not to worry Emma and keep her from her work."

Honor ignored her and pulled me toward the door.

"They tell me you brought a cat with you?"

I felt the spasmodic leap of Honor's pulse before the words registered with me. "Yes." I whirled about, impaled by her stabbing glare.

"Get rid of it, then. I won't have pets in this house."

"Oh, please, Mrs. Southwick, he is a good cat. I have had him for eight years and I can't get rid of him now. He's a good mouser and I'll keep him out of your way."

"We don't have mice, and I don't allow cats in this house. Get rid of it."

But Honor ranged herself passionately on my side, and, to my surprise, her mother grudgingly gave ground.

"Very well, you may keep him so long as he stays out of the

house. And out of sight. But I won't answer for the consequences. Don't come whining to me when he is savaged by a dog."

But I saved his life for two weeks before her prophecy—or was it a promise?—came true; before sweet William was found, ignominiously tied in a sack and drowned, then deposited triumphantly, and with a calculated malice, upon the kitchen doorstep, for me to find.

Honor flung herself into my arms, wild with sobs, and I flew in to confront her mother, assuming that hers had been the order that sent William to his death. Her first question took me aback by its unexpectedness: "How was he killed?" Her face was a conflict as she listened to me; then, without a trace of pity in her voice, "How is Honor taking this?"

I told her how Honor was taking it, incoherently, passionately, and when I had finished, she said flatly, "Well, I told you not to come whining to me. I told you to get rid of the cat yourself, before it was done for you. You are just lucky that it was done mercifully. It could have been—ugly. Honor will have to take many disappointments. This isn't her first, nor will it be her last. Now, Emma, get back to your work, and try to control your grief before the child. You have wasted enough time with me on the subject."

"You mustn't take on so, sweetheart," Mrs. Margate said comfortably that night as I wept in my pillow. "He was just a cat, and all the cryin' in the world won't bring him back."

"But who—who—could have been so cruel?" I sobbed. "At first I thought she gave the order to one of the potters, but then I saw she was taken by surprise, and even seemed *slightly* concerned about the effect on Honor! But not concerned enough to have inquiries made."

"Maybe she already has a good idea, and the less said, the sooner mended," Mrs. Margate said wisely.

"What do you mean?" I asked, raising a drenched face.

"I haven't been here much longer than you, lass, but I hadn't been in this house a week before someone told me about the murder, and someone else about the witch," she explained. "Havin' been raised a Roman, as I was, I learned about witches, although Father—and the Church—doesn't like to hear such talk nowadays. But, bless his soul, he knows he can't stop talk. There are too many people who believe in witches. I'm thinkin', lass, that someone believed your cat was a witch's familiar, it bein' from this house an' all. And caught it out and drowned it!"

I listened, aghast to think that poor William could have been killed because of such a superstitious belief.

"Mrs. Margate, surely you don't believe in that nonsense!"

She was silent for a long time. "Not of your cat."

CHAPTER I

Marcus began my portrait the day that I learned I would see Joanna again. Her letter, incoherent with crossed lines, informed me of the impending visit even before Mrs. Southwick told me of it.

"You're different today. Excited, I think." Marcus, posing me carefully, stepped back and eyed me consideringly. "You've lost that look I want. Never mind, it will be back. I am only working on the outline today, anyway. Talk if you must," he added, "but for God's sake, don't expect an answer, and try not to distract me," and thereafter he became blind to all but the canvas before him.

I smiled as I watched him and thought of Joanna. Of the last time I saw her, when she slipped the bracelet upon my wrist and said good-by. Seven years ago. Would she find me so changed? I was no longer the fearful, timorous girl who shivered when told by her employer to speak or be silent. I was now aware of my own worth and importance in the management of this household. With my wages, presently a dazzling sixty-five dollars a year, thriftily banked against the future, I had become independent, could hold my own with Silence, and frequently came under her fire, even as she astringently appreciated my staying power.

I had remained as reclusive as ever in the social clime that was Joanna's world. In that, she would find me unchanged. Church attendance, yes, that was mandatory in this house; but the balls, the turtle feasts, the ladies' tea parties, and the theater parties at Faneuil Hall found me run to ground as an animal would to its burrow. No, Joanna would despair of me when she arrived to find that I now had two worthy suitors, both of whom I had rejected.

The first was the minister, Reverend Wilford, a strange, intense gentleman of about thirty-five years, who had assumed the pulpit upon the death of old Reverend Monkshire, who had preached himself into an apoplectic fit one Sunday. The new minister had lost his wife five years earlier; he had a small daughter, and though pursued unceasingly by the widows and spinsters of the church, had so far resisted their ploys, until his eyes fell upon me. Now, delightedly abetted by Silence, who had revealed matchmaking depths heretofore unsuspected, he was a frequent visitor to the house.

My other suitor, Judge Dashwood, a contemporary of Silence's, had buried four wives and would not hear me say that I would not be the fifth. He was importunate, aggressively so, waylaying me at every opportunity, and I had begun to desperately suspect that only my marriage to another would discourage him from assuming that I welcomed his suit.

Just so would Joanna not take my denials seriously, when she arrived, I thought ruefully.

"No, no, not that look! I want you pensive. What are you thinking of, anyway?"

"Joanna."

"Oh, yes," he muttered absently.

Marcus knew of Joanna and Thomas but not yet of their pending visit. They had business, apparently, with Silence, and the final disposition of Joanna's father's estate, which seemed to be securely tied into the Southwick interests. Before his death, I had frequently met the gentle, frail old man, with his shaking, paper-thin hands. He had always paused before entering Silence's office and spoken to me graciously of his daughter, and I had never failed to be uncomfortably reminded of an unwary fish circling the jaws of a waiting shark.

Years ago, I had believed that I would return to New York and Joanna when I had the independent means to do so, but my reason for staying on could be put into one word: Honor. My little water sprite was now eighteen, but she needed me as desperately as ever, just as I needed the reassurance of having someone to love. She was the little sister I had never had, the child I would never know, and I stayed on to befriend her, for I had learned very early that she would always rank below Patience in her mother's affections.

I had never conducted my own battles as fiercely as I did Honor's, and Silence, in her cold, self-contained way, allowed it and sometimes paused to listen. Our first head-on clash came about because of Honor's school. She was sent away at the end of that first summer to a school in Salem that was recommended by the minister, Reverend Monkshire. It was a school noted for its stern disciplinary methods even more than its Godliness and the piety of its master. I attempted to intercede on behalf of the tearful, pleading little girl.

"Here, in the paper, is advertised another school in Salem, conducted by a lady who furnishes impeccable references. It sounds less rigid and far more pleasant than the one you are considering. She promises to teach needlework, tambour, embroidery, as well as writing and ciphering. Also, how to wax flowers—"

A snort. "I hear nothing about the Bible. I can imagine the idleness there."

"But a most impressive list of references is furnished—"

"Anyone can find fools to write references. No, the church school comes personally recommended by my minister and teaches good, fundamental skills that she will need. And it is presided over by a Congregationalist minister and his wife. I haven't the money to throw away on extravagant nonsense. . . ."

I gave this statement the contempt it deserved. She had the money to keep Patience in luxurious idleness, to provide her with rich clothes and expensive baubles. That winter I burned with resentment as I watched Patience's complacency and thought of little Honor at school, homesick and unhappy.

"Is the fire too hot, sweetling? Piper, move the screen a bit; our darling is feeling the heat. Now try, dearest, to set the stitches straight this time."

Patience would create a tangle of her embroidery, and then yawn with boredom as one of us carefully picked it for her, then reinstructed her in placing the stitches. She loved to sit indolently, her vacant blue eyes heavy-lidded, while the fire turned her fair curls to red-gold and flickered its light upon her pretty, plump countenance. Or she would lift a rounded arm and watch with simple pleasure the glittering jewels in the bracelet she wore.

There was an endless procession of beaux, young men of good family, with solid family fortunes of their own, to match hers. So long as they could sit and watch Patience, her eyes demurely downcast, while the firelight cast its ruddy glow upon her pale face, they were under her spell. But let Patience talk and the enchantment vanished. Let Patience raise her eyes and the emptiness was unmistakable. Allowing even for the silliness expected of a young lady of her class, Patience's words bordered on the inane. Most of the young men, accustomed to a sister's simperings, bore with it very well at first, but even the most determined suitor, prepared to overlook much in the lady of his choice, could not help but view her with open eyes, sooner or later.

She was not altogether stupid; in those attitudes of others which she could sense, as an animal would, she was even clever, but let a beau speak of the weather and Patience would prattle about her hair ribbons, or let him direct a languishing look, and she was petulant and babyish with her mother, making nonsense of his gallantry. Silence tried, that first winter, until finally she admitted to herself what had become clear to me: that Patience and her goods were not for peddling in the average market. One by one the young men fell away, and Silence, in her despair, commented on it once to me.

"It is an inherited weakness, Emma. My mother-in-law, Anne Pride, was confined to the attic of this very house, a raving maniac until she died. I did not know the truth about her until after I was married to her son. She had been a witness at the Salem witch trials, one of the children who claimed bewitchment. A tortured child, with a mother who aided her delusions. It was not until she met my father-in-law that, with his help, she saw the evil she had done. By then, however, she was nearly thirty years old and it was too late. Remorse drove her mad. It would have been better if he had never helped her to repent, for in later years she raved of her victims, seeing their dead, reproachful faces all around her as she begged unceasingly for their forgiveness. She finally hung herself from a beam upstairs by tearing her clothes into strips and knotting them into a rope.

"When my husband, her only child, was born, she was forty years old and already showing signs of instability. He waited until his middle years before marrying, to be sure that he had not inherited her diseased blood. He died before we knew that it had merely bypassed him to his child."

So much for the talk of witches! This, then, was all it had been: a mad woman confined to an attic bedroom, and because she had once been involved in a notorious witch trial, the good citizens of the city had attached to her name the brand of witch. Of such ephemeral substance was the explanation commonly surrounding Captain Southwick's death, and given to me in the story of the gate that did not squeak and the alley that was empty.

I asked Silence if she did not think marriage would be unwise for Patience, if she would not pass on the inherited taint as her grandmother had done. "The doctor thinks not," she replied stolidly. "He believes the madness merely a deficiency that can be cured by a placid life and children. She is, after all, not really mad but merely simple. There is no viciousness in her nature."

I shrugged, knowing that there were always doctors to be found who would say precisely what one wanted to hear. And Silence was desperately quick to clutch at any reassurance that her favorite child could eventually lead a normal life. She had confided in me in a moment of weakness, and did not repeat her confidence until that summer, when Honor came home from school and found me in the kitchen, preserving jam.

"It was a horrid place, Emma, with no fires. We had to break the ice in the pitchers to wash every morning. We had chilblains from the cold and our feet cracked and bled. Sundays were the worst days, because you spent all day on your knees, asking God to forgive your sins, and sometimes one of the girls toppled over in a faint. I never knew I had so many sins until I had to think of all of them before I was allowed any supper."

We spent a certain amount of time on our knees, too, at morning and evening prayers, but they were conducted by Silence in the comfort of the parlor. Fortunately, she saw for herself that the school was a punishment, so she chose another minister, another school, and Honor was boarded out again, this time at

Marblehead. The minister's wife was kind and motherly, but Honor felt her expulsion keenly.

"Why must I always live away from home, Emma? Is it because this house belonged to Patience's father and my father was only a sea captain? Am I a charity child, like those in the orphanage in Boston?"

Silence answered me with characteristic honesty when I indignantly demanded an answer. "Honor is by way of being a charity child, Emma, when her prospects are compared to Patience's, but she is by no means a pauper. However, word has gotten around of Patience's mental deficiencies, and I must concentrate all of my energies upon her future. I can see no solution but marriage for her, for otherwise how, after my death, will she be taken of? That is why I send Honor away, to give Patience her chance. Patience is not at her best around her sister; Honor frets her, and Patience feels the contrast between them. I shall continue to send her away to school until she is older, or Patience marries. When she is at home, I want Honor to be your charge, Emma, with your first duty to be keeping her out of Patience's way. Honor is strong; she can take the rejection, and someday she will understand why I had to sacrifice her for her sister."

It was a cruel decision, to deliberately place one child above another, and I sometimes wondered how she could make it. It was at such times that I was thankful that the vagaries of mother love were beyond my understanding. When I reflected upon Silence's cold objectvity, I knew that Honor was better off with the minister and his wife in Marblehead than in the reluctant arms of her family.

"I like that look." Marcus was working furiously. "What are you thinking of?"

"Honor."

"Ah, yes, Honor." His voice warmed.

Honor had been living at home for a year now, but under a cloud. No one had warned Silence that the minister's wife, with her staid background, was also of a frivolous, romantic disposition, so that when disaster struck and Honor formed a connection with an ineligible suitor, she had to be sent home under severe restriction. It was left to the minister to deal with his wife, who had innocently fostered Honor's acquaintance with one whom the minister described as an out-and-out fortune hunter. For a few months Honor had been stormy and given to bouts of weeping, but gradually she grew to accept her banishment more calmly.

Marcus was putting away his pencils now. "That's enough for today. I'll work on the background for a while without you."

Perhaps the best description of Marcus Goddard's position in this house was that of a nonpaying boarder. He was not expected to confine himself to his attic studio; he had complete freedom belowstairs, having his meals and attending church with the family and spending evenings at chess and conversation with his benefactress, Silence. He had come to her attention through the efforts of a family friend who saw in the young man a talent to be encouraged and persuaded her that he only needed a sponsor to be a success. It was a role she had never played, and it was possible that she had taken him in with the thought that he would be useful as a designer of pottery. But to everyone's surprise, her own included, she had become interested in Marcus as an artist, and he had lingered on for months now, painting extravagantly flattering portraits of Silence and Patience, and later, a wildly beautiful one of Honor against a stylized Baroque background of Grecian columns and windy sky. Recently he had asked permission to paint me, and Silence had given grudging approval so long as the sittings did not interfere with my work.

"You do need subjects for practice, and Emma has good bones. I suppose you can pose her so that her scars won't show," she had added with thoughtless cruelty.

Afterward, he set to work patiently to undo the harm her words had done. With great tenderness he explained why he wanted to paint me.

"You do have good bones, Emma, and haunting eyes and a mouth as seductive as Eve's. I want to paint your portrait because you are beautiful, for, in spite of the few scars that smudge your forehead, or perhaps in contrast to them, your skin has the fine quality of silk. When I have finished, I think this portrait will be the best thing I have ever done."

I did not believe him, of course, but I thought that his words were the kindest I had ever heard, and he the kindest man I had ever known for uttering them. Was it any wonder, then, that I loved him? And could I not be excused for wishing that he might love me back? Watching him yearningly as he bent over the canvas, his lean brown fingers delicately handling his brush, a lock of black hair dangling over the fine, thin face, I felt my bones melt with tenderness. But he was no less concerned about Honor, and in my saner moments I told myself that the light I occasionally beheld in his dark eyes was no more than an artist's appreciation of his subject.

"Emma. Come to my office. I want to speak to you." It was days later, and my portrait was almost completed. I was idling on the stairs, still bemused after a session with Marcus, and I found my employer waiting for me in her wheelchair. She preceded me, the wooden wheels creaking loudly on the polished floor, to her neat little office. Although the day was only moderately chilly, a fire burned in the grate.

"Jacob has just returned from Cornhill Street with good news. A notice has been posted at the Customs House that the *Salem Lady* will dock tomorrow at the Long Wharf. She is one of the Murray Line, you know, and we may expect a prompt docking. That means that our guests, the Eatons, will be here for dinner tomorrow night. But I have just received a letter that we will have an additional guest, a gentleman, arriving with them. That is why I wish to talk to you." To my astonishment, I saw two spots of hectic color burning in her cheeks, and I realized that she was excited. "He is coming at my invitation."

"Who is he, ma'am?"

"A cousin. Distant kin, but the closest male relative I have. I haven't seen him since Captain Southwick's death. He was a great comfort to me in those trying days. I want the best bedchamber for him. That means putting the Eatons into Marcus's bedchamber and sending him upstairs to the attic to sleep. Piper will occupy a trundle bed in my room to ease the arrangements. I want a desk for my cousin, and plenty of sharpened pens and ink. And, oh, yes, a good fire, Emma. Start it now so the room will be warm when he arrives." My eyes opened wide at this lavish ordering of fires.

"Why? Is he from the South?"

"Oh, no, he was originally from Salem, as all of our family was. But he has lived for years in New York and has become accustomed to their soft winters."

I smiled slightly. "He will be alone, then?"

"Yes, he is not married." The flush rose, she started to speak, then bit off her words impatiently: "You might as well know, Emma, I have written asking him to come and look into the matter of the diamonds." She met my eyes defiantly.

I was conscious of shock. Weeks ago, a chamois bag of uncut diamonds, brought home by Honor's father on his last voyage, had disappeared from Silence's bedchamber, and although the house had been ransacked, they had not been found. After years of careless storage in a drawer, the loss had been so suggestive, following as it did upon the heels of a quarrel between Silence and her daughters, that I had become convinced that Silence had hidden them for reasons of her own, then chosen to call it a theft. The quarrel had been launched by Patience's idle boast that the diamonds were to be made into "a pretty necklace" for her, and grew with Silence's flinty assertion that the diamonds were left unconditionally to her, to be used as she saw fit. Her stance was so unjust, particularly since Honor had always viewed the diamonds as her only legacy from her father, that Honor had grown increasingly more violent as the gates to years of smoldering resentment were loosened in one fell swoop. It was the first time Marcus and Usher Tournais, Silence's lawyer, had known of the diamonds, and they had listened in appalled silence as Honor's tantrum burst its bounds.

But Honor was nothing compared to Patience when the theft was discovered. Even Honor was shaken by the sight of her sister in a full spate of hysterics. It had taken a liberal dose of laudanum to soothe her to sleep and make her forget her grievances.

"I know you think I put them away myself to settle the argument, but I am not in my dotage yet. Since you seem determined not to take me seriously and have influenced Usher Tournais and even my loyal Piper to think your way, I had no recourse but to go to someone else for help. And since I don't intend to have my business bandied about the streets, I am calling in a relative."

"That is wise, ma'am. But why all the way from New York?"

"He was glad to come when I wrote him for help. I explained all the circumstances, even your unwarranted interference, and since he had other business to conduct in Salem, he promised to stop here for a few days and remain with me until we can clear this up. It was a privilege, he wrote, to come now, when he could have the company of the Eatons on the voyage."

"Then he knows them?"

"Yes." She looked at me cautiously. "I will confess, while I am about it, that I used the diamonds partly as an excuse to bring him here. I am thinking of him for Honor, Emma. She seems to be recovering from that unfortunate Marblehead affair, and even enjoys her work in the shop these days. This man is personable, and although twice her age, is very eligible. If only she doesn't ruin her chances with her moods. That is where I hope you will be able to talk to her about the importance of making a good impression."

"He wouldn't do for Patience?" I asked, not much liking what I was hearing.

"No, not this man. He knows her background, remember, and has no need to marry an heiress. I believe I have already settled Patience's future, if you will recall."

Yes, I recalled. Patience's future had recently been settled to Silence's satisfaction in precisely the same high-handed manner in which she was now proposing to settle Honor's. The unwilling candidate chosen for Patience's hand was Obediah Watson, one of the potters. That with Patience would go the pottery, Obediah found the most galling condition of the proposition he had been offered, since he had been taught by his father to think of himself as its part owner already. The elder Watson had begun the pottery in partnership with John Henry Pride, but after their deaths, Silence had repudiated the claim. Now, she had at long last agreed to honor her obligation if Obediah took Patience as his wife, an unequivocal business arrangement that he had, so far, scorned.

I could have felt more pity for the young man if I could have found it within myself to like him at all. He was sullen and disagreeable, without a single prepossessing charm, and recently I had begun to suspect that he was nurturing a passion for my beloved Honor, which he covered by a possessive, overbearing manner. He must have known for himself that his ambition was foredoomed, for what Silence might accept to safely establish her deficient daughter, she would not tolerate for Honor, upon whom she had begun to pin her more ambitious hopes.

"I have had this match in my head since Honor came home, for I realize if she is not settled soon I may have a scandal on my hands," Silence mused. "He will be impressed with her—how could he be otherwise? And he will provide the strong rein she needs. The diamonds seemed a good excuse to bring him here to meet her."

Her words pricked at me. As casually, and with the same ruthlessness with which she was bending Obediah to her will, she was planning Honor's future.

"I don't believe they were stolen," I cried, determined to pierce her complacency.

Her eyes flashed. "Fortunately, your opinion no longer counts. I do not have to depend upon you—" She whirled about, muttering to herself, but I caught the remainder of her sentence.

"What do you mean? I am a suspect? Suspected of what? Do you mean that you believe I stole your precious diamonds—Honor's legacy? That I could—would—do such a thing?" I was choking with rage.

"I know that you didn't steal them, you silly girl," she was hasty to appease me. "But if I brought in your good friend Judge Dashwood to investigate and make an honest analysis of the theft, you might find yourself the first suspect! The outsiders always are. At least, in this way, I have chosen to keep the matter contained, so far."

I knew that her words were true. It was not consideration of me that held Silence's hand, however, but the possibility that one of her own daughters was guilty. Would Judge Dashwood think of that? I thought of the pompous little strutting man and his deferential treatment of Silence, and I knew that he would look for a thief outside her family circle first. It was a measure of the world's injustice that because of my inferior station in life I would always be considered one of those outsiders. For the first time, I was touched with a shiver as I thought of the cousin who was expected tomorrow.

I leaned my head exhaustedly against the kitchen door and paused to gulp breaths of the cold night air, which stung my lungs with its icy purity. It smelled of damp leaves and frosty winter nights to come. I had been driven from the kitchen by the hot, close atmosphere, with its rich, heavy odor of cooking jam. It pursued me even out here, for the arbor hung heavy with grapes, and the cooking fires had been kept burning all day. Inside, the McNab sisters helped Mrs. Margate prepare dinner, flitting noisily back and forth, swinging the dining-room door open with a careless hip, their skirts crackling, giggling and whispering breathily as they leaned over to reach a slipping, cascading stack of plates. This, and the candlelight dancing dizzily in the shadows and the greasy haze from the cooking pots had all been enough to send me fleeing to the fresh, clean air outdoors, followed by Mrs. Margate's warmly sympathetic eyes.

I had no room of my own, for my bed was in the kitchen and my clothes kept in a damp, unfloored shed room off the buttery. I could be sure, however, of being alone if I left the house. Silence regarded the sickening effects of night air with suspicion and most of the household followed her reasoning. But tonight there was no hope of a quietly pensive hour on the garden bench, for the wind was up, rising in short, fitful gusts, and only a brisk walk could ward off the chill. I shivered and turned to go.

"Emma." It was Marcus. "I saw you from my window. You come here often, don't you? Is something wrong?"

I wrapped the concern in his voice around me like a blanket as I found myself telling him of my conversation with Silence, with her reminder of my position and her possessive plans for Honor. He listened thoughtfully.

"I too was present when the argument over the diamonds was raging," he said wryly. "It was the first I had known of them, but I saw for myself that they were extremely valuable, so I would be a suspect."

I stared at him, shocked. I had not thought of suspicion falling on anyone else. Marcus, the servants, even the potters might be accused. The ripples from Silence's words were widening.

"And little Honor has been used by her mother too long," he added. "Do you realize, Emma, that there is no one—"

"To care about Honor but you and me," I finished. "Yes. This marriage may suit Honor, but if it doesn't, I don't intend to stand by and see—"

"I know." We were both silent for a time. "Did I ever tell you about my brother?" he asked abruptly.

"No."

"Actually he was my foster brother, since his parents adopted me from the city orphanage when I was a child. They had known my father, who had been an artist too, and a teacher. He had been gay and charming, but improvident and feckless, and had left me penniless. My foster parents took me in. They were elderly, and my brother was much older than I, so that when they died he was like a father to me. He was proud of my talent and saw to it that I went to London to study. I was a stripling lad at the time, homesick and frightened, but he made periodic trips to London, and saw to my support and comfort, until gradually I was commissioned for a few portraits and began to find my feet. My career had reached a critical stage; I was making great strides in learning new techniques when I received a letter from him, asking me to come home. It was a casual letter, on the surface, but beneath I could sense the appeal. However, selfishly, I chose to ignore it, and wrote that I would be ready to leave London the following year. Time passed: I heard nothing, and believing that he was angry, I stayed on like a sulky child. Later I learned that he was dead, had died within weeks of writing me. The letter, in fact, had been one of the last ones he had written. Since then my guilt has been immense."

I waited but he said nothing more.

"I am sure that he forgave you," I said hesitantly.

"Ah, he died before he learned of my callousness. For that, at least, I am thankful. But that is not the point. I never forgave myself."

At last I thought I saw the point of his strange little story.

"Honor and I need help now," I offered timidly.

He turned swiftly, the brooding look gone in a blaze of response. "Yes, I know. Both of you. And in helping you I feel that I can, somehow, help my brother. You do understand, don't you, Emma? I have never felt it so strongly, that this is where he would want me to stay and this is what he would want me to do. Never again will I turn my back on those whom I love." He hugged me to him and my heart gave a joyful little beat.

The kitchen was a warm and welcoming room; in fact, the only one in this cheerless house. Mrs. Margate's comfortable presence helped make it so. Our bed hung behind wooden shutters on the wall and could be dropped to the floor at night. In the winter I was thankful for the vast hearth fire, which was banked with ashes at night, but in the summer it so overheated the kitchen that frequently, in searching for a cool breeze, I took my pillow and quilt to lie in the open doorway and sleep.

My clothes were stored in my trunk on a shelf in the small shed; I had another, narrower shelf for my comb and brush, with a cracked mirror overhead, and there I dressed, shivering with cold, before hurrying back to the friendly kitchen.

It was a large room with a low, smoke-blackened ceiling and a brick floor covered with braided rugs. A scrubbed oak table stood squarely in the center, to be used for the preparation of vegetables; here, bread was set to rise and the potters were seated to eat their meals. The brick chimney with its baking ovens and large open fireplaces took up one end of the room, and the leaping flames glinted on copper, pewter, and black iron skillets alike as they hung from hooks on the walls. At most times a black iron pot, smelling rich and savory, hung suspended from a swinging crane.

The mantel was the repository of all of Mrs. Margate's worldly possessions, accumulated over a lifetime of working in other people's homes: her painted clock, the family Bible, which she could not read, the blue vase of pipe spills, and her pipe, blackened and worn smooth by her fingers. The mantel wore a gay, ruffled prawn of red calico, which was echoed in the window curtains and did much to add to the cheerfulness of the room. Here was the only touch of red in the house, for Silence considered it a sinful color, its brightness a temptation of the Devil, but she allowed Mrs. Margate undisputed reign of the kitchen.

It was pleasant to sit by the fireplace after dinner, idly watching the flames, sharing the company of Marcus and Honor. Usually Mrs. Margate would go to bed, her snores a gentle background to our conversation. She allowed one final invasion from the potters after she had cleared them out of the kitchen, and this would occur late, sometimes after she had braided her thin, grizzled hair for the night. Before dossing down, they returned for their bedtime flip, but she sternly forbade any lingering, and they usually took the smoking mugs back to the shed with them. She would have the ingredients assembled, the rum, the sugar, the pot of quince jam, and the poker heating among the coals, to be thrust red-hot into the mixture, sending up a cloud of alcoholic steam.

Tonight, as I wearily prepared for bed, I noticed one cup of flip yet to be made.

"Obediah's not come up yet, lassie," Mrs. Margate groaned. "Do you think you could take it to him, or he'll be knocking us out of our bed after we're asleep."

I could not refuse, knowing how tired she was. Clutching my shawl and the toddy cup, I held the lantern aloft with my other hand as I picked my way carefully down the dark path. The potters slept in lean-to rooms off the kiln room, but tonight I found Obediah still at the wheel, bent over his wet clay. He was an artist in his way, choosing often to ornament his pieces with a bunch of grapes or a curving handle.

I had been repelled from the beginning of our acquaintance by Obediah's sneering unfriendliness. It was his way to select his friends for their usefulness to him, and he had decided early that I could offer him nothing. He was surly and uncouth when he spoke, but usually he ignored me pointedly as beneath his notice. Contrasted to Jacob's cheerful garrulity and Mog's bashful, stammering silence, his manner was like a blow. I often tried to excuse him by reminding myself that he had had the misfortune of having grown up under Silence's thumb; that, plus a cankering sense of injustice, could combine to make an already sullen nature thoroughly unpleasant.

Now, he barely glanced at me as he growled, "What d'ye want?"

I shrugged and put the toddy on the table.

"Wait! Ye kin tell me what I wanta know." I paused, held by the first agreeable tone he had ever used to me. His shock of ragged hair, powdered with clay dust, almost obscured the mean little eyes as he straightened his large, hulking form and reached for the cup. "I learned ternight that *she'd* ast a fancy rich cousin from New York fer a visit ter marry Honor. Is't true?"

I frowned. He was not yet her brother-in-law and I thought his familiar use of Honor's name offensive. His success in learning secrets always surprised me, but I suspected him of pumping Patience, who often retained odd bits of information she had overheard. "If I knew," I snapped, "I wouldn't tell you. It is none of your business!"

"Oh, yis, you pock-faced little jade, I calc'late if it's about Honor, then 'tis my business! Ye've managed ter ferret out th' way I feel about yer precious little Honor, right enuff! I seen ye watchin' me when I watches 'er! Wal-l-l, that's all right, too; no harm ter ye knowin'. Soon, an' they'll all know! But anythin' concernin' 'er *is* my business, an' th' quicker ye learn it, th' better fer both o' us! Oh, yis, Missus High 'n' Fancy, ye kin read an' talk like a lady, an' look down on a low potter, *if* I gives ye a chancet, but I've known about yer kin' from th' beginnin', givin' yerself airs, an' in spite of all, ye ain't nothin' but a servant yerself!" He surveyed me with a glint of humor. "Watched yer lordin' it over us pore ignorant souls down 'ere in th' pottery shed, an' I've bided my time, so long's ye stayed outa my way. But I'll be in charge up there 'n' 'ere in th' pottery, too, soon, an' yer'll 'ave ta learn quick like who's boss then!"

I felt a spurt of pure rage at both his arrogance and the venom in his words. "You're only a potter, you stupid fool! And though you may become her son-in-law, don't let it go to your head, for so long as Silence Southwick lives she will never delegate any authority to you! And long before she dies, I'll be gone, and Honor, too, for I'll see to that myself!"

"Big talk from a servant who can't do more'n look after 'erself!" he sneered. "I'll be a son-in-law, true, but not by sharin' my bed 'n' board with a fool! I know a secret, somethin' that'll bring that family ter its knees an' I know jes' where ter strike ol' Silence where it hurts th' most. I would'a told long ago, but I waited ter see 'ow it could be put ter use, an' it loses no power by bein' a *old* secret! It's jes as important now as't ever was! I've talked ter a good friend, one who knows th' importance of what I've got, an' the law, an' been told ter 'old off awhile, an' I've agreed ter do it. But I ain't intendin' ter wait forever, an' see Honor married ter another man."

"What is this great secret?" I asked scornfully.

"Wouldn't she like ter know, eh? Wouldn't she now?" His knowing smile was sharp, gleaming. "Then she could use it 'erself! Oh, no, I knows yer sort, thank ye! But yer'd better learn where yer buttered bread lies, Emma Ashton, an' start workin' on Honor, bringin' 'er 'round, teachin' 'er ter favor me. Ye do that, an' yer'll find me grateful when I holds th' whip. Cross me, an' I pushes ye out to starve!"

"You poor fool," I said slowly. "I would leave tomorrow if it weren't for Honor. She doesn't love you and I couldn't make her do so even if I tried!"

"It ain't important if she does or not," he replied indifferently. "If 'er mother tells 'er ter marry me, she'll do it, an' I 'ave th' means ter make 'er mother knuckle under ter me."

I shivered. "You know, don't you, that what you're saying sounds like blackmail? I'd be careful of publishing threats like that if I were you. Blackmail is a criminal offense and you can be put into jail for it."

"There ain't no one who's goin' ter bring charges against me," he jeered. "They'd be th' last ones ter want ter bring th' law into it. I jes might make sure of 'avin company in jail if they did. I've sat on my secret a long time, but I 'ave my rights comin' ter me, an' Honor, too. An' I intend t' 'ave both or bring thet 'aughty family down with me!"

I experienced a familiar revulsion as I stared at him, and realized that I was thinking of my father as he must have once been, shrewdly bartering for my mother just as Obediah was prepared to do for Honor. Oh, not with threats of blackmail— that would have been too uncouth for my father—but with the smooth lure of worldly advancement and riches. In both cases, my mother's feelings and Honor's did not enter into it for either man. A thousand years of breeding and culture might separate my socially urbane father and this hulking, foul-speaking lout, yet under the skin they were brothers.

A footfall outside on the path alerted us both.

"It's th' loony," Obediah growled.

Patience was wearing a cloak over her nightgown, which she made no attempt to conceal from Obediah's knowing eyes as she drifted in with an absent look and over to one of the wheels.

"Has she done this before?"

He sniggered. "All th' time. Th' other potters an' me 'ave ter take 'er back ter th' house an' put 'er inside more'n oncet. Long after everyone's asleep, we 'ear th' wheel runnin'. 'Er mother'd be het up, don't yer think, ter learn 'er favorite daughter visits th' men in th' pottery shed after they're abed?"

I said nothing, and Obediah, as though a little ashamed of his implication, added, "It's th' wheel, o'course. She can't keep away from it. Since we shipped in thet new shiny clay, she can't leave it alone. I'll say this much fer 'er, she's got her father's way with clay."

Patience had discarded her cloak, indifferent to our words, and now, with a swift movement, she dived into the vat of wet clay, bringing up a handful.

"No, Patience, it's too late, dear. You must go to bed."

She looked at me wistfully. "Please, Emma."

"No, dear, come with me now, and I will allow you to come back tomorrow when Jacob is here." This, too, would not suit Silence, but I felt confident that she would be more amenable when she realized that Patience's midnight forays were probably occasioned by her frustrated attempts to work the wheel during the day.

Obediently Patience dropped the clay and came forward to wait dumbly for me to wipe her hands.

"Some o' th' best pieces are made by 'er," Obediah added. "But we 'ave ta save them at jest th' right time, fer she ain't got a notion o' 'andlin' them careful-like, nor 'ow ter cut 'em off th' wheel oncet they's finished with."

"Get your cloak."

The light shone through her thin gown, and I saw Obediah looking at her covertly. I would have to warn Piper to watch her, I thought, for though Obediah sneered at sharing a bed with a "loony," I no longer trusted him, and Mog, too, was an unknown factor. Patience, unconscious of undercurrents, brought me her cloak and waited while I put it around her, then took my hand and like a sleepy child followed me home.

CHAPTER II

Joanna found me in the kitchen, my hands in the flour, and fell upon my neck, laughing and sobbing, until I led her to her room. It was there that Thomas found us both, indulging in a tearful orgy.

"Well, Emma, are you coming home with us?" he asked me benignly. "Joanna needs you, and as for me, I shall be glad of your company, my dear."

Joanna's sobbing, incoherent words and her bursts of laughter and tears had begun to alarm me, but Thomas regarded her stolidly and seemed to see nothing amiss. I eyed her warily as I answered, "If Honor marries, as indeed she soon must, I will go willingly. Did he give you any indication of how he felt about the prospect?"

"He?"

"Yes, you two were with him on the ship from New York. You must have formed an opinion of his suitability for Honor?"

Joanna looked dazed; then, surprisingly, her face crumpled. "Oh, Emma, I thought you'd be unhappy about it!"

"Hush now, dear, no more tears," I soothed. "Of course, I would be happy for Honor if she is happy. Particularly if she is to live in New York! Didn't you know that?"

"Exactly what I told Joanna," Thomas approved. "Didn't I tell you, Joanna, how sensible Emma is? But when Mrs. Southwick hinted in her letter of a possible marriage, asking us to be her ambassadors during the voyage, Joanna was sure you'd find the prospect hurtful. Now, see, dear, how foolish you were to worry? You're overtired and must rest now. Let Emma go about her duties. Leave her to me, Emma, and I'll see she rests."

The matter seemed better left in Thomas's capable hands. With a last kiss, I left her, slightly frightened by her volatile emotions and more than a little surprised that she would misinterpret my ambitions for Honor so far as to believe that I would envy her a happy marriage.

But I had other duties. A company dinner was a task to try Mrs. Margate's culinary talents, and she had already been thoroughly flustered by a rare visit from the mistress of the house. I found her in the kitchen, her temper stretched to the breaking point, snapping at the McNab sisters, both of whom had been called into service for the night. I sent them out of the room and set myself to soothing the troubled waters. We worked together without speech, anticipating each other, and before long, after I had complimented her upon her gravy, which was as smooth as silk, and ladled her best cherry preserves into an exquisitely fluted silver container, she was smiling, and suggested that I go along and make myself pretty for the guests.

By this time my face was flushed from the heat and my hair was curling in damp ringlets about my face. Knowing how anxious Silence was to make a good impression, I put on my best dark blue silk, with the white muslin cross collar, and a fresh white apron. The house keys dangled at my waist, as they always did upon these occasions, Silence having been once embarrassed by a guest who, misled by my accent and manners, had assumed I was one of the daughters of the house.

There was a burst of conversation as I entered the parlor, and Honor's laughter over the others. Thankfully, I thought, she is making an effort to please her mother. Marcus came forward to take my hand and draw me into the center of a group which parted to reveal Silence's cousin, whose eyes, alight with amusement, smiled directly into mine.

"Come and meet Mr. Murray, Emma," Honor called. "He has been making us laugh with stories of their voyage from New York."

I had never seen her in such looks as she was tonight, I thought from some detached corner of my mind. Vivid in primrose silk, with her black hair gathered up into a careless knot of dangling curls on top of her head, her dark beauty stripped the color from

Joanna's and Patience's pale cheeks, and I, of course, was no match for her. She wore no jewels, of course, but they were unnecessary: her brilliant eyes sparkled like gems.

"Emma, you are like a ghost. Is something wrong?" Marcus asked in a low voice.

"Stay by me, Marcus. Don't leave me," I whispered, clutching his arm and stepping forward to acknowledge the introduction. Edward Murray answered my curtsy with a slight bow.

"Miss Ashton," he repeated expressionlessly, and I saw his eyes indifferently note my hand clasping Marcus's. At that moment it seemed to me that he had changed hardly at all in seven years, which meant that he was still, somehow, very young. Yet I, knowing his age to be thirty-six, was aware of how much I myself had changed. He was still tall and broad-shouldered, with sandy hair and a powdering of freckles across his nose. He wore an air that somehow suggested salt breezes and the sea, which was not so surprising since he had been captain of his own ship from the age of nineteen. His eyes were a shallow, light blue, and they looked into mine with the guileless innocence I knew they were capable of assuming when he was least guileless. With an effort, I struggled to mask my emotions, and as I did so I noticed one obvious difference in him. At one time he had worn nothing but the drab, homespun clothing of a Puritan; now, although clad in sober black, his coat and breeches were rich and unmistakably well-tailored, his waistcoat was a masterpiece of finely embroidered satin, and a waterfall of delicate lace fell gracefully from his collar.

Judging by his blank face, I thought he did not remember me, or that the blankness was assumed to ward off familiarity on my part, or merely the result of boredom. Then I noticed the Eatons watching me with covert anxiety, and I stiffened my backbone and determined to behave with tolerable dignity so that he would have no cause to inflict a snub. Dropping my hand from Marcus's arm, I looked around coolly.

"Dinner is served."

Just an hour, or two at the most, until I have served coffee in the parlor, and I can escape, I promised myself desperately as I sat in my accustomed place, well below the big silver salt box in the center of the table. Obediah and Piper were included with me, by virtue of their special positions. Usher Tournais, the minister, and Dr. Dashwood and his lady had been asked out of courtesy to the house guests.

There was not much conversation between the three of us who were at the end of the table; at one point I dazedly realized that Obediah was suffering torments of jealousy as he watched Honor, and briefly, I felt a reluctant pity. I derived a small amusement from Usher, Silence's man of affairs, who as usual was dressed in dandified fashion. Tonight he was even more ridiculous when contrasted with the subtle good taste of Mr. Murray and Thomas. Usher had chosen to wear a pea-green coat of satin, with a waistcoat lavishly embroidered with pink and green fleur-de-lis, a concession to his French heritage. His knee breeches of lavender clashed glaringly with Patience's puce velvet beside him.

For the most part, however, my head whirled like a spinning top, and the candelabra's bright flames made my eyes ache. It had been seven years since I had seen Edward Murray, and I do not think I had thought of him a dozen times since. I had assumed that he was long ago married and lost to me forever. Now, I knew that the old hurt, crushed so ruthlessly once, had merely been waiting to spring up, reviving. Why did I feel so restless; why did I persist in remembering? At seventeen I was foolish, gauche; even now, I wondered anew at my ignorance. When did I begin to see myself as I really was, in contrast to the daughters of my father's friends, who could coax a favor so winningly, whereas for me there was only a frown or a punishment? Yet, too long I continued to persist in my daydreams, until I awakened to the fact that, at almost eighteen, nothing had changed, nor would, and I was destined to remain the spinster daughter of a father who barely tolerated me.

Obviously, strong measures were called for. My father could provide a dowry, if he cared to make the effort, so that I could be disposed of like so much merchandise. But he did nothing. Thomas, prodded by Joanna, and unknown to me, attempted to intercede on my behalf, only to be repelled with a powerful snub.

When my father finally aroused himself to do something about me, it was abruptly, without warning, and in the most humiliating manner possible. That afternoon I was in my special retreat, the back parlor, when he sent word that he was bringing a gentleman home for dinner and my presence was required at the table. It was our usual custom to dine separately; at times, as long as a week might pass without our seeing each other, and when we did, after such times, meet briefly, I would be struck anew by the distinct look of repugnance upon his face, as though he had forgotten for the time being what was thus unpleasantly recalled. Occasionally I acted as hostess for him, my ordeal a penance for us both, but then only when he found himself compelled to return a social engagement. I was not encouraged to add to the conversation and I wondered sometimes if his guests considered my stupidity a mental deficiency.

Now I sighed, put away my sewing, and went upstairs to dress myself in my best frock. With strangers I affected a certain mode of hairdress, pulling forward my ringlets to dangle on my forehead, thus hiding, to a degree, my pockmarks.

I remember that I wore a cool white muslin with yellow ruffles and ribbons and matching kid slippers, and I looked all of seventeen. When I entered the room and curtsied to Father's guest, Edward Murray, I glanced up to see upon his face a look of shock, before he returned a jerky bow. He was young and apparently, I thought, Father had not prepared him for my face: nevertheless, his obvious surprise showed a lack of good manners. As a result, I found myself freezing into self-consciousness.

Father usually permitted discreet candlelight, to spare not me but himself, but tonight he issued new orders: the dining room was to be well lighted and the table shortened. So, there we sat, a cozy threesome flooded in strong candlelight, and I never guessed the reason. I had already learned from their conversation that Father and Mr. Murray were business acquaintances, and as they talked I stole surreptitious looks at him.

He was handsome in a boyish, fresh way, and I thought him to be not much older than myself. He had a pair of innocent blue eyes, and a sprinkling of freckles across his tilted nose attested further to his youthfulness. He wore neither wig nor powder but his own light brown hair, pulled back and tied carelessly with a black string. His clothes were severe and extremely simple, of a style I recognized as worn by the Puritans, which was rather stark when compared to the overdressed fashions of the day. All in all, I wondered indifferently how my father could take him seriously in a matter of business, but considered that such a green young man would find himself ripe for the picking in the city, and should not whimper at the experience if he persisted in playing an adult game.

Gradually I became aware that my father was taking pains to include me in the conversation and I wondered idly at it, but had no intention of being drawn out of a conjurer's hat and made to talk merely when it suited his fancy to do so. Thankfully, I saw an end to the meal draw near, when I would be released for the remainder of the evening. However, when I arose with the customary "I'll leave you now, Father," he astounded me by adding, "We'll join you in your parlor after we have had our wine." I blinked, only partly aware that Mr. Murray was directing a look of amusement toward me.

By the time Father and his guest arrived I had worked myself into a state of nervous anxiety, wondering just what Father expected of me. Surprisingly, the thought of Edward Murray as a suitor never entered my head. Even when Father suggested that I entertain them with music, I was merely thankful to escape so lightly, since performing on the spinet was one thing I did well. With my back to them, I could lose myself in my music and I persevered diligently, until Father testily suggested that they had had enough and I might join the conversation now. But I sat in dumb silence for the short time that Mr. Murray lingered.

Father wasted no time in coming to the point.

"How did you like that gentleman?"

"He seems pleasant enough," I said cautiously, "but rather young for you to enjoy his company, surely, Father?"

Father chuckled. "And how old do you think he is? He is twenty-nine!"

"Twenty-nine?"

For some reason, Father seemed pleased by my surprise. "That boyish look has deceived many who have considered him a fool. Underneath it all, he has a very shrewd brain: he cultivated it and that yokel air, I believe, on the many sea voyages he has taken. At nineteen he was a captain, and has owned his own vessel at least these past five years."

I was impressed and said so, though not greatly interested until Father added genially, "I am glad you like him. I want to warn you that you may expect him back here tomorrow or the next day with a proposal of marriage. I have already given him permission to address you."

I stared at him, openmouthed, and he, being Father, depressed my pretensions immediately when he enlightened me.

"He needs money desperately right now. With the upsurge in shipping, the vessels cannot be built fast enough to keep up with the demand. He has heard of such a one for sale but does not have the money to pay the purchase price, although he has found the captain, and can get the crew. There is a cargo in Barbados, if the right man comes along to trade for it, but it requires two ships. He could float a loan, of course, but that takes more time than he is able to allow right now. I have put a high price on you, one that would give any man pause, particularly a man with a pressing need for money. I told him before he arrived tonight what to expect, so that you were no surprise to him, and I showed your deficiencies honestly. When you left us to our wine, I was prepared for a negative reaction. You could have been more than he could tolerate, but he surprised me by asking for permission to approach you." Which shows, his unspoken words said, what a man will do for money.

"Do you hate me so much, then, that you would sell me?"

"Don't sneer at money, Emma." He eyed me coldly. "Just be thankful that you are an heiress. How else would you get a husband? You might have an improvident old age to look forward to, but as it is you will be provided with someone who will continue to care for you after my death."

"Did you have anything to do with Mr. Murray's failure to get a loan?"

He laughed, his good humor restored.

"You have a sharp brain, Emma. Possibly I put a word or two out in the right quarters, but if he is going to survive in the business world he must be prepared for such contingencies. And with your face, I would have difficulty in finding you a husband who did not need your dowry badly. Therefore, I felt justified in engineering a situation to fit the circumstances, but I was careful to show you as you are. He can't later claim that he was tricked. He has promised to make no demands on you as a wife, a stipulation that I am sure he was glad to agree to. You will continue on in a role almost like the one you assume here, as daughter of the house. In return, upon my death you will receive my estate, which will make you a rich woman." Noticing the look on my face, he added sternly, "Spoil this for yourself if you like, Emma, but I warn you, if you do, I don't intend to worry my head with you any more."

I left the room without replying. I was not shocked by my father's cold manipulation of my life, but I was sickened. I had not expected him to interest himself in my future at all, but since he had, he would not fail to do so in as humiliating a manner as possible. By reducing everything to the level of money, by tearing away all of the small illusions that made such callous marriage bartering endurable, he had left me without pride or self-respect. I found myself thinking of Edward Murray with a cynicism worthy of my father. Well, why not? He could not be worse than Father, and the life he would offer might be slightly more bearable than the one I had now. At worst, I would only exchange one prison, one warden, for another.

Edward Murray was not received by a blushing girl when he called the next day, but by a cold, composed woman. When I saw that he was embarrassed I instantly felt more at ease. I met him in the cluttered little back parlor and wore my oldest dress, for, as Father had said, he should have no illusions about me. After a civil inquiry as to his health, I showed him a chair.

When he showed no signs of stating his business, I did it for him, baldly: "Have you had second thoughts about me, Mr. Murray?"

He was taken aback but did not pretend to misunderstand me. On the contrary, his mouth twitched as he answered blandly, "No, I was merely hunting for a tactful way to allow you an opportunity for those second thoughts yourself, Miss Ashton. Or perhaps I should say, an opportunity to freely express them. But there is no place for tact here, is there, so let us be frank. I was aware, last night, that you were ignorant of the reason for my presence at dinner. And you were not at all what I expected. Your father was so—uncompromising—in his portrayal of you that, although he told me your age, I was prepared for a much older woman, with an extremely plain countenance. Instead, I found that your age was apparently the only truth he told! And, rather than the aging harpy I was expecting, I found an extremely shy young girl who obviously had no idea of why I was there."

I appreciated the kindness whch prevented him from quoting exactly my father's words, but I did not mince my own. "I am seventeen, sir, and that is a fact. My father believes in facts. Other than that, I am sure he described exactly what he sees when he looks at me. If there is a fault in his description," I added bleakly, "it can perhaps be attributed to the fact that he looks as seldom as possible."

His eyes narrowed. "If that is the case, Miss Ashton, I begin to believe that you can do worse than marry me."

"Are you sure that it is worth it?"

"Worth it?"

"The money you will get when you marry me."

He smiled slightly. "You plead my case for me too well. Are you being forced to accept me?"

"Not precisely. I was given a free choice. But were you? My father's wickedness does not surprise me, but you are too young and inexperienced to be forced into this bargain—"

His smile widened. "How old do you think I am?"

"I know that you are twenty-nine, but you have been following the sea since you were a boy. You cannot have had much experience with men such as my father. He is accustomed to using his money to manipulate situations and people, ruthlessly."

He had been watching me steadily, but now he answered dryly, "You tell me nothing I do not already know, Miss Ashton. Your father considers himself a master of intrigue, but I have found his machinations childish these past days. When I grew tired of his evasiveness I obtained the loan he thought to deny me for a second ship. I came to your home last night in a spirit of revenge, intending to humble his arrogance by rejecting his offer. Also, I was curious. It had occurred to me that a man who would describe his only child as he did you might be something of a tyrant. Then, when I saw you, I abruptly changed my intention."

"I don't understand, Mr. Murray. You cannot wish to marry me merely to rescue me from my father?"

"I could almost believe that I did, Miss Ashton. I don't like him and I would enjoy crushing him. However, to set your mind at rest, I will admit that I will find your dowry of great benefit. One never has so much money that one cannot use more."

I burst out laughing and after a moment he joined me. "Then it is a bargain—Emma? May I tell the disagreeable gentleman that we have accepted his proposition?"

My father called him shrewd, a young man with a future in the financial world. Time proved my father correct; I soon learned, even in the little backwater that was my world, of the power he exerted through his shipping line, of his ships that slipped through the blockade time after time, when others to the north were landlocked by ice and those to the south stifled in their ports. This might have been due to his rare talent for choosing captains with a touch of piracy in their blood and a complete knowledge of the harbors and inlets from Salem to Charlestown, then turning them loose, with a sizable share of the profits as their prize, to play tag with the pursuing British, during their seasonal forays on American ships they suspected of trading with the enemy. He also had another talent, that of knowing the right blockading captain, who might be willing to become deaf as well as blind on any named foggy night.

Yes, he was shrewd and young and brash. And how quickly he brought me around without injury to my pride and allied us as fellow conspirators bent on circumventing a common villain.

Or did we? I often wonder if Father foresaw the final jest. The jest, of course, was inevitable, but did he entirely misread our characters? Did he anticipate wrongly that I would cling, Mr. Murray reject?

The betrothal had scarcely been announced before Father's suicide. In those confused days that followed, although he called to extend his sympathy, I hardly thought of him until I heard about the money.

"Does Mr. Murray know?" I asked Joanna at once.

"Yes, dear, he has known for several days. It is fortunate that your future is secure, Emma."

"What do you mean?"

"By your betrothal, child."

"But I thought you said the money was gone." I frowned in an effort to understand. "Doesn't that mean my dowry too?"

"The dowry? No, you won't have a dowry, Emma, but that hardly applies now. You have made a contract of marriage, and no gentleman would back out now while you are in trouble. That would immediately label him a scoundrel. Thomas has already spoken to him about it, and he has agreed to honor his pledge."

I cringed. "Thomas exceeds his authority," I said crisply. "I won't marry him now, under any circumstances. I must see to it at once. Given me a pen and paper, and I will write him, severing our engagement."

"But, Emma, you can't! What else can you do but marry?"

"I don't know. Scrub floors, perhaps? But I won't marry Edward Murray," I promised grimly.

Undoubtedly, Father foretold what would be the outcome when he left me penniless, abandoned. But did he, perhaps, knowing Father, hope for a reversal of the roles, with Edward spurning me, the supplicant? If so, in that small detail he misread my character as mistakenly as he had misread my mother's before me. The terminated betrothal was accomplished with dignity and pride on my part. I made no demands, and when he called, upon receipt of my letter, I was "out" to him.

But I had not expected him to be still unmarried, just as I had not known he was a cousin of Silence's. I comforted myself with the thought that his visit was to be of short duration and my duties would not bring me into his company often, if at all. Apparently he felt the same, for he made no attempt to seek me out as I hovered behind the coffee urn in the parlor after dinner.

As I watched him from afar, I was captured by Reverend Wilford, who seized this opportunity to push his suit. It did no good to embarrassedly plead with him to desist, for with bland arrogance he saw my present position as one I would gladly exchange instantly for marriage: my protestations he took for coyness or an indication only that his rival, the judge, had gained an ascendancy.

"I beg of you, Miss Ashton, think prayerfully upon it before you leap into wedlock with one so ill suited to yourself," he intoned pontifically. "As your spiritual adviser, I would be remiss if I didn't remind you of his past record—his four wives—"

"But an old man's darling, sir," I murmured wickedly.

"Surely, madam, you jest! I know you want to tease me to make me jealous, but I am sincere in thinking only of your welfare. You should heed my words." His voice rose slightly and the group surrounding Mr. Murray looked our way.

"Please, sir, you are making us conspicuous." I signaled Marcus desperately.

"So long as I have my distinguished parishioner's approval, I don't feel that I am committing a social error in remaining at your side."

"Wouldn't it be more to the point to have my approval, sir?"

"No, you are too young to know the right or wrong of it, Miss Ashton, and too unused to society's ways." Above the beaked nose, his gleaming eyes watched me avidly; a tongue touched the sensual lips, too full for the thin, cavernous face. "Your timidity, your withdrawal from society, your—innocence, if you will, is one of your most refreshing traits, as a matter of fact. Therefore, you must let yourself be guided by someone who is your superior in social usage."

"Then Mrs. Southwick was aware of your intention to renew your suit when she asked you here tonight?"

"She was," he replied.

I began to appreciate what I was up against. For the first time, I considered disgusting Reverend Wilford by flinging myself madly into a social whirl. It might almost be worth it, I thought whimsically.

Marcus strolled up, obedient to the appeal in my eyes.

"I was reading some of Cotton Mather's sermons the other night, sir," he began, "and I wonder if you can tell me—"

I made my escape. Courtesy required that I at least bid Joanna good night. She was standing with her husband and Mr. Murray, listening to Usher Tournais hold forth on one of his favorite subjects, the rough treatment accorded the legal profession by the press. With litigation increasing since the Revolution from returning Loyalists fighting in court to regain their property, many lawyers had been busily enriching their pockets by the collection of overripe fees, a practice that endeared them to no one.

As I listened to Usher's spirited defense of his profession, and waited politely for an opportunity to break in, I was struck for the first time by the similarity of our positions. Usher too had received a gentle upbringing: his accent and manners spoke of an environment of good breeding. The family funds had not extended to the luxury of college: he had received his legal training by the more direct route of reading with an older lawyer. Like me, he had fallen an easy, early victim to Silence's greed. I had watched his entrapment myself. From an occasional deed or mortgage, Silence had progressed to where, now, he was handling all of her business, had long ago given up all other clients in order to devote his time to her interests, and was, I felt sure, grossly underpaid for his work. In fact, as I listened to his bitter comments I was sure of it.

He was a neat-looking young man, rather swarthy in coloring and appearing slim and undersized in contrast to Mr. Murray's towering height and Thomas's bulk. He was spoken of as handsome, for his clothing was always colorful and his wig carefully curled, but the look of petulant discontent that marred his features destroyed the pleasant expression he should have worn.

"A lawyer who is forced to beg for a fair fee when he has saved his client many thousands of dollars is justified in his resentment," he burst out, then suddenly he was recalled to a sense of his whereabouts and looked hastily at Silence, whose attention, fortunately, was engaged with the doctor and his lady.

He turned to me in relief, seeing me as a distraction from his careless words. "Yes, Miss Ashton?"

"I merely wanted to say good night to Mrs. Eaton," I replied coolly.

During the next few days I spent as much time as possible with Joanna, permission having been granted by a gracious Silence. In fact, Silence was so filled with beneficence these days I was confident that, with her usual aptitude for attracting good fortune, she had attained her dearest wish, and Honor had indeed taken a great liking for her cousin Edward, just as her mother had hoped. I assumed from Silence's air of quiet satisfaction that an announcement might be expected shortly.

Shamelessly, I took advantage of the rare tranquility to spend extra time in the studio, and my portrait suffered while Marcus and I shared our hours with Joanna and Honor, who were with us more often than not these days. I was worried about Joanna, however. She chattered feverishly when we were alone together, and became skilled at avoiding personal conversation, in spite of my repeated requests to know what was troubling her. When possible, she arranged for us to be in the company of others. Sometimes, when my old twin imps of doubt and insecurity rode my back, I wondered if she was ashamed of my diminished station in life. If so, there was nothing in Thomas's attitude to warn me: he remained his usual comforting and dependable self.

Business took Thomas into the city often, as it did Edward Murray, who also spent much of his time about Silence's affairs in her office. At night, hidden behind the coffeepot, I was anonymous, ignored by the company whose gaiety was not impaired by Silence's doting restrictions.

This state of affairs lasted until Saturday evening, when Jacob and Mog appeared early at the kitchen door for their supper. Mr. Murray had hired a hack and driver that morning, Jacob told me, but the afternoon had been spent in the pottery, while he closely observed its operation.

"Missus' nevvy be a knowin' one, all right," Jacob commented. "Not much gets by him. He was down at me pottery this very afternoon, askin' questions of Mog and meself, inquirin' as to the operations of the same."

"He's a cousin," I corrected absently. "Why was he there?"

"Now, there, 'tis the strangest part of all, lass, and not one I'd be expectin', nor you neither, I'm thinkin', knowin' *that* one as you and me do." He jerked his head in the vague direction of the office. "The mister's on the brink of a partnership with that one," another jerk, "since he is bought into a pottery like ours in New York, and knows enough to recognize a growin' business when he sees it, he says. Hisself has in mind bringin' over a skilled artisan from England, if he can talk herself over to his way of thinkin'." Jacob's voice was rich with irony.

"Hm." It wasn't surprising news, knowing Silence's plans for Honor. "That must have infuriated Obediah?"

Jacob and Mog exchanged chuckles as they hunched over their plates. There was no love lost there. " 'Tis angry Obediah is, right enough, but he kept his mouth shut and a decent tongue in his head until the mister left. Said his quarrel was with the missus, not her nevvy. He plans to face her tonight, he says, and find out if the hand he holds is worth anything. 'Tis time now, he says, to find out if he has a winnin' card. Funny way to talk!"

"Not so funny," I said scornfully. "It's blackmail! I hope you two don't take him seriously."

"No, lass, Obediah is always one for talk, and spoilin' for a fight, as usual. Tonight is Saturday, and himself, here, and me are headed for a night at the tavern, and hopin' he'll not follow us."

Saturday night the potters went down to the docks to the grog shops that lined the wharves, and joined other boon companions on their rounds, their safety from the impressment gangs lying in their numbers. Tonight, apparently, the delightful memory of Obediah's discomfort would spur them on.

Usher entered the kitchen almost upon the heels of their departure. He seemed slightly embarrassed by my astonishment at finding him so far from his customary realm of Silence's office, but he quickly explained.

"Has Obediah been in here? Recently, that is?"

"No," I said wonderingly.

"That man's a fool," he said irritably. "You will know it all soon enough, so I may as well be the first one to tell you. There has just been a mighty argument between Mrs. Southwick and him. I left her prostrate, under Piper's tender care. It was no place for me, then. I was discussing business with her when he stormed in, without permission, and demanded that she deed him over half of the pottery immediately!"

"What happened?" I asked curiously.

"What one might expect would happen! She became furious and he followed that demand with a threat to go to the magistrate with certain information he had! You can imagine the result then! Her temper knew no bounds, nor did his!"

"What information?"

He glanced sharply at me. "He didn't make himself clear. I don't know what the young fool expected to gain, for as I had warned him earlier, Silence Southwick is not a woman to hold still for outright blackmail. He was so loud and abusive that he attracted the attention of the family, who were assembled in the parlor. He can't hope to return here now, for if she does not have him arrested, her cousin will! And Marcus Goddard is likely to knock him flat the first chance he gets, if no one else does it for him. I told the stupid idiot this would happen—I tried to talk patience to him, but—"

"You are his friend in court!" I cried.

Abruptly his talk ceased and his face shuttered of all expression. "What do you mean?" he asked cautiously.

"Obediah spoke of a friend—one who was advising him—"

Usher smiled slightly. "Oh, I see what you mean. Of course," he said carelessly, "I have tried to advise him to be careful in his dealings with Mrs. Southwick. He has had a small legitimate claim on her estate for years, and I have been prepared to advise her to settle it and rid herself once and for all of a minor nuisance. But the wilder threats, the nonsense he poured out a while ago, he can find himself hailed into court if he isn't careful!" He looked at me fixedly, as though to test my reaction to what he had said, then, as abruptly as he had entered, he quit my kitchen without another word.

Why haven't you given Obediah that good advice, my man, I thought severely. From what Obediah had said to me, I thought he had been flattered into thinking his claim had magnitude, and also had been encouraged to believe that his threats would bring Silence to her knees. You can't serve two masters, I told myself, but it looked as though Usher had tried to do just that. For the first time, I seriously wondered about Obediah's threats, since they had interested Usher, who had picked up his employer's wiliness, through propinquity to her.

He passed Mrs. Margate in the dining room; I heard him speak briefly and she hurried in a moment later, panting in her haste.

"Jane Piper wants some brandy and she's squawking like a gaggle of geese! Mrs. Southwick has taken a turn, so hurry, lass!"

"A turn" could have meant anything, and when I saw Jane

Piper bent over her mistress, agitatedly chafing her hands, I feared the worst. However, although Silence was pale, she did not seem to be in breathing difficulties, and I attempted to reassure Piper. Fortunately, she had had the presence of mind to empty the room, although I had seen from the grim, anxious faces outside the door that the quarrel had been overheard.

"If he has harmed her, I'll kill him myself," Piper moaned. "He brought her into a spasm—she almost had a heart attack! She said he nearly struck her once, that he raised his hand to her!"

"Ungrateful boy," Silence muttered, glaring at me.

"Keep still, Mrs. Southwick, and sip this brandy."

"I'll never allow him near you again, Miss Silence. He'll have to cross over my dead body first!"

"He's to be out by tomorrow, or I call the Watch!" Silence's color, as well as her usual irascible disposition, was returning rapidly.

"I'll ask Mr. Murray to come in now," I said tentatively.

"No, no, not necessary." She closed her eyes wearily. "He'll never be a son-in-law of mine," she rasped, and I knew that she had not meant Mr. Murray.

CHAPTER III

Katie McNab awakened us before daybreak with the news that the potters, drunk and disorderly, had been thrown into jail by the Watch.

"Was Obediah with them?" I asked, throwing on my clothes.

She smirked. "No, mum, they didn't say." Katie lived with her mother and sister in a shanty near the docks and seemed to be on intimate terms with the Watch. She was a sensual girl and that, as well as her behavior around the potters, made me suspect that her activities after work would not have been approved of by her employer. Surprisingly, Silence, who was usually acute in her pursuit of sin, did not sense what had always seemed obvious to me.

"Ask Marcus if he would see to bailing them out and apologize for embroiling him in my concerns on a Sunday morning."

Silence, in her nightcap, was sitting up in bed. She and Piper were both heavy-eyed, as though neither had slept well, and Piper was bent over the hearth, boiling their early morning medicinal drink of sassafras root.

Marcus was not in the dining room when I returned with the tray. Instead, Edward Murray sat alone at the table, dressed in somber Sunday best, while he awaited his breakfast and perused his newspaper. He arose at my entrance and pulled out a chair, but I waved him back.

"Sit down, sir, and I'll bring your breakfast. I am looking for Marcus—Mr. Goddard. Have you seen him yet this morning?"

"No, I haven't." He eyed me oddly. "Will I do, or do you have some particular reason for wanting the artist?"

I thought his words and voice sarcastic and answered him in the same tone. "It's hardly a job for you, sir. Mrs. Southwick asked me to see Marcus about bailing our potters out of jail. They were thrown in by the Watch last night for disturbing the peace."

"A frequent sin on their parts, I assume?"

"Yes."

"Well, no need to bother Mr. Goddard. I'll take care of it myself." He folded his paper as Mrs. Margate came in with his breakfast. "Any other problems, Miss Ashton?" he added, and I realized that I had been staring.

"No, sir, I apologize, but I was surprised. It is a rather—er—humble task for you, surely?"

"But not an unfamiliar one." His long brown fingers curled around the handle of his porringer. "I have bailed out many a drunken sailor, as any sea captain must when assembling his crew after leave in a foreign port. I believe I have a passing acquaintance with most of the jails in every seaport of Europe and the Americas, as well as China."

"Yes, sir."

I had been routed, and he, eyeing me with amusement, knew it. I had been prepared to be slightly arrogant with the Edward Murray whom I did not think would care to soil his hands by contact with the city jail, but instead found the tables turned by his calm acceptance of what Marcus had always considered a distasteful task.

As I was dressing for church I thought again of the scene between Obediah and his employer last night. Now, while he was in jail, would be the opportunity to search his room that I would not be granted again. My motives for so doing were mixed, but chief among them was a wish for a lever whereby I might protect Honor and, possibly, Joanna.

Mrs. Margate was still at Mass, but I had peeled the potatoes and left them to soak in cold water. I would have time, if I hurried. Tying my bonnet in a slapdash fashion and snatching up my Book of Prayer, I sped through the kitchen and toward the pottery.

The pottery wheels, lined in a row, seemed strangely silent in the large bare room that echoed the sound of my footsteps. A fine layer of clay dust covered the contents, which included a jumble of discarded broken crockery as well as the vats of smeary golden liquid and large crocks of shining clay. Occupying a sizable portion of the room was the kiln, an enormous brick beehive still warm to the touch from yesterday's firing. There were too many hiding places here for me to consider plundering among the crocks and churns. Obediah's lean-to room would be the only practical place for me to search.

Predictably, I found it occupied by Edward Murray, who, warned of my approach, calmly awaited me. He had discarded his coat and the sleeves of his shirt were rolled up, displaying muscular arms glinting with golden hairs.

"Ah, the redoubtable Miss Ashton. I should have expected you," he said ironically.

"Yes, sir. I had the notion to search Obediah's room, too," I replied tartly. "I was told about his threats last night and was curious to see if they meant anything."

"Yes, they were extremely interesting. His voice has a carrying quality, and although we could hear only part of what he said, the effect on cousin Silence was violent, I thought. I wanted to see if there was written evidence of this blackmail."

"Why?"

"I hardly know how to answer that, Miss Ashton. I might ask you the same thing. Why not? My cousin is old, sick, and—alone. And I don't like bullies."

"She may be all of those things," I agreed, "but she is the most capable person I know. Of the two of them, I would back Mrs. Southwick in any quarrel they might have. Obediah feels that half the pottery should be his, from his father, and so far she has kept him working for her without giving an inch."

"Yes, I heard all of it last night," he replied impatiently. "But that happened years ago. Why hasn't he seen a lawyer about it before now, if he has a legal claim? He has delayed too long."

I thought of Usher, who apparently had been his adviser. "He was—persuaded to wait. Mrs. Southwick is not above a little blackmail herself."

"Is that so?" He was shrugging into his coat now, which had been hanging on the back of the chair. "What do you mean?"

"She made no secret that she wanted Obediah as her son-in-law and would reward him afterward with half of the pottery."

"Then she is indeed a scheming old woman!" He flushed with anger. "How could she even think if yoking Honor to that stupid lout?"

I looked at him thoughtfully. "I am not speaking of Honor but of Patience."

"Oh. But why, then—ah, I see now. Obediah objected, of course?"

"As was his right," I said stiffly.

"Quite. And understandably so, Miss Ashton, so soothe those indignant feathers. You have a tender heart for that unpleasant young man."

I shook my head. "I don't even like him, but I too don't like bullies."

"Umm. Perhaps they were well matched after all. Come now, I left bail for the potters, and they will be rolling in shortly, so this is no place for you," he added briskly. "Obediah wasn't with them, but he will be returning anytime for his things." He put his hand out to take my arm.

I resisted. "But what did you find? You've been searching the room, haven't you?"

He grinned. "Some filthy clothing, and some French pictures—equally filthy. I am only trying to spare your blushes, but if you insist on seeing—?" He paused provocatively.

I backed off. "No, thank you. Is that all?"

"That is all. I promise you, I found no secret I am refusing to share with you, my coconspirator. There is probably nothing to be found. His secret, if it exists, is in his head, and, I am sure, of minor importance. If he continues with his threats, I intend to see him clapped in jail with an extortion charge, if cousin Silence does not."

"Do you not feel pity for him, then?"

"I think not. You are too soft-hearted, Miss Ashton. I did not know of my cousin's plans concerning Patience, but last night I heard that impudent blackguard demand Honor—Honor, mind you—as the price of his silence, and the words he used were quite brutal and explicit. It was all that I could do to keep Marcus Goddard from flinging Piper aside and storming the room, or, for that matter, myself. Obediah is an offensive young man, I think, and personally I am glad to see the last of him."

"Yes," I said reflectively, "he is single-minded about Honor. He calls it love, I am sure, and for him it passes for it. I am not in sympathy with his ambitions there, but I do feel he has some justice in his claim on the pottery."

"Don't let cousin Silence hear you say that. You may wrong her in thinking it," he added abruptly. "John Henry Pride had the opportunity to make the debt good, if Obediah's claim was a fair one, and he did not. Perhaps she is justified in feeling as she does. Now, may I have the pleasure of walking you to the carriage for church?"

"I walk to church, Mr. Murray. It isn't far. Mrs. Southwick hires only one carriage on Sunday morning, and that is filled with her family and guests. But she will expect you to join her."

He pushed me firmly ahead of him. "Indeed! One carriage. Too crowded for me, then. Since it is not far, I will walk with you."

But he changed his mind when he saw Marcus and Honor awaiting me, and after turning me over to them he disappeared.

The meetinghouse was a simple white structure with a turret and a shiny weathercock that glittered in the thin autumn sunshine. The weathercock, with admirable Puritan thoroughness, served a dual purpose, that of reminding the unwary of Peter's fall from grace as well as predicting the wind and weather. No cross and spire, symbols that smacked of Popery, would do for the staunch Massachusetts Bay faithful who worshipped within the plain interior with its hard-benched pews and austere pulpit.

A narrow, green lawn, enclosed by a picket fence, surrounded the meetinghouse, with a churchyard next door, which had only recently been abandoned in favor of the burying ground near the Common. However, for Silence there were strong ties to the churchyard, for it was here that her two husbands were buried, side by side, with a proper resting place between them for her.

She had chosen to await us alone at the door, and when we approached she called sharply, "Where is Edward?"

Honor replied vaguely but there was no time to talk further, for Silence's progress down the aisle on her canes was a tedious one, and she was panting heavily by the time we established her in the family pew.

Struck then by the damp chill that penetrated the church, I remembered with a sinking heart Joanna's susceptibility to colds. A stove would have done much to contribute to the comfort, but a stove was forbidden in this particular meetinghouse. Recently this quarrel had divided similar congregations throughout the state, for with the invention of Mr. Franklin's stove, some churches had adopted them; it was only in others, such as ours, that the members most resistant to change had prevailed. Silence had ranged herself, predictably, upon the side of the minister, against the stove, and the argument had been as long as it was foolish: foolish, that is, to those who, like me, saw nothing heretic in being comfortable while worshipping. In the end, however, the minister's group had carried the day: he had prevailed when he foretold fiercely of the hellfire which awaited those who felt they needed a fire in their meetinghouse, and the lesser souls among them had quailed before his forecast of doomsday. I was not allowed a vote: Silence, as head of the household, represented all of us. Once, timidly, I had asked why listening to the Word of God in comfort would alter one's concept of Him, only to be met with a chilling reproof that sealed my objections permanently. But then, Silence's God was a stranger to me, as was the tenet to which she adhered: that one must mortify the flesh in order to achieve purification of the spirit.

As for the minister, his dogmatic righteousness had been a shock to me, accustomed to a softer and less demanding faith. Young as he was, he was a part of that group of Congregationalist ministers who were called the New Divinity men, clerics who had undertaken to seek out wrongdoing and bring their flocks back to the faith and discipline of the earlier Puritans. The war had brought about a laxness among the young people, which they deplored, and there had been a certain amount of backsliding among the older members too, which they hunted down and denounced with relish from the pulpit each Sunday.

After three exhausting hours, it was a relief to leave the damp chilly church and go next door to the tavern, where we found a simple hot meal awaiting us and could thaw out before the fire.

Mulled cider was served as a matter of course; perhaps it was this that gave all of us the courage to leave the warm, genial atmosphere of the taproom and return to the meetinghouse for another three-hour sermon.

It was an unfailing routine, and one that Silence, who could ill afford the endurance it took, expected of her household and guests alike. But Joanna's white face reproached me, and I wondered how I could appeal to Thomas, who had said nothing about taking her home. It was left to Edward Murray to make the move. He was mingling with us in the taproom, although I suspected he had not been in the church, and now, with a neatness I had to appreciate, he cut the pair of us out of the crowd and hustled us into a waiting carriage.

"Don't let us keep you from the afternoon service, Mr. Murray," Joanna said timidly as he followed us into the carriage.

"No, Mr. Murray," I added maliciously, "you mustn't let us prevent you from attending."

He grimaced at me. "I could see that you were near fainting, Mrs. Eaton, and apparently your husband had not noticed."

"Thomas and I cannot afford to offend Mrs. Southwick just now," Joanna sighed.

"I see," he said thoughtfully. "I wasn't aware of that. But even he must have seen you couldn't go back into that cold church. I have grown away from my faith," he added, "and I had forgotten how cold those meetinghouses can be, even in such moderate weather as this. It seems to me that one of those new stoves wouldn't be amiss. It can't be from lack of money—the people sitting there today easily own half the city, so why must they sit and shiver?"

I told him the story of the stove controversy. "The minister felt that his congregation could better attend his sermon if they weren't lulled by creature comforts."

Mr. Murray shouted with laughter and even Joanna chuckled a little.

"I said that I had grown away from my faith, Miss Ashton," he said, sobering, "but that is incorrect. I mustn't give you the wrong impression. It is more that I have embraced a new faith. I have become a follower of the New Method man, John Wesley, and his brother Charles. You may have heard of Francis Asbury, and here in New England, of Jesse Lee. I had the divine experience of hearing Wesley speak in Bristol, where I too had my heart 'strangely warmed.' Even now I am astonished at the miracle that led me through those church doors. Since that time, I have found my Saviour anew through Methodism, and my salvation in a tenderer, gentler religion. I will have to confess that I attended church this morning after all, but you were right to be skeptical, for I have just returned from hearing Jesse Lee preach."

I stared at him in astonishment. What a man of contradictions he was! Convinced as I had been that he had deliberately avoided church through disinterest or slothfulness, I was made to feel ashamed of my prejudice.

"Does Mrs. Southwick know?" I asked weakly.

"No, I have carefully avoided telling her, and trust that you two will not either. It is a fault of the elderly to find it difficult to accept what is new. Perhaps I flatter myself to believe that she would be hurt, but I know she would not understand me and I would avoid giving her pain if I could."

No, he did not flatter himself, nor did he minimize her reaction to the news. He must surely be aware that it might be a violent refusal to entrust her daughter to a man who had embraced such a reactionary new faith.

"I would rather not quarrel with her just now, for she needs friends very badly." Yes, he saw the difficulty for himself, and had, apparently, decided upon evasive tactics. I wondered at his putting such a weapon into my hands, but he seemed unworried.

He was peering out the window, puzzled to see Jacob hovering in the doorway. "Is that one of our potters? I wonder what the trouble is?"

Jacob's relief when he saw Mr. Murray was pathetic. "It's Obediah, sir, he's dead," he stammered, and dragged Mr. Murray to one side to hold a low-voiced conversation.

He was grave-faced when he returned to us. "Jacob and his partner found Obediah's body in the kiln when they opened it this morning. Mog is with the body now. From what Jacob says, he may been killed and placed there by someone. At any rate, I am sending Jacob for the law, and I must go straight around to the pottery and stay there until the Watch comes. Will you let yourselves into the house?"

"What about Mrs. Southwick?"

"For the present, we won't interrupt them at church. They'll be home soon enough."

Katie McNab screamed and threw her apron over her head and Mrs. Margate had to be eased gently into a chair, when I told them the news, but I was thankful to see Joanna efficiently taking charge of the tea while I calmed the two women. Obediah meant nothing to her, and I was grateful for her coolness, for to have had her on my hands as well would have tried my capabilities to the limit.

The next few hours passed confusedly for me. Judge Dashwood, apparently because of his connection with the family, had been placed in charge of the investigation, and at one point he came into the kitchen to question us. I found myself reluctantly impressed, seeing in his present capable handling of his duties little trace of the lover who had been pursuing me these past weeks. But it was not until Silence returned from church that I learned what had happened. She had fainted upon hearing of Obediah's murder and was revived with burned feathers under her nose, after which she demanded a full account from Edward Murray.

"It was undoubtedly murder, cousin Silence. He was killed with a blow upon his head sometime last night. He was struck with a heavy piece of pottery, just as the Captain was, then dragged to the kiln, which was still hot from yesterday's fire, and flung inside, with the hope, I suppose, of either hiding the body or burning it beyond recognition." Seeing the looks upon our faces, he added hastily, "He was already dead and was not burned badly, or what would have been fatally, at all."

"The murderer must have been a strong man," Silence whispered.

"Strength—exceptional strength—would not have been required, although the murder must have been done by a man. It would have been beyond a woman's nature," he added kindly, and with a fine lack of knowledge, I thought ironically, of woman when propelled by her primitive nature.

Silence was showing a slight return of her spirit. "It must have been a tramp, Edward, just as it was the other time. I want to see the judge, to tell him."

"I don't think this murder can be dismissed that easily, cousin Silence," Mr. Murray said gently. "The judge doesn't intend to write it off as another tramp. The coincidence is too strong. He has already made a case, but I will let him tell you about it."

She received the judge from her bed. If he noticed the pallid cast to her face, he put it down to ill health. He was a short, comfortably stout man and usually wore his wig slightly askew. He and his brother, the doctor, were frequent guests in this house, and now, although he treated Silence deferentially, he was firm when he denied her suggestion that a stranger was responsible.

"I wish I could spare this house further distress, Mrs. Southwick, for inevitably this will bring the other sad business to everyone's mind. I wish, too, that it hadn't happened in the pottery, for that reason. But that is where the quarrel occurred. That is where the murder was done. Apparently, he was struck in the heat of the moment, and afterward, the thought of delaying discovery by putting the body in the kiln came to the murderer's mind."

"You talk as though you know who did it?" she asked.

He looked surprised. "Why, yes, ma'am, I thought you had been told. There is no mystery about it. We have already arrested your potter, Mog O'Shaughnessy!"

"Mog!"

"Yes, indeed. It will be a speedy trial, with as little publicity as possible, I can promise you that. But we can't stop people from talking, and I fear they will be bringing up the old murder."

"Yes, I realize that." The color was creeping back to Silence's face, and I could see how frightened she had been. "But what happened? Did Mog say why he killed him?"

"Mog isn't admitting anything just yet. But the facts are against him. He left Jacob to go on to the tavern alone last night, while he returned to his room for money for drink. He was gone for quite a while, returning pale and shaken, and told Jacob that he had fought with Obediah, who was in a mean mood earlier. Jacob admits that Mog drank throughout the evening as though the Devil himself were after him. We have plenty of witnesses to his state of mind, his resentment against Obediah. He'll break down and confess after twenty-four hours in jail, I have no doubt of that."

"I see." Silence was complacent now that the danger of questions about her own quarrel with Obediah had been averted. "What do you think of it all, Edward?"

He was standing at the mantel, frowning, and twirling a wine glass between his fingers. I knew he was thinking of the same thing and debating whether to speak of it to the judge. In the firelight, the cherubic look had been stripped from his face; his eyes were tired and shadowed. "I don't know either man well enough to hazard an opinion, cousin Silence. Jacob denies that Mog would have been foolish enough to kill Obediah. I myself would have expected him to show a clean pair of heels once it was done, rather than linger on here."

Judge Dashwood smiled condescendingly. "Ah, there, sir, you don't understand the mentality of this kind of brute, whom I come up against every day in my work. He was too frightened to run. All he could think of was getting his dram to bolster his nerve, and, being stupid, he drank too much and was thrown into jail until this morning, when it was too late to run."

"But he remained with the body this afternoon until I joined him."

"Yes, indeed. He thought he could bluster it through."

"It seems to me, Judge, that you can't have it both ways. It was the act of a cool man, or of a stupid, frightened man, but not both. I warn you," he added coldly, "if he's innocent, I'll not stand by and watch him sent to the gallows."

"No one doubts Mog's inherent good nature, Edward, nor the provocation that Obediah no doubt offered him," Silence said appeasingly, rightly interpreting his words to be aimed at her. "I intend to see that Usher does everything possible for him, and I will provide the money for legal counsel. But, if you please, Judge, let's have as quiet a trial as possible."

I saw Mr. Murray eyeing her wryly, but he said nothing more. The judge's mind was made up and Silence was eager to accept his version. The opportunity, the motive, and poor Mog himself were all there, available for the taking: it would require a man irrevocably committed to Mog's innocence to look elsewhere for a murderer.

With Obediah's brooding presence lifted and his murder so painlessly solved, the air of relief overcame the sober, funereal atmosphere and Silence's pious morning prayers for his soul. If Mr. Murray had doubts, he did not make them known, but went about the grave business of arranging for Obediah's burial without allowing his activities to intrude themselves upon the sensibilities of the household.

In fact, I seemed to be the only one to regret Obediah's passing, and that only due to the cost to my nerves, which grew raw from answering the door and fending off curious visitors. Even with the shop closed and the door knocker draped in black, they continued to call. By early afternoon I was glad to flee to Marcus and the comfort I found with him, but even here I was denied solace.

He had obviously put aside his work on my portrait to console Honor, whose bent back remained stubbornly toward me as he sent me away.

"Please leave me alone with her, Emma," he said urgently. "She has been upset by the curiosity seekers who have been calling all morning. She will be all right soon. Please." He escorted me firmly to the door.

I eyed him sadly. From the set of her shoulders, I could see that she had been crying, but she had endured no more than I had. I felt a twinge of jealousy to see how easily she commanded his sympathy, whereas for me there was no such freedom of appeal. I too longed for a shoulder to cry on, not from grief for Obediah but merely for comfort. Not even Joanna— Yesterday, during the judge's questioning, Joanna's attitude had been as one who twitches her skirts away from a sordid encounter, and she had been at pains to emphasize her casual relationship to her hostess and her household.

When I thought of her I wanted to weep. "Ah, Joanna, once you would have knocked over all obstacles in your rush to my side, but now—!"

Descending the stairs, I came upon Usher, who had just emerged from Silence's office and stood watching me speculatively. Since the night of the murder, when I learned that he was

Silence's man, body and soul, I had noticed him watching me covertly. Now, he looked as though he might speak, but did not: instead, giving me a slight bow, he clapped his hat upon his head and went out, through the shop.

Nevertheless, he had worn an unmistakable air of triumph, which was explained when Silence, that night, broke in with the festive announcement that Usher and Patience were betrothed. She was received with varying degrees of shock. Honor's wondering exclamation, "But, Mama, only yesterday she was engaged to Obediah!" signaled the attitude of all of us.

Silence's color rose angrily. "Honor! You overreach yourself! Your sister was *never* betrothed to Obediah! It was suggested at one time, but nothing came of it and her affections were never engaged! She is free, in God's eyes as well as man's, to make whatever commitment she and I so desire!"

Joanna was recalled to her good manners with a start, and rose and touched Patience's cheek briefly with hers, murmuring felicitations.

Of the three members of the small, mean little conspiracy, Patience was the only blameless one. She was unaware of any undercurrents of distaste, and smiled with simple happiness at the good wishes, while her mother and her future bridegroom wore identical looks of defiant guilt. How soon, I thought, Usher had moved in to consolidate his position, once Obediah was removed as a rival. Now I thought I saw a reason behind his method of discouraging Obediah from seeking legal counsel, while never questioning his ability to squeeze from Silence his "rights," and never, above all, doubting the goodwill of his friend, Usher Tournais. How long had this pot been boiling? Had Silence known of Usher's strategy, with this betrothal his reward, or had she been approached just today, and leaped at the opportunity to secure Patience's future?

It had been an exhausting day, and I excused myself early, driven to the kitchen and Mrs. Margate by the sight of the betrothed couple holding hands while Usher spoke fawningly of their future together.

"You look tired, dearie. 'Tis ready we'll both be for our sleep tonight, but Madam said today we must begin warmin' the beds—

she found the sheets cold. I'll do her room while you do the upstairs. Jacob will be wantin' to linger and talk with his flip tonight, but I'll give him short shift."

Thus it was that I found myself in Mr. Murray's bedchamber
for the first time since his arrival. It was neatly kept, the silver
brushes on the chest and a crumpled towel the only signs of occupancy. I knelt and built up the fire, then filled the warming pan
with coals.

Flinging up the feather puff which was topped by a stack of
quilts, I burrowed beneath to pass the warming pan back and
forth over the sheets, and wondered, as I did, if Mr. Murray was
as susceptible to the chill as Silence believed. I was submerged to
the waist between the feather bed below and the puff above when
I felt a light slap, administered familiarly as I bent over, and a
pair of strong hands grasped my waist and hauled me bodily out
from the bed to set me with a thump upon my feet.

"Be careful." He was laughing, his eyes on the dangling warming pan. "You'll drop your hot coals." He looked up and a deep
flush spread over his face. "Miss Ashton! I beg your pardon! I
didn't recognize you with that brown coverall thing on. I assumed
that it was one of the maids—that giggly one, perhaps."

"It is one of the maids, sir," I gasped, too discomposed to speak
rationally, "but not the giggly one. You are upstairs early."

"Yes, I was tired of the conversation—pious hypocrisy bores me.
What do you mean—one of the maids?"

"A figure of speech only. Good night, sir."

"Why are you doing this sort of work? Cousin Silence speaks of
you as her housekeeper."

"What is a housekeeper when there are no maids?" I backed
off. "Excuse me, sir."

"No, I won't excuse you. I order you to stay. What about those
two women whom I've seen about the place?"

"Mrs. Margate doesn't climb stairs because of her sore feet, and
Katie McNab leaves early." I didn't explain that wild horses
would not keep Katie McNab in this house after dark. "Pardon
me, Mr. Murray," I added, his determination beginning to alarm
me, "you are a guest. You can't possibly be interested in Mrs.
Southwick's domestic arrangements."

"But I am, and stop pulling away." He gripped my arm. "I intend to get to the bottom of this. Why are you, a gently bred young woman, working as a maid in this house? It isn't necessary. There is no lack of money here, my girl. It wasn't for this that you left the sheltered home you had been accustomed to. Have you always done this sort of work for her?"

"Then you do remember me?" I asked involuntarily.

Now it was his turn to look blank. "Remember you?" he repeated in astonishment; then with impatience, as he understood my question: "Remember you? Of course I remember you! Do you take me for a fool? Or possibly you thought, because I did not pay you an unusual amount of attention when I first arrived, that I had forgotten? Were you piqued then, because I did not call up the circumstances of our last meeting? Or the details of our betrothal?" He watched with narrowed eyes the flow of blood to my cheeks.

"Of course not!" I cried. "I merely assumed—"

"Not that I couldn't recall it easily if I wished to. As I remember, you owe me an explanation. I called at your home with the intention of demanding one, after receiving your letter, and was refused entrance by a servant. According to all the rules of etiquette I have read, the young lady at least accords the gentleman the honor of an explanation in person—"

"Mr. Murray, please. You are teasing me. I owe you no explanation, and our stations in life are too far apart now for there to be anything other than distant civility between us."

He looked startled. "Indeed! And what is your station, then?"

"My duties take me all over the house, Mr. Murray. I bake and clean and make fires—nothing very difficult, as you can see—and tend the shop— No," I corrected myself, with a confused notion that I should praise Honor in his hearing, "Honor now tends the shop since her return, and is very talented, too, incidentally—"

"Quit trying to be evasive," he snorted impatiently.

"Evasive?" I was genuinely bewildered by this time. "I don't understand you. I was minding my affairs when you pulled me—"

He laughed. "My affairs, surely. My bed, anyway. But I have explained why I did that. I should have known, though, that those ankles would not belong to the maid, but—"

"Then this familiarity would be excusable if it were the maid rather than the housekeeper?" I asked slyly.

Too late, I remembered his Puritan background. He frowned, but more in exasperation than offense. "You are right, of course. This conversation is absurd. I should speak to cousin Silence, not to you. But wait—first, tell me if there is anything to read in this house, beyond these long-winded religious tracts!" He flung the book he had been holding down upon the bed. It was a copy of Foxe's *Book of Martyrs*. "The piety that saturates the atmosphere is enough to choke a man and send him fleeing, to search out a fresh breeze!"

I suppressed a smile. "I have joined a social library which has recently begun here. It is similar to the one started in Philadelphia by Mr. Franklin. If you can wait until tomorrow, I will see if I can find you something to read that won't be quite so dull."

"What? Cousin Silence permits novels to be brought into the house?" He eyed me with a gleam of amusement.

"Your cousin does not supervise my reading so long as I do not contaminate Honor," I replied. "I cannot promise you a novel but I think I can find a volume of Shakespeare."

"I accept your offer, Miss Ashton, with thanks. Now, show me to my cousin's chamber."

I led the way downstairs, and left him rapping smartly upon her door. After reviewing our conversation, I was nettled by it. What had possessed the man, I thought uneasily, to question my duties? Was he possibly going to Silence about my work, and turn our smooth household arrangements awry? And for what reason? Apparently he had been given a free hand to look into whatever he liked, as witnessed by his inquiries Saturday at the pottery, and having already precipitated a full-blown crisis there, which had climaxed in a murder, he now was turning his attention to the house and my domain. In the kitchen, I found Mrs. Margate already in bed.

"Jacob just left, sweetheart," she quavered. "He asked that you approach one of the gentlemen here on Mog's behalf. He doesn't believe Mog is guilty, and he doesn't trust that Mr. Tournais to do his best for him."

I nodded dumbly, too sore and unsure of myself to venture an opinion.

"Tonight reminds me of the unsettled way things were when I came to work here," she went on. "Mrs. Southwick had gotten rid of the potters and every servant in the house, except for Obediah and Piper. She said they were all gossipin' about the murder, so she brought a new lot in, and I was the cook. She was in pain, and had not yet learned to use her chair very well, and little Honor lay upstairs with a broken arm, with only Piper to nurse the two of them and look after Miss Patience, who was fair beside herself, worryin' about her mother."

"I didn't know that Honor's arm was broken at that time."

"No, she wouldn't have told you," she agreed. "She forgot it herself and most of what happened durin' that bad time. Just wiped it from her memory, the doctor said. I felt sorry for her, poor little mite, her bein' so quiet and still and givin' no trouble to anyone. Piper was tendin' to the mistress and Miss Patience, fair worked up about them, she was, and payin' no attention to the little one. There was a cloud of darkness over this house, lass, for it was a month before I had more than a glimpse of the mistress, her buryin' herself in her work as she did. I didn't know at first that she was hidin' her grief; I thought her a cold, unfeelin' woman, but Piper told me she'd been madly in love with the captain."

"Really? If that's true, then why does she hate Honor?"

"Aye. 'Twould seem that way, but she doesn't hate Honor so much as she favors the weak one. Like any mother. And Honor suffers for it. The mistress is strong; she expects likewise of Honor."

"Perhaps. Mrs. Margate, did Obediah resent the captain?" I asked, a glimmering theory in my brain.

"No. Not he! He liked him, as well as such as that Obediah could like anyone. He told me, he did, that when the captain died, he lost a good friend. Wanted her to sell the pottery, the captain did, settle up with Obediah, and move to Tremount Street, where Honor could have room to run and play. If he'd lived, 'twould've been done, too, for she'd already agreed to give up her business and do as he said."

"It's hard to imagine her submitting to another's will."

"Aye. It just shows you. Love can make fools of us all."

And Mrs. Margate, to whom the late Mr. Margate was merely a dim memory conveniently called forth upon suitable occasions, closed her eyes and dismissed it all from her mind.

CHAPTER IV

The result of Mr. Murray's interference was to put Silence into a rage. The following morning when I carried her breakfast tray to her room, I felt the backlash immediately.

"Has Katie McNab arrived yet?" she snapped.

"She just came in. Do you want her?" I trembled for poor Katie.

"Not I! But I will see her if you feel yourself overworked," she added sarcastically. "She must be persuaded to remain overnight so as to relieve you after dinner from further chores."

I sat down abruptly and eyed her puzzledly. She had waved aside her breakfast tray, usually an eagerly awaited event, as of no importance, and now, with Piper's aid, she was attempting to heave herself out of bed. Her grizzled hair, streaked with powder and topped with corkscrew paper curlers, trembled with the effort. Piper sent me a look of burning reproach while I, in an attempt to apply reason to Silence's demand, counted the bedchambers, all of which were already swallowed by the extra guests. Even Marcus was sleeping in the attic on a cot. Also, I knew the hopelessness of trying to persuade Katie to remain overnight in a house she firmly believed to be haunted.

When I pointed this out to her, Silence agreed grimly. "I suggest you see about a cot in the kitchen. I understand the difficulties perfectly, even if you didn't when you whined to my cousin last night!"

"What do you mean?" I stammered.

"You took your grievances to him instead of coming to me with them," she said flatly. "He has demanded that I set matters right. Obviously, you are unaware," she added with a snort of irritable impatience with my stupidity, "that he wrote me after your father's death, asking me to find some employment for you in this house, preferably as a companion. I could not have old Piper supplanted, and I could not afford the wages of an indolent society miss, and so I wrote him. However, I owed him every courtesy, and I answered his letter in as gentle a manner as possible. That is when he suggested that I take you on to train you, so that you might become useful to yourself and others. He offered to pay your wages and expenses himself, and suggested that I submit the bill to his bank. That is what I have done each year, until it has become so commonplace that I forgot about it, and assumed he had, too. When you showed no particular reaction to his name, I believed that his acquaintance was with your father, and he felt a duty to him. But Edward has now chosen to remind me of my obligation to him, and to suggest that if I do not care to make new arrangements, I release you at once, at a time when I can ill afford to do so!"

Evidently finding my dazed stare unnerving, she said sharply, "Why do you look like that, Emma? You may object to the unpalatable truth, but I can't see that an agreement between my cousin and myself is any of your business. If so, don't voice your objections to me! I won't be criticized!"

"I am thinking, Mrs. Southwick, that I don't know you. Nor anyone. I have been proud of the success I have made of my work and of my rise in wages, but now I find it has all been a sham," I added in a stifled voice.

"A sham! Nonsense! You worked for every cent you got."

I rose and smoothed down the skirt of my snuff-brown housedress with trembling hands. Worked for every cent I got! Yes, and more, I thought fiercely.

"But not for him, ma'am." I faced her proudly, returning glare for glare. "It is not pleasant to find myself an object of charity after all these years of pride in my ability. I don't like the feeling, I think. I will be returning home with the Eatons when they leave." I wondered wistfully if Marcus would follow me. "Joanna needs me," I added.

Her eyes flashed, and momentarily I quailed before that dangerous sparkle. When she spoke, her voice was icy with fury barely held in check. "So you intend to trail back to New York, following Edward Murray now that you know he has taken a personal interest in you? I thought better of you than that! Shame, you wicked little baggage, to try to supplant Honor!"

I was struck dumb by her unfounded charge. That, and the hot, airless room, stale with the odor of sour bedding and the two old women's pungent medicinal potions, threatened to overcome me, and I found myself at the door, fighting to reach the knob. Silence's sharp command stayed my hand.

"Wait! I haven't said you may go!" she snapped. "You may intend no harm to Honor," she conceded in a milder tone. "If so, you can prove your good faith by remaining here instead of scuttling back to New York, where you might inadvertently cause trouble between Honor and her new husband. I can use you here with Patience, for her marriage will not solve the need for a strong woman to remain with her, and Piper grows old, as do I." She smiled as though, having quenched my small revolt, she could afford graciousness.

I hovered near the door, silent, while my mind rejected the words she was saying. Remain here, in a house that would be a prison without Honor and Marcus? Never! I wanted to shriek my refusal at her. Earlier, I had thought myself strong, and proof against any attack Silence might muster, but I saw now that I was no match for her in fighting form, as evidenced by the way she had sensed immediately where to lodge her venomous charge. Unfounded though it might be, it yet contained grains of possibility. Would it appear thus to Honor? Surely not! It was merely that Silence was quick, in her jealousy, to perceive Mr. Murray's interest in me, although she could have no idea of the cause, our onetime betrothal. Yet, I thought, would Honor, learning of it, as she must eventually, attribute my return to New York to the same motive?

"Stay on here," Silence went on swiftly, "at my expense. If you cannot suit Patience, or if she seems jealous of you, then I myself will find you another position. I don't wish to offend Edward, so make what temporary arrangements you can with Katie McNab, and help me with Honor until she is wed. Remember, too, if you leave this house, you leave Marcus Goddard!" I heard with horror that she was aware of the feelings I had thought so carefully hidden. "Spend as much time as you like with him. I will commission him to do another portrait of you after he finishes with this one. And I'll put in a pleasing word about you whenever possible." She smiled wolfishly. "What do you say to that, Emma?"

I said nothing. My sick silence she took for assent.

"Then it's settled! Good! And, Emma, don't let Edward know I mentioned our little arrangement to you. He would be angry."

"I certainly don't intend to bring up the subject, ma'am," I said faintly. "I would find it too humiliating."

"That is wise. Avoid him if you can. He is persistent and, strangely, feels responsible for you. You could, possibly, damage Honor's chances."

"How?" I quavered.

"Oh, some men are very susceptible to pity, so much so that they lose all sense of proportion." She looked me over appraisingly. "Oh, you would do it unknowingly, I grant you that."

"I am glad you said unknowingly, ma'am." My lip trembled.

"I know I tend to be cruelly frank, Emma, but I give you credit for preferring frankness to that muddled sort of sentimental nonsense Joanna Eaton deals in. I think you know yourself that your face inspires pity, and I don't think you would want to sleep with pity in your marriage bed. Now, go along and talk to Katie, and we will speak no further of this, now that we understand each other."

She looked tired, as though she had narrowly averted a disaster, and I knew she had no idea of the effect her shattering words had on me, nor would she have cared if she had known.

I had always sensed that someday, under the guise of mother love, she would tighten the lines of filial duty that bound Honor to her. After years of neglect, her sudden access of sensibility toward her daughter came too late to ring true of anything but overweening ambition. Silence had always possessed an uncanny sensitivity to the vulnerability of others: thus, her quick, vicious attack on my loyalty to Honor, her telling blow at my timid love for Marcus. I found her motives confusing, and hidden within the hurt she had inflicted, although I easily recognized her panic at my suggestion of leaving. She had never spared my feelings in the past, and I was frightened to think that with her heavy hand she might destroy the fragile thread of my relationship with Honor and Marcus. Thankfully, she was not armed with an additional weapon, knowledge of my previous betrothal to Edward Murray: therefore, armored by our mutual lack of interest in each other, I could meet with tolerable composure her charges there, so long as Honor did not heed them.

By this time I had wandered into the parlor, which bore a slightly intoxicated air from last night's revelry, with the chairs pulled out of place and sticky coffee cups about on the tables. Ineffectually, I began stacking them, when one of the subjects of my immediate difficulties strolled through and paused to leisurely check his watch by the clock. I pressed back into the shadows, but his sharp eyes caught my movement and he peered in.

"Taking your ease, eh?" he asked coolly.

"No, Mr. Murray, recovering! From the effects of your interference last night. I have been accused of exciting your pity purposely, with the result that you have made impossible demands upon your cousin. By meddling you have made my position even more difficult, so that I cannot do my work if you insist on supervising it."

He was not disturbed. "Nonsense! I don't see wherein I caused you any difficulty, Miss Ashton. I merely suggested that you be relieved of some of your duties by keeping a servant in the house overnight."

"And where would she sleep, sir? There are no extra rooms."

His lips twitched. "Must I plan it all for you, Miss Ashton?" he asked wearily. "Surely you can manage the details yourself? A half hour's thought to it, a little practical management, and the problem is solved! I wonder at you! If you are this incompetent, perhaps I should transfer that pity you scorn to cousin Silence."

I glared. I knew that he was deliberately provoking me. Making a strong effort at self-control, I frigidly invited him into the kitchen to himself talk to Katie McNab.

Katie proved my point by refusing steadfastly to sleep overnight, even when Mr. Murray, of whom she was obviously in awe, added his powers of persuasion to mine. I watched with amusement as, with a rare stubbornness I had not known she possessed, she sat at the kitchen table and resisted all his efforts to change her mind. Her blunt face was set, and her reddened hands twisted in her lap, as her "naicklace," a tenpenny nail she wore on a string around her neck, rose and fell with her quickened breathing.

Mr. Murray was extremely gentle with her, a side of his nature never before shown to me. "Is it because of the murder, Katie? If so, it's absurd to be afraid now. The murderer has been caught."

"There's murders an' there's murders, soir."

"Could you mean—Captain Southwick's? But that was long ago, and you weren't even here then. How could you be frightened of what happened almost ten years ago?"

" 'Tis more to it than that, soir. Miss Emma knows what I mean. She knows what's to be feared in this house!"

He glanced up quickly at my blank face. "Could she possibly mean the ghost theory?" I asked. "Katie, do you believe in that nonsense? If so, you are mistaken to think that I agree with you."

She dropped her eyes. "There's some things best not talked about."

"Aye, and there's some fools who don't know when to stop, either!" Mrs. Margate added sternly. "And 'tis you, Katie McNab, who's one of them. 'Tis better off without you, we are, if you're goin' to hint and scare decent folk who are doin' just fine as they is!"

Katie burst into tears.

"Now, now, Mrs. Margate," Mr. Murray said soothingly. "Katie has a right to her own opinion. You two need her badly, so don't scold her."

So, by blatant flattery and promises I was not sure Mrs. Southwick would keep, he persuaded Katie to stay on until her work was finished each night, when Jacob would walk home with her. Softened by his deference, Katie then disclosed that she had slightly more than mere superstition to strengthen her fear. Reluctantly, she told of how, as she was leaving Saturday night, in passing the darkened pottery shed she had overhead the Devil talking with Obediah's voice, but in such an icy whisper as to be almost unrecognizable. The voice had threatened and spoken of punishment and public disgrace, all the while in the darkened room. As she hovered near the gate, transfixed by the malignancy of the threats, she heard a crash within the shed, followed by a *whoosh* and a sound of beating wings overhead, which sent her scrambling out into the street. To suggestions that she might have heard a bat or an owl, she remained unconvinced, and implicit in her unspoken words was her belief that she had heard the Devil flying away after a conversation with the already dead Obediah. To queries about the hour, she could only generalize: it was late and dark and she did not know, and would not guess, the time. To suggestions that she should tell her story to the judge, Katie turned stubborn and frantically refused to say a word.

I mentioned my doubts about her story to Mr. Murray when we were alone.

"Of course she was telling the truth, as she knew it," he said impatiently, "but so long as she believes it was a witch or a devil, or anything supernatural her credulous little brain can conjure up, she will refuse to tell her story officially. But what can you expect, when one who is superior to her caters to her foolishness?"

"Are you referring to me?" I asked indignantly.

He snorted. "Don't tell me you are innocent of pandering to her when you wear that ridiculous bracelet?"

I looked at him wonderingly, then at my little iron bracelet, which had become so familiar as to be almost invisible to me. "Joanna gave it to me years ago, but I didn't know it had a supernatural meaning."

"Is it possible? Surely, sometime, someone has mentioned to you the significance of your bracelet, Miss Ashton? It is iron. A metal that in the Middle Ages was considered strong enough to protect the wearer from evil spirits and demons. And still thought so by the superstitious, particularly in that part of Europe Katie hails from. Have you never noticed her necklace, or Mrs. Margate's horseshoe over the kitchen door?"

"Good-luck charms," I said feebly.

"Exactly. With a special meaning. If you don't wish to be considered the same as Katie, Miss Ashton, get rid of your bracelet!"

"But why did Joanna give it to me?"

"Because Joanna is credulous too. A natural result of having lived in Salem, I suppose. Witches—this country's witches, that is —were invented there! Apparently she was frightened for you, and concerned about where she was sending you. A woman who is

popularly believed to have been a witch committed suicide in one
of the upstairs bedchambers, and the house has been avoided as
haunted ever since. I should have thought by now the old stories
would have died, but as it is, with one unsolved murder, and
another pending, to its credit, it will be impossible to quiet the
gossip."

Joanna did not deny it when I taxed her with his charge after
breakfast.

"I wore it for protection when I was a child and I gave it to you
for the same reason. I am sorry if you resent it, Emma, but it was
the only way I knew to protect you," she added, shivering.

"I think you should leave this house," I said gently. "I can see
that you are terrified."

"I am, I am," she cried. "I know that Thomas is worried about
me, and I can see in your eyes that you are too. But we can't
afford to leave, and offend Mrs. Southwick. We are under obligation to her."

"What hold does she have over you, Joanna?"

She answered me evasively. "Business affairs of my father's. He
—owed money to Mrs. Southwick, and she is pressing us. I know
of only one person who might be able to influence her, Emma,
and that is Mr. Murray. Could you ask him to help us?"

"Mr. Murray would not do it merely because I asked him," I
said slowly, convinced now of what I had suspected this morning:
Joanna had known the reason for my inexplicable offer of work in
Silence's house. "I would have more influence with Mrs. Southwick myself."

She hesitated, then reluctantly said, "Please do whatever you
can, Emma. We're desperate. Legally she cannot harm us, but if
she persists in ruining my father's good name, it will kill my
mother and disgrace me."

I thought her fear of public censure excessive, but I said nothing more. She had been pacing the garden paths when I found
her, as though driven from the house by her fears. The morning
was clear, with a hazy sun that promised warmer temperatures by
noon, but now the ground was hard and struck cold to the feet,
and Joanna, with her usual disregard for practicalities, had come
out shod only in thin slippers. She smiled wanly when I pointed

this out to her, and I was pleased to see my gentle scolding bring color to her pale cheeks.

The reproachful words, the accusation of duplicity, that I had been saving for her died on my lips. Wryly, I understood why Thomas wore a driven look: the task of bringing order from the muddle Joanna's father had left, as well as dealing with her fanciful fears and starts, could not be an easy one. How long had she been like this? I wondered. Gone was the strong, supportive Joanna of my childhood, if indeed she had ever existed. For the first time, I surveyed her with the wisdom of adult eyes.

I was glad to escape to the kitchen, where the week's bread, set aside to rise, was ready for the baking. A fire had been burning in the Dutch oven since the night before: it was dying now, and the bricks were glowing hot. I swathed myself in an enormous apron and began to knead dough, hoping that the familiar task would work its usual magic and still the strange, disquieting thoughts I was having about Joanna, and even Honor, as I felt them both slipping away from me, leaving me alone and bereft.

"None of that flimsy bakery stuff," Mrs. Margate was saying, the same words she used every baking day. "My bread has some chew in it, and plenty of stayin' power."

She clanged open the oven door and, balancing her loaves on a long-handled paddle, set them inside. As I watched I thought of the kiln door clanging shut on Obediah, and the kitchen whirled in bright, shifting patterns as the waves of heat from the open oven hit my face.

"Mrs. Margate—"

"Put your head down between your knees." I was in a chair, my floury hands hanging down. "'Tis takin' all the troubles of others on your shoulders that's done this to you, lass, and I've been expectin' it to happen." She seemed to be talking above my head to someone.

I looked up and saw Edward Murray. His face was stern.

"What is the matter? Are you sick?" he snapped.

So many questions, and so angry, I thought dully. Mrs. Margate pressed me comfortingly to her broad bosom.

"You should be in bed. Where is your bedchamber?"

"Here." I began to distractedly brush flour from my hands. Bed in midmorning, indeed! I could imagine the state in which his dinner would reach the table, if Mrs. Margate, whose nerves were not of the best, anyway, had to work around an open bed, with me lying ill in it.

"Here?" He was bewildered. "Do you mean in the kitchen?"

"Why not? Over there—the wall bed. Mrs. Margate and I sleep together and keep our clothes in a little room off the buttery."

"That little room?" he said dazedly. "But it is unheated and has a dirt floor, I remember."

"Yes."

His face assumed a controlled look. "Obviously," he said tightly, "it will not help you to be put to bed in here. I think it will do more good for you to get away for a while. I was looking for you, to go on an errand with me, and I think you need the outing. Be ready in fifteen minutes. I have rented a curricle, and the weather is not cold if you dress warmly. See to it that she does," he added to Mrs. Margate.

It was not cold at all beneath the luxurious fur rug which he tucked around me. And I found that I did indeed need an outing, for my senses responded immediately, with leaping pulses, to the crisp, cold air, the delight in the high-stepping pair of spirited horses, and the heady exhilaration of a holiday away from the house.

He did not say anything as he guided the fresh, restive team through the crowded streets, for a strong hand was needed to calm their nerves as they shied at a flying scrap of butcher paper and the unexpected noise of the muffin man's bell. I wisely held my tongue while he concentrated on avoiding scraping wheels with the conveyances we passed.

Our way led us down Anne Street, which took a gentle curve toward Dock Square. We passed the cupolaed Faneuil Hall, with its bookshops and market stalls displaying the latest London trinkets. It was opening hour; the shopkeepers were unshuttering their windows as we went by. Already the housewives had dumped their morning's refuse into the gutters, where squealing pigs and scavenging dogs fled beneath the passing wheels to reach scraps of food.

We rounded the curve beyond the State House, where the

street widened and became more fitting to the scene of a famous shrine of liberty.

"Where are we going?" I asked as soon as the turn into Tremount Street had been successfully negotiated. By now we had pulled free of the heaviest traffic.

"Cambridge," he answered absently. "I have an errand there."

"Cambridge!" I repeated in awe. I had lived in Boston for seven years, within a stone's throw of that little town that housed Harvard University, yet I had never had an opportunity to visit it. Now, in just such a casual manner, on a casual errand, wearing my old brown calico and my second-best bonnet, I was to see it for the first time!

Under the deep-piled furs, I wriggled and shivered with excitement.

"Are you cold?" he asked quickly, noticing the shiver.

"Cold? Oh no!"

But he had his mind on other things, and he spoke of them abruptly. "I have been wondering what your life has been like, working for my cousin. I don't think it could have been very pleasant?"

I smiled slightly. That conscience of his Silence had spoken of! But his concern was no longer necessary, in view of the fact that most of the difficulties I had experienced seven years ago no longer existed. And I had no intention of being an object of pity to Mr. Murray any longer, so I answered him with asperity.

"Please don't worry about me, Mr. Murray! It has been a better life than I might have had in some situations I applied for, and no worse, I promise you, than it was with my father! Mrs. Southwick has a difficult disposition, I will admit, but I have grown to understand her. And, too, I am in the company of liberal-thinking people—"

"Liberal-thinking!" He sounded almost amused. "Cousin Silence?"

"Well, no, I was thinking particularly of Marcus Goddard."

"I see. You take a great interest in that young man, don't you?" He glanced at me.

"Yes. He is my friend," I said simply, not knowing how to dissemble. "He is painting my portrait," I added.

He scowled.

"I know you think the idea is absurd," I faltered.

"Why should I think it absurd, Miss Ashton?"

I was silent, unable to make the obvious answer.

"It is not, at all. As an artist, he would naturally want to paint you. I can see that for myself, and I am not artistic. And if he is in love with you, he would have another reason for wanting to paint you."

"He hasn't said he is in love with me," I said in a small voice.

"He will, I am sure. He is merely waiting for the right time. I would like to see that portrait," he added reflectively.

I said nothing, unsure of myself and shaken by his putting into words what I had never dared to even tell myself. If such an analytical observer as Edward Murray could think that Marcus loved me, could he possibly be mistaken? I asked myself. I could not trust my own instincts, but I wanted badly to trust his. I threw him a sudden look of such delighted pleasure that he blinked.

"Are you cold?" he asked again.

I shook my head, laughing joyously. Cold, when he had just given me such a gift? "I am too happy to be cold! This is too much fun!"

"Fun?" He smiled. "You haven't had much fun in your young life, have you? When was the last time you rode in a curricle?"

"The last time? I have never ridden in one!"

"Then I am very glad that I had this idea."

We were proceeding at a faster pace now, the traffic confined to an occasional carriage or horseman. Our way lay along the Charles River, a broad expanse of water separating the tadpole-shaped land that made up Boston from the town of Cambridge. Out here in the countryside, I noticed that autumn would soon be gone. Those trees that had not already given up their leaves of scarlet and gold glowed with color. A row of pumpkins, forgotten and left waiting to be stacked away for the winter, made a brilliant splash of orange against a stone wall. Juniper bushes, friend of the housewife and candlestick maker, grew in thick clusters along the roadside, their purple berries gleaming waxily.

My companion was unusually quiet and I respected his silence. We were in Cambridge before I asked him about his errand.

"I am on my way to a small shop behind the college. It occurred to me that having a lady accompany me during the coming interview might allay this gentleman's suspicions, at least long enough to get me in the door! I hope I haven't guessed wrong and brought you into trouble. I believe he would be too cautious for that. I am not afraid of a fight, but I don't want to involve you in one."

"Dear me. It sounds mysterious."

"Not so mysterious. The gentleman conducts an unsavory little business dealing in stolen and pawned goods, mostly pawned. The students frequently run into money difficulties when their quarterly allowances from home fail to catch up with their gambling debts. But I am seeing him on a matter of uncut diamonds, which he purchased from someone who surely stole them from cousin Silence."

"Good heavens! Then you have succeeded in tracking down the diamonds, and they were stolen, as she said they were? Is the man a criminal?"

"You didn't believe it, did you?" He grinned at me. "Cousin Silence told me you did not, and indignant she was about it, too! Yes, he deals with criminals, although he undoubtedly calls himself a businessman. He would not be found lurking in a dark alley, himself, with a truncheon on the ready to stun his victim, but he would readily buy the jewelry taken by the thief! That is his trade —the buying and selling of stolen articles."

"When did you find out about him?"

"When cousin Silence wrote me about the diamonds, asking my help, I in turn wrote to an inquiry agency here in Boston. I had occasion to use their services once before, and asked them to make discreet inquiries for me. They are not an official agency, as the Watch is, and whatever they discover will not be disclosed unless we wish it to be. The information was ready for me when I arrived, and Saturday I interviewed a man who had been employed to find a sea captain without too many scruples, who would transport some diamonds to Paris: we think—hope—the Southwick diamonds. The inquiry man and I, between us—um—persuaded him that his best and safest course lay in being frank, so he gave us the name of his employer. I received a note from the inquiry man early this morning that his shop was now open, and I could talk to him if I came on right away. He said he would be lurking outside somewhere, in case of trouble, but you and I will go in alone at first."

To my surprise, the shop was in a respectable section of town, although the street was small and narrow and crowded with little shops, their doors open for business. As Mr. Murray helped me from the curricle, he directed my attention to a poorly dressed individual lingering nearby, repairing the wheels of a pushcart. Tossing a coin to a boy to watch the horses, Mr. Murray led me inside.

I thought the shop empty until I noticed a furtive little man hovering in the back, peering at us cautiously through the gloom as we paused to admire some oriental jewelry displayed in a showcase.

"Are you Blott?" Mr. Murray asked casually as we drifted slowly in his direction.

"Who wants to know?" the man said uneasily.

"Captain Murray of the good ship *Salem Lady*, docked in the Boston harbor."

Mr. Blott relaxed. "Oh. You don't look like a sea captain to me."

"I assure you that I am. When I come ashore for a leave, I like to dress like a gentleman and get the smell of tar and brine out of my nostrils."

He had not introduced me, and after a first leering look my way, then a second, closer look, Mr. Blott apparently decided that I was not the captain's fancy woman after all, but a respectable lady who perhaps might be his wife.

"Might I have a private conversation with you?" Mr. Murray asked.

Blott glanced swiftly at me, and Mr. Murray said easily, "Oh, don't let my wife's presence bother you. She'll not talk, I promise you, for she has felt the back of my hand often enough to know she'd better keep quiet when I say so." He squeezed my elbow and I dropped my head with an air of spurious dejection. "I was told that you were looking for a courier to transport some rough diamonds to Paris."

"I told that fool to be careful how he talked!" Blott burst out exasperatedly. "Did he mention the cargo to you?"

"I got it out of him," Mr. Murray replied meaningfully. "I don't like to start off in a deal of this sort without knowing the full deck of cards from the beginning. If that's the way you do business, then cut me out. Diamonds, yes, I'll take on, but not opium nor slaves. I have my principles, you know," he added righteously. "So be honest with me and you will have a partner you can deal with, but cross me just once and it's the end for us!"

Blott beamed. "You're a man after my heart, and I can appreciate your feelings on the matter. It is diamonds, as he told you, and bought under the counter from a member of the family who owned them, so there will be no outcry nor questions raised, it being an inside job, in a manner of speaking! I have connections with a gem cutter in Paris who can find a market for the stones afterward, and I think we can work out a fair three-way cut, with more business for you in the future, laddie, if you do this job right for me now."

"Let me see the merchandise first, then I'll tell you if it is worth the risk."

Mr. Blott snickered. "Oh, it will be worth it, right enough!" He carefully drew out from under the counter a chamois bag. I recognized it instantly, even if I did not the dozen large, irregularly shaped stones he rolled onto the counter.

"Well, well," Mr. Murray hissed, then gave my curls a painful tweak which yanked my face around to his. "Take a look, Emma, my girl, and tell me if you think you'd like a necklace made of a set of baubles like that!"

I met his laughing eyes. "They look very ordinary," I said primly, "much like another set of baubles I saw once. I consider the chamois bag they came in far more interesting, sir."

"Then that answers my question." Mr. Murray leaned across the counter and, with lightning speed, gripped Mr. Blott's black string tie, tightening it around his fingers until the little man was choking helplessly. With the other hand, he imprisoned both bony wrists in a paralyzing grip.

"Emma, suppose you step outside and tell the gentleman who is repairing the broken cart to come inside. And you, *my laddie*," he added, with a world of meaning in his voice, "are going to talk. To me."

By the time the agency man and I returned, the little man had already begun to blubberingly talk. The diamonds had been swept up and disposed of in Edward's pocket, and Edward was listening coolly, although he still retained a bruising grip on Blott's collar.

It only took a few sentences, stammered out in a trembling voice, to tell us who had sold the jewels to the dealer in stolen gems. Honor. He described even her red bonnet with the curling feather.

"You are in luck, my man." Edward released the tie and absently flexed his fingers. "I know your little thief. It will be up to the family to prosecute her, if they wish. But I can't understand how she summoned the nerve to do this alone. She is a brazen little housemaid, but I would have thought she would have a man along on such an errand."

Mr. Blott was crestfallen to learn that the thief, whom he had thought a lady, was merely a housemaid, but he added hopefully, "There was a man. He waited there in the doorway while I transacted the business with the woman. I can't describe him too well, for the shop was dark and the light behind him. He wore his collar up and his hat pulled down. I am used to that kind, who want to remain anonymous, and I would have almost thought he was disapproving, but he spoke once, while I was questioning the little baggage." His voice was vicious. "He said, 'Don't harass the lady! Either you do business with her as she wants or you won't have the opportunity to buy at all!' Well, under those circumstances, what choice did I have but to buy the diamonds?"

"I hope you weren't fool enough to pay much for them?" Edward asked carelessly.

"Only five hundred dollars, sir. That's why I thought her a member of the family, she accepted so little and seemed so new at this sort of thing."

"And the man didn't demand more?"

"No. I said he acted disapproving. He turned away while I paid her, and seemed to not want to have anything to do with the sale."

I was listening to this conversation with my heart in my throat, fearful of what it was revealing. I had guessed instantly the identity of her companion as soon as I learned that Honor was the thief. I only hoped, for the sake of Honor's future life with Edward Murray, that I could keep him from guessing the truth. Honor, of course, had continued to meet her Marblehead lover. I knew now how it had been done. There were many opportunities, for Honor worked alone in the shop for hours at a time. I remembered how eagerly she had assumed that duty, as well as other signs that should have pointed the way clearly to me: Honor weeping in her room for a month, then the resignation which gradually grew into cheerfulness. I had assumed that her new adaptability meant that she was reconciled: instead, it had meant that she had found a way to meet her lover.

It did not speak well for him that he had allowed her to pawn the diamonds, although I was cheered slightly to know that he had been disapproving. And no one knew better than I that Honor, with a determination every bit as powerful as her mother's, was impossible to control when set upon a course of action.

However, the past was unimportant. The future, Honor's future, was at stake. I could not doubt her affection and liking for her cousin Edward, and he had shown, by his concern, his interest in her. For the sake of a possible betrothal between them, I must keep him from guessing the truth.

"You're a thoroughgoing rogue," Edward was saying to Blott, "but I won't make you suffer for an error in judgment. Here is your five hundred dollars and another five dollars for that string of beads in the window my lady admired."

"Oh, no!"

"Why not?" he challenged me. "Why shouldn't the family owning the jewels be grateful for getting them returned, and give you a present for helping them in the enterprise? Wear them or not, as you please, but they'll go nicely with that blue silk of yours."

I took the beads without another word, too astonished by his reference to my best silk to protest further.

Outside, Edward and the inquiry man shook hands. "Although I did nothing . . ." the man said wistfully.

"But you were there, and I couldn't be sure he didn't have a strong-armed bouncer in the back room."

"You'd be a good man to have beside one in a fight. Have you ever done any, sir?"

"Fighting? Plenty! In every seaport around the world, I reckon, and without any polite rules governing the way it was done, either."

The inquiry man shook his head, gazing disbelievingly at Edward, whose face had regained its innocent smile.

I was silent as he tucked me into the curricle, until, giving me a sidelong look, he finally said wryly, "I meant no disrespect by my gift of the beads, Emma. I'll take back the paltry things if the gift distresses you."

I was startled, my thoughts a long way from the beads I still held loosely clasped in my hands. In my confusion, I did not notice his use of my Christian name, nor that I had begun to think of him by his.

"What? Oh, no, I wasn't thinking of the beads. That is—I should have been thinking of them, for it was certainly not necessary, nor expected, that you give them to me, even from the family. But they are very pretty, and I have never had a piece of jewelry, and—" I stopped abruptly, realizing that I had become hopelessly tangled in words.

He laughed, his face clearing. "If you weren't thinking of the beads, what then?"

"Of Honor."

"Oh, yes." He sobered. "We must decide what to do there. She should be protected from her mother's wrath, for her actions were those of a thoughtless child. But the man—what of him?"

I looked at him cautiously, no nearer yet to an explanation that I could plausibly give him. Wisely, I kept silent.

"I am aware that she was sent home in disgrace because of forming an unsuitable friendship with some man," he said impatiently, as though guessing my thoughts. "The question is, Was this he?"

"Oh. I didn't know Mrs. Southwick had told you about it."

"She didn't. Honor did."

"Honor!"

"Yes." He smiled. "She told me the whole story when she warned me that she had no intention of accepting my offer of marriage! She had become fond of me, she said, and she wanted to spare me the pain of having my offer rejected because her heart was already promised. Since I had no idea that I was expected to make her an offer, I was naturally interested in everything she had to say, and listened very closely. When I learned of the plan cousin Silence had afoot, it opened my eyes to many of the hints I had not understood before," he added ruefully. "However, Honor seemed relieved to learn that neither of us was bound by what her mother wanted. I have become fond of your little friend, Emma, but I am puzzled that you did not know anything about this. I thought you were in her confidence. Didn't she tell you about our conversation?" he said thoughtfully.

"No, she didn't," I said reluctantly, remembering Honor weeping to Marcus. I was also having difficulty in readjusting some of my ideas about Edward. Until now, I had not seen this second betrothal for what it was—largely a wish born in Silence's fertile imagination, for I had assumed that he would fall into her plan eagerly.

He too was having second thoughts, for he spoke deliberately. "I don't like keeping this business today a secret from her mother. Honor is under age, and there is, after all, a man involved, whom we know nothing about. But for the moral issue of the ownership of the diamonds, I would speak out at once. Honor is on a dangerous course; she is under the influence of a man who, apparently, has no principles, and she is badly in need of strong guidance and control. Until today," he added slowly, "I would have said I needed to look no further than you for that guidance, but after what I have learned, I see how little you can be trusted to provide it. It seems this love affair has been running full tilt for months, directly under your nose, and as Honor's chaperon you have shown yourself just as careless as the susceptible minister's wife in Marblehead. It throws a neat little problem into my lap. What must I do about it? How long can I keep quiet, in all conscience, knowing what I do?"

My face was flaming. I was stunned by his attack and could not reply immediately as I struggled for composure to meet his words.

They had been coolly delivered and I could not deny the good sense behind them. I was Honor's chaperon; Silence herself, years before, had told me that I must be responsible for Honor while she bent her efforts toward caring for Patience, and nothing had changed since that long-ago day. Yet, I had been careless of my charge; I had allowed her to get into trouble, even to the point of committing a criminal act. Yes, I, and no one else, was accountable for what had happened.

"I have always looked after Honor to the best of my ability," I said defensively.

"My dear girl, I am not arguing with that," he replied with a cool, weary logic that shamed me further. "I know how you feel about her. I merely question that your best ability is good enough. It is obvious that you are now out of your depth. My cousin, who is old and sick, has always depended upon you, and at one time her trust was within the range of your capabilities, but I don't think that is any longer the case. It is not unexpected: you are hardly more than a child yourself, and your knowledge of girls of Honor's type, as well as the tricks this man might resort to, is limited by your own inexperience. Added to which, you are apparently wrapped up in your own love affair. You mean well, but some new arrangement should and must be made."

His words, effectively reducing me to the character of a lovesick, undependable little fool, were devastating, but it was the last sentence that frightened me out of myself.

"Please!" It was a cry from my heart. I could see Honor torn from my arms and sent to another school, another strict disciplinarian. "Wait! Before you say anything to her mother, let me help. Tell me what I can do. I will do anything you ask!"

"I don't know that you—or I—can do anything," he said thoughtfully. "It seems that Honor herself has withdrawn from you. She has found herself someone else to fill the role of confidant and mentor. It may be too late already."

"Marcus might be able to help," I stammered.

"Goddard?" he asked quickly. "Does he enjoy her trust?"

"Sometimes I think he might have more influence with her than I have," I explained. "It is possible that she has told him something."

"I see," he said in an odd voice, but when I looked at him quickly his face was blank. We were in the city traffic now and his concentration was needed for the horses. He said nothing until just before we reached the house on Hanover Street. "You asked what you could do to help. For the time being, do nothing, and I will say nothing to my cousin. If Honor comes to you for advice, then try to persuade her to confide in you. I believe we will gain more ground if we find out the identity of her friend, and approach him first. In the meantime, you have a portrait to be painted, and only a few hours of daylight left. I suggest you get on with it, before the artist indulges in a fit of temperament," he added ironically.

CHAPTER V

Marcus greeted me with absent-minded impatience, his mind already on my portrait. Having been warned to say nothing about Honor, I hesitated to confide in him, although I longed to unburden some of the guilt and worry I felt. His concentration discouraged me, however, as he worked furiously at the canvas, until the fading light forced him to throw down his brushes with a sigh.

"There! If I don't have another sitting, it is not important. I have succeeded in capturing the look I wanted." He looked up, startled. "Hallo!"

My moment was lost; I stared, disconcerted, as Edward Murray strolled casually into the room. He ignored me and glanced around curiously, then walked over to the easel to stand behind Marcus, who, oftentimes temperamental with onlookers, said nothing. Edward gazed at the canvas with a face suddenly grown expressionless, then raised his eyes to me, and back again.

"Amazing."

Marcus shrugged and began to clean his brushes.

"Where did you learn to paint like that?"

"London," he replied laconically.

"My cousin tells me the portraits downstairs are your work also. They are excellent, but this is better, I think. Yes?"

"Yes. It has surprised me too. I had no idea it would go so well when I began."

"Why are you not out in your own studio then, taking commissions? I can't understand why you waste your time here, when you can paint like that." Edward sounded almost angry. "You're no itinerant artist grateful for crumbs. Why, man, you're the equal of the great Peale himself! Hang up your shingle. You'll be swamped with orders!"

Marcus eyed him warily. "As a matter of fact, I intend to make a move soon to my own studio. I have—personal reasons for remaining."

"I see." Edward nodded, and I believed that he suspected that I was the personal reason. "But I don't understand why that would prevent you from accepting commissions."

"I don't think you do see," Marcus replied. "I haven't been able to paint since learning of my brother's death. I came home as soon as I heard—" Haltingly, he tried to explain the apathy that had prevented him from serious work.

Edward listened politely, but I, who had begun to understand the emotions that dwelled behind his mask of bland innocence, saw that he was skeptical of Marcus's motives. As I listened, I too was struck by a false note in his story. He spoke of being unable to paint, yet he had painted steadily since living here. For the first time, I questioned the reason for Marcus burying himself in this house and hiding such an obvious talent. Surely the guilt he claimed was somewhat excessive? But when Edward probed too closely, Marcus, with all the obstinacy of a gentle man, retreated and refused to reply any longer to his questions.

"And you never learned why he wrote to you?"

"No," curtly.

"You should go back to your painting, you know, and try to forget it. You know that for yourself. I am sure he would have wanted that. Is it for sale?" he added abruptly.

Marcus was startled. "This portrait? To you?"

"Yes. What had you planned to do with it?"

"I don't know. I would like to exhibit it to important people."

"I can arrange for that if I buy it."

"Why do you want it?" Marcus asked curiously.

"I know an investment when I see one. Name your price. I'll pay it."

"No!" I leaped up and ran over to the easel. "Why must you sell it, Marcus?"

"Emma," he said pleadingly. "It is the best thing I have ever done. Mr. Murray is correct about that. Would you want me to lose an opportunity to sell it for a great deal of money and have it exhibited in Mr. Murray's home, where it will be seen by many important people?"

"Yes," I replied mutinously, "I do."

"But what did you expect me to do with it, Emma?"

Keep it because you can't bear to give it up, I said in my heart, or give it to me. But I was silent.

"Are you prepared to buy it?" Edward asked dryly. "Have you even seen it? Come around here, then, and look. See if you can ask him not to allow it to be exhibited."

It was not finished, for the background, my hands, and the fabric of my dress were yet to be painted, but, as he said, he had already captured me and reproduced on the canvas what he saw. Large, haunting eyes and a tender mouth were illuminated from overhead by soft light, leaving the rest of the face in dim shadows. And I, gazing with startled recognition, knew that I was beautiful.

Blinking, dazzled by the inconsistency, I turned, half frightened, to Marcus. "I don't understand," I faltered.

"I painted what I saw, Emma. I told you I would."

"Yes," Edward said smoothly. "The technique is superb. I have never seen it better done."

"It is the best thing I have ever done," Marcus repeated humbly.

"Those downstairs are fine," Edward added idly.

Marcus nodded. "Good, craftsmanlike work, but this is the best. It must be displayed."

I wanted to strike both of them as they calmly discussed the disposal of my heart, for now I recognized what had frightened me about the portrait. Marcus had indeed painted what he saw, which was my love. Each sitting had found me blinded with it, brimming full of it, as I gazed my fill upon his face. The look he had been seeking had been that, nothing more: I realized the truth, even as I saw for myself that he did not. Apart from Marcus's insensitivity, however, I burned with resentment to know that Edward Murray was perfectly conscious of the revelation of the portrait.

I deliberately arranged to be the one who carried the hot water to his room that night. He was in shirtsleeves when he opened the

door to my knock, and when he looked amused to see me I knew
that my arrival was not unexpected.

I had been forced to leave the two of them discussing the sale
of the portrait, one as oblivious to my feelings as the other was
blandly aware of them, as well as my seething rage and the struggle I was having to subdue it.

Now he greeted me politely and reached for the hot water, but
I slid past him into the room.

"Why did you buy my portrait?"

He sighed. "You insist upon a confrontation, don't you? Very
well—I wanted to see if he would sell it to me."

"Then I was right," I said scornfully. "That talk of an investment was a coverup and you are trying to prove something!"

He gazed over my head. "I think I had better shut the door," he
said evenly. "You may not want this conversation overheard. I
know that you are smarting because I bought your portrait, and if
I were a sensitive man, I might take it as a personal affront. But I
really have nothing to do with it, have I? You would be just as
angry if—say, Thomas Eaton bought it. It is because Goddard
sold the portrait, isn't it? It tells you something about him, something you don't want to admit to yourself. I apologize for having
told you today that he was in love with you. Don't place your
faith in that artist, my dear," he added gently, "because he will
always put you second to his work."

"I think I know Marcus better than you," I said steadily. "He is
sensitive, gentle, and kind. You had no right to tempt him as you
did today."

He shrugged. "I wonder why you resent so much my having the
portrait. You cannot have expected to keep it? It seems to me that
you should be the last one to have it. Even the person who pays
your wages has a better claim, surely?"

His eyes, looking straight into mine, were sardonic, daring me
to open that discussion with him.

"When are you going home?" I demanded furiously, too angry
to heed my words.

His eyes narrowed. "Why do you ask?"

"You have found the diamonds and that is what you came here

for, isn't it? So, unless you lied to Honor, and intend to marry her after all, you should leave!"

"I believe that is none of your business," he said gently. "I think you have been given so much freedom in this household, your sense of power has gone to your head. Your unbridled prying has become chronic, Miss Ashton, and I cannot allow you the same liberty to interfere into my business as you seem to have acquired with my cousin. Offhand, I would say that you must try to cultivate a sense of restraint where I am concerned. When I decide that I need your advice, you will be the first to know, I assure you."

My face reddened. It was an effective snub. My tongue chastened, I slammed the hot-water can down and flounced out of the room. I was burningly aware that I had deserved the rebuke, but that did not lessen my anger nor my sense of ill usage over the portrait. However, I had been rude to a guest in my employer's home, and although I did not entertain even the fleeting possibility that he would complain of my behavior, he would have been within his rights to do so.

I knew that what was between us would be fought out between us, without resorting to the unworthy tactic of bringing another party into our duel. Such a move would be beneath my opponent. That there was an unresolved issue between us I did not doubt: it was present in our sparring attitudes whenever we met, propelling us into instant battle. It had begun the day I terminated our betrothal; there were things that needed to be said before the door could be finally and irrevocably closed by either of us. Edward, in arranging to put me in his debt by placing me with his cousin and paying my wages, had kept the lines of communication open, in spite of having allowed seven years to elapse before seeing me again. I had no doubt that the battle would be decided, one way or another, before we parted again, just as I knew, with that uncanny knowledge one has of one's adversary, that the purchase of the portrait had been a deliberate move on his part to flush out a reaction from me. I wondered uncomfortably if, by my angry response, I had played into his hands.

Edward Murray was not present at dinner that night, and I squirmed uneasily to think I had driven him away. However,

Silence did not comment on his absence, and since her mood was an expansive one I assumed that his reason had been satisfactory. It was at the end of the evening, which I had spent at the spinet, idly playing, that he strolled in, elegant in court breeches and a satin waistcoat. To Honor's gay question, he explained that he had been dining with the governor, but had managed to excuse himself on the grounds of pressing business, when he saw the governor's wife and daughter preparing to make it a musical evening with a harp duet.

"He saw me to the front door himself," he added, "and I think was seeking an excuse to depart with me. Which reminds me, I believe these are yours, Honor." He leaned over and dropped the bag of diamonds into her lap. "They are intact, but I advise you to hold on to them for a while. I had them appraised for you, and the jeweler tells me they are worth a fortune, and one of them, the largest stone, is particularly valuable. But only if they are cut properly, mind, and there is no one in this country worthy of laying a hand on them. He advises that you take them to France and have a skilled cutter do it for you. If you would like, when you are older I will advance you the funds myself for you to do just that."

Honor was clutching the bag, and now she raised wide, frightened eyes to him. Apparently she was reassured by what she read in his face, for her eyes filled as she whispered, "Thank you, cousin Edward."

"The diamonds are mine, Edward," Silence said imperatively. "I think you know that. Give them to me."

"It does not seem a just division, cousin Silence," he replied coolly, "for you to deed all of Pride's estate to Patience, and divide Southwick's, which has suddenly become the more valuable."

I knew Silence's fury when her orders were questioned, but she kept her temper. "I have changed my will," she said sharply. "Just this afternoon! Usher has persuaded me of precisely the same thing—that I should divide all of my property evenly between my two daughters. And that is what I have done. Share and share alike. You can see now why the diamonds are mine, not Honor's."

"That is a coincidence," Edward said reflectively. "In less than a week after I learn the whereabouts of the diamonds, you are persuaded to change your will. You seem to have impeccable sources of information, Mr. Tournais, but why the haste?"

"No haste," Usher replied with smooth unctuousness, "and it has nothing to do with the diamonds. Mrs. Southwick's will provided for Obediah, and since his death it is out of date. Heretofore, her estate has been divided, giving Patience the larger share."

"Usher, as Patience's husband, lost by my doing so. Of course, at the time we did not know the diamonds had been found. I thought his decision was an unselfish one," Silence added defiantly, "and worthy of my dear child's future husband." She smiled at him. "So, only half of the diamonds belong to you, Honor."

With an angry sob, Honor flung them at her and flew out of the room and up the stairs. The interlude that followed was full of embarrassment for some, but for Silence and Edward it was obviously stimulating. The Eatons, who had been listening round-eyed, rose hurriedly to their feet and asked to be excused. Usher himself took advantage of their going to bid his employer a hasty, deferential good night, as he made a clearly relieved retreat.

"Mama, is Honor angry with us?" Patience asked with a puzzled frown.

"Yes, I think she is," Edward replied crisply.

A smile curved Patience's lips. "Then I shall go upstairs to bed," she said with satisfaction. "Good night, Mama."

Marcus and I eyed each other and decided simultaneously to leave the field of the coming battle. Neither antagonist needed my help; they were evenly matched and fully armored against any harsh words that might be flung by the other. I had already been too severely rebuked to remain when it was plain that the atmosphere was sizzling with speech barely held in check.

I was preparing to rise when the screams began, wild, hysterical, meaningless, one following the other with equal intensity. We were all brought to our feet and I was slightly behind Marcus and Edward as we three plunged upstairs. Honor was standing in her doorway, white-faced, as the screams continued to come with throbbing regularity from Patience's room. I reached her first, and dealt with her as I had seen her mother and Piper do, by slapping her face repeatedly until sanity returned to her eyes and the screams trailed off into a series of hiccuping sobs. Her body was trembling as she clung to me.

"Look at her clothes!"

Her wardrobe door was standing half open and her dresses had been taken out and flung onto the bed. But there was more than that. They had been systematically turned inside out and tied into knots. The muslins, the silks, the pretty new velvet walking suit, all had been reversed and savagely knotted, the arms, the necks, the hems of the skirts, and in some cases, where knotting was impossible to secure, the laces or ribbons had been ripped off and used to tie the garment. Her bureau drawers had been left open, too, to tell their story of destruction. The gloves, each finger tightly knotted; the stockings, the white silk as well as the wool ones; the pretty corset cover, tied as tightly as though a vindictive hand had vented its wrath on the garments in place of the wearer. No attempt had been made to destroy, save that destruction accomplished by the savagery of the knots. I saw the same look of stupefaction on the faces of the others that I knew mine must be wearing.

"It was you! You did it!" Patience launched herself upon Honor in a frenzied effort to claw both her face and clothes, and it took the combined efforts of Edward, Marcus, and Thomas to pull her free before she ripped the flesh with tigerish fingernails. This time, Edward dealt with her as I had, slapping her until she collapsed, sobbing, a rope of foam trailing from her open mouth.

"Get Honor out of here," he said briefly to Marcus, as he wiped his hands distastefully with a linen handkerchief. "What do you usually do with her after these bouts of hysteria?" he asked me.

"Give her laudanum and put her to bed. Piper will know," I added distractedly. "What is this all about? Who would want to destroy the poor girl's clothes?"

Joanna tittered "Dear me." She leaned forward to finger the dresses lying on the bed, but a low feral snarl from Patience jerked her back.

"What is the meaning of this? Why was Patience screaming?" Silence stood in the doorway, leaning heavily on Piper. Her mouth was blue and she was breathing heavily. It was the first time in more than a year that she had been upstairs.

She lowered herself into a chair and looked at the pile of clothing on the bed with an expressionless face. "Piper, take Patience down to my room and put her to bed. Drug her. You know what to do. But don't leave her until she is heavily asleep, for she can't be allowed back upstairs and at Honor. Edward, Emma—stay with me. I believe we can excuse you others." They filed out silently. "We must get to work and get these things untied."

When we were alone we worked swiftly, without words, the only sounds Silence's heavy, panting breaths. I saw Edward watching her anxiously, but he said nothing. She was working over the contents of the bureau drawer, which had been poured into her lap, while we attacked the garments on the bed. Halfway through, she gave way to the strain with a sharp cry and swayed as though she was about to faint.

"No!" She held me back. "Give me—a moment. Let me recover myself, then I think I will go to bed. I am not strong, after all."

"No, ma'am, I don't think you are," I said compassionately. "You can't manage those stairs again, however."

"I'll carry her down," Edward said. "Or perhaps you would want to sleep in here, cousin Silence?"

"No!" The revulsion in her face and voice startled us both. She smiled wanly and added, quietly, "No, Edward, dear. Thank you. But I will sleep with Honor tonight. Call Honor, Emma."

"Have these clothes been ruined?" he asked me later, after she had been led off by Honor.

"No, most can be ironed smooth. But that's what I can't understand," I said wonderingly. "What was the point? Why the knots?"

"If you don't understand the significance of the knots, then apparently you are the only one!" he said shortly. "Even Patience knew it. But then, all along I have been amazed by your ignorance on the subject.

"Witches, my dear girl!" he added explosively, as I continued to look blank. "Someone, and I suspect that housemaid, believes that Patience is a witch! In any witch hunt it is the naturals, no matter how simple and harmless, who are the first to be accused. And considering the recurrent theme of witchery that continues to crop up here, I expect anytime a delegation to call upon her, demanding that she recite the Lord's Prayer backward, or that she strip to be examined to see if she suckles a familiar!"

"Sir! I grasp your meaning, without the need to be so graphic!"

"Pardon me, but tonight I find myself singularly inconsiderate of the delicate sensibilities of a female, particularly when I think of how, in the past, the females were always the most rabid witch hunters!"

"But—but—I still don't understand why someone knotted her clothes."

"To drive away her familiar, Emma, which is said to inhabit a witch's clothing during the day. If one can lock it out of its hiding place, then it is rendered harmless!"

I was frightened by his low-voiced savagery, and I wondered how he could be so violent abut a belief that I could not view with any more than a tolerant disapproval. It was unhappy, yes, and annoying and almost pitiful that anyone would believe Patience could be a witch, and be driven to knot her clothes, but surely it could not be taken seriously, and to do so was to invest it with a significance that would gratify and encourage the credulous.

I tried, hesitantly, to point this out, but he shook his head impatiently and did not stop his taut prowling around the room.

"I have heard all the arguments before, Emma. How we have seen, as recently as the Salem trials, the tragedy and shame brought upon a town, a state, by a mindless fear of witchcraft, and therefore we would never be driven to repeat such a senseless mistake. How we are on the verge of a new century, and have shaken off all the superstitions that ruled the last one. How man has ascended and ridden above this earth in a balloon, and sailed a ship upon the water without the aid of the wind, and how we have now become too scientific-minded to believe the old superstitions of the past. But all these arguments mean exactly nothing when faced with something like tonight's viciousness. Don't you see that people still do believe in witches and demons, and the Devil in human form? And so long as one person believes it, and has the power to sway others to his thinking, no one is safe? You have seen for yourself how the tentacles reach out to poor, stupid Patience, haven't you? Even you, yourself, continue to wear that bracelet." His face was satanic as he stopped his hungry pacing and glared at me.

I stared down at it in revulsion. "I can't seem to remove it."

"Try again tomorrow. You may find it easier now, and if not, it is merely an iron band, not a magic circle, and can be cut off. In the meantime, don't take me to task for finding the odor of superstition nauseous," he added wearily, pausing to take his favorite stance at the fireplace, elbows leaning on the mantel.

I hung my head, unaware that the firelight successfully revealed the shame I was aching to express. I had not known many men: this had been, on the whole, a household of women. But there had never been a time, while in the company of a man, that I had not been painfully aware of my scars, and rigidly in control of myself and my actions. Now I was confusedly out of my depth and I acted instinctively, without self-consciousness, leaning forward and placing a hand sympathetically upon his arm. It was the first time I had so touched a man in my adult life, and the shock sent a quivering tremor through my body. He seemed to notice nothing, however, although his face softened at my obvious distress.

"I am aware that my reaction is extreme," he said gently, "but so are my reasons. It is in the blood, you see. My family has suffered much from the effects of superstition. Not my cousin's, but mine, on my father's side. Did you ever wonder about the families of the Salem victims? My father was a grandson of the John Proctor who was hanged, just as Patience is the grandchild of Anne Putnam, who was only twelve years old when she accused my great-grandfather of witchcraft! She and seven other children —young girls—were responsible for the deaths of more than thirty people. One old minister was almost a saint. Another old man was pressed to death. Do you know how a person is pressed to death, Emma?"

His words evoked a recollection of an incident long forgotten and buried beneath the layers of memory that was my only legacy from my mother. I had been no more than six or seven years old when taken to the Bowery by "Nursie," dressed in my best velvet

walking suit with a sealskin muff and cape, for I had been the
spoiled darling of the house, then. "Nursie" had bought a book
from a furtive man selling them on a street corner: I could still
remember the sharp, piercing wind from the river riffling the
crudely illustrated pages. She had shown the pictures of gory tor-
ture scenes and Indian massacres to me, to the accompaniment of
sibilant breaths of mingled horror and pleasure. Nightmares, and
the subsequent dismissal of "Nursie," had been the end of the
story until now, when I remembered one of the pictures. Some
persons, two or four, dressed in flowing judges' robes, were placing
stones on a large, flat board, while sandwiched between it and
another board, his hands, feet, and head projecting like those of a
squashed bug, was a man. The title beneath the picture read:
"The publick tryal of the Witch, Giles Cory, and later Execution
of Same, in Newe England. The manner and date being—Pressed
to Death, September 19, 1692."

Slowly, I nodded.

"Then shall I tell you about witches, Emma, and about one in
particular, Anne Putnam? It isn't a pretty story, but I think you
might understand it; having the father you did, you can perhaps
appreciate the deviltry of Anne's mother. Goody Putnam seems to
have led a dull enough life. In Anne, whom she manipulated as
cold-bloodedly as Satan would have his puppet, she saw a way to
make her life more exciting as well as pay back old scores and rid
herself of old enemies! There was proof, after the hysteria, the
blame, and the fault-finding died down, that she might have mas-
terminded the entire plot, and was the one who guided the girls,
although she herself never took the witness chair, nor openly accused anyone."

"What about your great-grandfather?" I whispered.

"He was a good man, religious, upright, thrifty. He employed
one of the girls on his farm as a housemaid, and he attempted to
apply reason in his dealings with her, which was tantamount to
accusing himself of witchcraft! He had noticed, he said, that if he
whipped her and set her to work at the spinning wheel, she forgot
her silly hysteria and behaved normally, so he suggested that all
the others be treated in the same manner! A madly sane remark
for anyone to have made at such a time! Consequently, he and

his wife and their five-year-old child were thrown into jail; he went to the gallows, and his wife was released only because she was with child. The five-year-old was confined to a dungeon in chains, for months, and understandably was of feeble mind afterward. I am sure that John Proctor died full of astonishment that he was not believed by his good neighbors. I hope that he died still believing in the God whose teachings they professed to be following."

By now he had thrown himself into a chair opposite me, with his long legs stretched out before him and his hands, which he had thrust into the narrow pockets of his satin breeches, riding upon his hip bones. In court attire, ruffled and laced, he looked both elegant and dangerous, incongruously so for such a large, amiable man. He reminded one of a massive, tawny-maned lion, hiding behind a deceptively mild manner the sleek power and cruelty of a jungle king. I could have believed him capable of fiendish revenge when he spoke of Goody Putnam, but at this moment his face expressed nothing more than sad regret for the passing of a man who had been in his grave for more than a hundred years.

"What happened to Anne Putnam?"

"By the end of the summer madness, for such it was, the girls began to lose their audience as sanity returned to Salem and the shamefaced judge and jurors regained their senses. The girls grew up and their fate is lost in obscurity. My grandmother was the child Elizabeth Proctor bore after her husband's death. At twenty-six, Anne Putnam publicly repented in church and asked for forgiveness from her victims' families. Family rumor has it that she did so at the insistence of her future husband, who married her afterward and brought her to live in this house. John Henry Pride was their son, and after his birth she began to slip into madness. It is a measure of God's retribution that toward the end of her life she was believed to be what she had charged her victims with—a witch. I heard the hints when I was a boy, but assumed the story had died, until I saw the irrational prejudice that sprang up when Nat Southwick was killed."

"Patience doesn't help matters," I said. "She used to boast to Honor that she was a witch and could wish anyone to death."

He had been watching me steadily, but now he rose and went over to the window, where he twitched aside the curtain to gaze out upon the dark street. His answer, when it came, was absent, as though he no longer had his mind upon his words.

"Poor fool. She is a hysteric, of course."

"Hysteric?"

"A girl, usually—who lies to gain her ends, performs hysterically when balked or discovered in lies, which are often so outrageous they are believed. She will talk incoherently, laugh, cry, irrationally, convulse sometimes, when excited, and is inclined to violence and abnormal behavior. Anne Putnam was one also, and given the same climate, Patience would behave the same way. But there was never any doubt about Anne's intelligence, however. Foolish, isn't it?" He smiled wearily. "And you think I am an alarmist to fear what Patience could do, or what could be done to her by a frightened person, aren't you?"

"No."

He had shown me how easily mass hysteria could attack a town, and it could attack us, too, within this house. I believed his story and shared his fears. I was ashamed, too, of how long I had contributed my part to it by wearing the bracelet, and resolved to put it away first thing tomorrow.

CHAPTER VI

"Rain, sweetheart." Mrs. Margate awakened me during the night.

And, I thought dismally, it spells the end to our Indian summer, that fabled season that was so named by our grandparents to indicate not the pastoral, waning days of summer, but rather the time of burning corn and raids of unparalleled savagery by the hostiles.

When I arose, shivering, to kindle the kitchen fire, it was to a dreary dawn and a steady drip of raindrops down the chimney, hitting the hot ashes with a spat and hiss. The garden was beaten beneath the drenching downpour and the trees that had heretofore managed to retain a respectable dressing of leaves stood naked and shivering, the wind rattling their branches like dry bones. The garden paths ran yellow with mud, and the ground was covered with sodden maple leaves, beached like drowned starfish in drifts beneath the trees.

"Emma." Silence stood in the doorway, braced on her canes.

"Mrs. Southwick!" I stammered, shocked to see her up, fully dressed, before having her sassafras-root tea and her early morning cosseting by Piper.

"Never mind your solicitude! Honor helped me downstairs; it was not difficult." She smiled grimly. "I'll go straight to my office and remain there. Will you see to a fire and notify Piper? I will have some instructions for you when you bring my tray."

She looked ill. Two spots of color burned feverishly in her cheeks, and when I brought her breakfast tray I found her eyeing me defiantly, as she always did when she had determined upon a course of action that was questionable.

"I want you to witness my temporary will that I drew up last night. You and Piper. It is a matter of urgency that I cancel out the will I made yesterday. My days—my hours, even—weigh heavily upon me, and I do not wish to delay a moment longer than necessary. In the meantime, I want you, Emma, to send Jacob to Judge Dashwood's home and ask him to attend me here. At once. I want him to draw up a new will. You might include that information in your note to him."

"Judge Dashwood?" I faltered. "Not Usher?"

"No, not Usher. He is too close to the family now." She indicated the handwritten will, and Piper, her face expressionless, bent over and affixed her signature. I had no choice but to follow. She gave no indication of its contents, but I suspected Piper of knowing them. I signed reluctantly, aware of a keen disappointment that Honor was so soon to be disinherited again, and hoping that Edward, or perhaps the judge, would be able to redirect Silence's purpose.

Patience was as gentle and tractable as a child when she held up her face for the damp washcloth, and only mildly puzzled to find that she had slept the night in her mother's room. After her breakfast, I set her to work sorting ribbons in the parlor before the fire, and hastened to the kitchen to learn if Jacob had succeeded in finding the judge.

"Yis, mum, I found him." Jacob, warming himself at the kitchen fire, eyed me warily. "An' I found somethin' else, in a manner of speakin'. 'Tis sure I am that I'll not have your approval, though what ye think I'd be doin' with her," he added righteously, "whin th' poor lidy was in th' family way, an' large with expectation, yet might say, that I'd not be knowin'!"

I tilted my head. "Jacob, please get to the point! What lady are you talking about?"

Pared of its Irish rhetoric, Jacob's tale was nothing more than that of the rescue of a lady in distress, whom he had found lingering at the shop door, frantic with anxiety to see Mrs. Southwick. Appealed to, no doubt, by a fragile, defenseless manner, Jacob had used his key to open the shop door and surreptitiously escort her to Silence's office while I was busy with Patience. Apparently, however, the visitor had found Silence in a complaisant mood, for there was no shouted "Emma!" nor irritable tinkling of her bell, as there would have been if she had wanted to rid herself of an un-wanted visitor.

The judge's knock, when it came, was at the closed and shut-tered shop door. I let him in and shook his coat free of raindrops while he dried his shoes before the parlor fire.

To my surprise, I found him hostile and suspicious of his sum-mons, and he questioned me closely about his old friend's change of mind, and her reason for a new will as well as a new legal ad-viser.

"You know how she is, sir." I smiled jokingly. "As changeable as a weathercock and about as predictable."

He eyed me sourly. Yesterday, my slightest witticism would have brought a smile to his lips, but he was in no mood now to be amused. There was none of the chucking under my chin, nor the surreptitious squeezes in empty corners, by which he had made former visits miserable, and I could only conclude that he linked me with his suspicions.

"I don't like it at all," he snapped. "She has not dismissed Usher Tournais as her lawyer, and he will have a right to resent my interference in his client's affairs. Why didn't she send for him?"

"She wanted you, sir," I said mildly.

"Humph! Oh, very well, I know what a strong-minded old gel she can be when she puts her mind to something. I assume she *did* ask for me—the notion wasn't suggested to her?" he added suspiciously, and I realized amusedly that he suspected me of deliberately—and illegally—throwing business his way in view of our warm relationship. "No, no, I guess not," he added hastily. "Absurd idea, that! Nevertheless, I don't like to think I am being used. Well, take me in—let's get it over with! It may be nothing more than a matter of a garnet brooch, or her gold-headed cane, eh?" Chuckling now at his wit, he went into the office, his good humor restored, and prepared to be tolerant of the notional ideas of an old friend and gently guide her in the proper direction.

His mood, when he returned, had changed to his former belligerence, as though he darkly suspected that he was being ma-nipulated, and would find it hard to forgive me for my part in the trickery. My fall from grace seemed complete.

"I don't like being involved in this sort of thing," he fumed testily. "Usher Tournais should have been called. They are not married yet," he added, nodding toward Patience, "and he might have been able to talk some sense into her head! She won't listen to me." He glared at me. "I don't like it! It smacks of collusion, and I have my reputation to think of! Does she understand the implications of this?" he added, nodding at Patience.

"No, sir, she has no interest in wills. She leaves that to others," I said shortly. I was puzzled by his offended attitude. Surely even the judge, to whom his dignity was a precious commodity, would not believe that I would conspire with Silence to defraud Honor? With a vague thought of making my own position clearer, I added, "She has always been her mother's favorite, and therefore never worries about her future. It is Honor who suffers an injustice when her mother makes a new will. Unfairly so, sir, if you ask me!"

He glared at me fixedly, and I saw that I had only made matters worse, and perhaps given him the impression that I was fishing for information. "What say you, Jane Piper?" he asked coldly, ignoring me. "Do you think your mistress is herself? Could she have been pressed to do what she has done?"

"No, sir!" Piper was affronted by the suggestion. "Have you ever known her to listen to anyone when she made up her mind? Didn't she seem right-headed to you?"

"Hm, perhaps. Well," he pulled on his coat, "I can dawdle indefinitely about drawing up this new will. I wouldn't be surprised if she changes her mind again before this afternoon."

"She's in a hurry, sir." I reminded him, leading him out through the shop.

"I know. I know. And so, apparently, are you," he added coolly as he left.

"I don't see why my lady has to have his approval of what she decided to do with her money!" Piper snapped at me when I returned. "Prosy old fool! He should never have been called, although I am perfectly aware of her reasons for doing so. But Usher Tournais would never have dared to argue with her as he did! He used the privilege of an old friend and consequently put her into one of her spells. If she's not ill as a result of this, I'll be surprised."

It was the longest and most agreeable speech Piper had ever had with me, delivered as it was in anger, but for once we were united in our disapproval of the judge. I too thought his censuring air toward me, as well as his manner of questioning Silence's competence, beyond the bounds of friendship. I wished uneasily for someone to talk to who would be on Honor's side. More particularly, I wished for Edward Murray, for his cool sympathy and clear-headed logic were preferable at this time to Marcus's fierce loyalty, which, though comforting, was of little practical use. Unfortunately, he was not at hand, however, and I had not been granted the opportunity of a private word with him at breakfast time. He had left the house early, as did Marcus and Thomas, bracing the cold, driving rain on business errands.

Joanna remained in her room, her door closed to me. Added to my other worries was this small, niggling one of her recent remoteness. Honor opened the shop early, shivering in the plunging temperature, and trade seemed brisk after yesterday's closing. I heard the bell tinkle repeatedly, and her bright voice reached me through the closed door.

Shortly after the judge's departure, Katie sought me out, anxious to reassure me of her innocence in last night's witch baiting. She did not seem insulted to be suspected, although she had apparently been sternly dealt with by Edward, for whom she held no animus, but instead a grudging appreciation for his perception.

"'Tisn't that I wouldn't't've done it, Miss Emma, if I'd had th' courage," she assured me earnestly, "but as I says to th' mister, knowin' how Miss Silence feels about Miss Patience, an' th' money she's put into her fancy wardrobe, 'twould've been beyond th' bounds of me doin', an' that's a fact! *That* took a deal o' nerve, Miss Emma, now, didn't it?" She shook her head admiringly. "'Tis a deal safer *I* feel in this house, knowin' 'twas done, but fer all that, 'tis not me doin'!"

I knew all of Katie's little mannerisms when she was lying, and this awed respect for the enormity of the crime did not indicate guilt. But I was not to know if Edward shared my belief, for he did not return that morning.

However, Usher appeared before noon to request an interview with Mrs. Southwick. Something about the grim demand made me suspect that the judge had sent him a message in which he had communicated his doubts about me, but twenty minutes later he had lost his militant air as he stood before the fire, warming his coattails and thoughtfully watching Patience's bent head and busy fingers among the ribbons.

"Miss Ashton, do you have any idea why her mother is disinheriting her?"

"Disinheriting her?" I asked blankly. "Honor?"

"Honor? Oh, no! Patience. You didn't know, then? Judge Dashwood seemed to think you knew all about it." He looked at me searchingly. "Apparently it is no secret, for she has just admitted it freely to me. Judge Dashwood hinted at influence, but I found her remarkably clear, although she didn't explain why she had made such an about-face decision. She gave me permission, however," he added whimsically, "to break my betrothal, since Patience is not to be an heiress, but I am not such a turncoat as all of you seem to think, nor do I wish to lose Patience."

I liked the wryness with which he made the confession. "I am sorry, Mr. Tournais," I said sincerely. "I think such a will is just as unfair as her earlier consistent mistreatment of Honor. It is a whim, of course, as you must know. She will change her mind again, soon."

He did not dispute it. "Ah, well." He shrugged. "At least it doesn't matter to her." His eyes rested contemplatively on Patience, who smiled at him. "I wonder if you will allow me to see Patience alone," adding teasingly, "after all, I am her betrothed, and you may leave the parlor door open."

I nodded and left the room, but he did not remain long.

The rain continued to drum monotonously on the roof and I stuffed rags in the windowsills and placed crockery pots about to catch the drips in the empty attic, where my portrait stood in solitary splendor. I stopped before it and gazed thoughtfully, my mind harking back to the oddity of Edward's expression when he first saw it. In spite of our spiteful little exchange, I could not rid myself of the notion that he had been pleased, on the whole, by my angry rejection of his purchase.

Before the fire, Honor, Patience, and I shared a light luncheon consisting of baked oysters in a pie, whole new potatoes, a few slices of broiled chicken, and a quivering, jellied blancmange filled with cream and fruit. Piper and her mistress apparently preferred their own company, and Joanna continued to remain aloof upstairs.

Honor spoke of her continuing absence but casually. Her attention was more taken up with the grievance of the damp, cold shop, "where Mama positively refuses to allow a fire!" She shivered. "Doesn't she realize how the customers hurry to get their business done?"

I smiled ruefully. "Your mother believes in mortification of the flesh—for others," I added dryly, for the little office stayed warm as toast throughout the cold months.

"Where is your bracelet, Emma?" Patience asked abruptly.

I started and glanced at my bare arm. "I put it away forever," I said lightly. "It was a wicked old thing."

Piper found me at tea time while I was trimming the Betty lamp for Honor's use in the shop. I was surprised to learn that the judge had not yet returned. She was in an irascible mood, exacerbated, no doubt, by her mistress's temper as much as by the judge's continuing absence. "I shall tell him exactly what I think of his treatment of her when I see him," she raged. "He knows she is anxious, yet he continues to dawdle! He knows she is not a well woman. She is perfectly aware that he thinks of himself as merely humoring an old lady's foibles, but she doesn't intend to be balked in this. If his dawdling puts her into a fever and makes her ill, I shall haul him into one of his own courts of law, with a suit!"

"You'll be in a fever yourself, if you don't rest," I said soothingly. "Go and take a nap, and I promise to call you when he comes."

"Very well." Piper was slightly mollified by my obvious sympathy. "The mistress sent me out to rest. She said she would answer his knock herself. But don't call me—send him right on in, and then tap on my door."

"Emma! You are just in time to give your opinion! See what cousin Edward brought us from a shop near Clarke's Wharf."

Honor was not alone in the shop. Marcus, whom I had thought to be in the city, was painting with watercolors in the corner, and from the appearance of the papers spread about him to dry, was well settled in. But it was to her cousin Edward that Honor was directing her attention. He stood in the doorway, his cloak stained and streaming with moisture, while the water collected in a puddle at his booted feet. He ruffled his hair free of raindrops and laughed at both of us. To my horror, my senses responded immediately with an aggressive tingle, stiffening me with the same sure tautness of a dog pointing at a covey of birds.

"Cousin Edward has given us an interesting idea to use in our shop. He saw it done in New York. While he was out, he bought this length of velvet to put in the window as a backdrop to our pottery. What do you think?"

I moved forward slowly, frantic to hide from his sharp eyes this alarming new awareness, but he took the lamp from me and strode over to the window. Marcus flung down his paintbrush and followed grudgingly. When Edward hung the dark blue velvet behind the rusty-brown and yellow earthenware, we all had to admit it was effective.

"It needs strong sunlight," Marcus said morosely, "but something can be done with it." The artist in him took over. "Draped in folds, with perhaps fewer pots, placed at different heights. Get me a box, Honor."

"Cousin Edward says we should import a few pieces of Meissen to give the shop an elegant touch," Honor added.

"I have always thought the shop could have a larger success," I said quietly, "but you won't find Mrs. Southwick agreeable to expansion."

"But I can bring her around." He grinned wickedly. "Don't you know what a persuasive and charming rogue I can be?"

If he was jesting, I was not amused. I knew that he would find it easy to win Silence over to an idea I had sought for five years to persuade her to accept.

"What do you think of this?" He had taken up Marcus's sketch pad as we stood apart from the two engrossed in the window display. "These horses are realistic, aren't they? Did you realize he could draw this well?"

"No," I said warily. "He has always been secretive about his work." He turned the pages rapidly, dividing his attention between the sketch pad and my face. They were filled with idle, meaningless drawings, such as Marcus might have done to employ his free time: a page of flowers, another of costumes, a carefully detailed design for a necklace, a caricature of Silence, accentuating the lines of ill temper and unpleasantness in her face, and, lastly, a page of Honor's, lovingly drawn. I frowned uneasily.

"A man of many talents," Edward said dryly.

He took up the watercolors, handling the wet pages carefully. They were obviously patterns to be painted on china: flowers, the Boston harbor done in blue wash, a ship with sails unfurled, atilt in the wind. "Hardly applicable to the pottery that is turned out here, surely? And that is what cousin Silence expects, isn't it? Designs for the pottery?"

My nerves snapped, aggravated by the long drawn-out day, and further irritated by the sight of the large brown hand in the immaculate lace cuff so close to my shoulder. I was in no mood for his vaguely sinister pleasantries.

"Surely you do not begrudge him a bit of idle doodling in his spare time?" I whispered fiercely. "Are you so selfish about your cousin's interests that you can't see how quickly his talent would become stifled if he devoted *all* of his freedom to designing her pottery!"

One eyebrow raised. "You react violently to any criticism of him, don't you? Your point is taken, but does he do any pottery designing at all? An honest man would spend an occasional hour on it," he added sarcastically.

Ignoring me, he strolled over to the window. "I like what you have done there, by using fewer pieces and placing them at different levels, you've made the display more effective."

Marcus shrugged. "We need sunlight to bring out the sheen of the velvet, but it will pass muster."

Suddenly, with startling violence, a body hurled itself against the door, sending it flying open, and Patience fell into the shop, bringing a shower of freezing raindrops in her wake.

"Patience! Where have you been?"

She looked up, blinking, and smiled with pleasure to see all of us.

"Patience," Honor continued, slowly and carefully, "you know Mama doesn't like you to go outdoors alone. Where did you go? Were you alone?"

Patience said nothing. Her eyes roved, then fell on the swathed window display, and she moved forward eagerly to stroke the smooth velvet. "It's pretty. Is it for me?"

"No, of course not, foolish girl," I replied sternly. "Your cousin Edward brought it to use in the shop window. You mustn't always be so forward, asking for presents. Now go inside and get off that wet cloak. I'll go with you to hang it up."

Patience pouted but moved away obediently. Edward's eyes were unreadable as he watched her.

"I have noticed a strange thing about Patience," he said slowly. "I wonder how the impression got around that she is unteachable."

"But she is," Honor responded.

"For most things, yes. But this is not the first time I have observed that although she is not intelligent, she is, nevertheless, clever. Did you notice how successfully she turned aside yours and Emma's questions?"

Judge Dashwood's arrival was attended by all the consternation he had failed to discover on his earlier visit. Signaling me from the shop door, where I was once again alone in the parlor, Honor's eyes were round with wonder.

"The judge has arrived, Emma. He says Mama is drawing up a new will? Is that true?"

"I suppose she hasn't changed her mind, Miss Ashton?" the judge asked me pompously as he bustled into the passageway and handed me his coat. "If not, then I suggest you summon Mr. Goddard and the potter. I'll need witnesses."

Edward was right behind me as I opened the office door for the judge.

"What's this about a new will?"

I turned on him furiously. "You heard the judge," I snapped. "Mrs. Southwick has drawn up a new will today. If you had returned this morning, as I expected," I added coldly, "I would have told you about it so that you could talk to her and perhaps moderate her revisions!"

He looked amused. "I'm flattered to be missed, for whatever reason. However, this rank injustice, to cut out Honor merely on the strength of Patience's hysterical accusation last night—"

"It isn't Honor who is being disinherited this time," I replied, "but Patience."

He stared at me, then his eyes narrowed with suspicion. "How do you know?" he demanded.

Before I could answer, the office door swung open, striking the wall, and the judge tottered toward us, his face ashen with shock, his wig, as usual, tilted on his head. He saw Edward and relief overspread his face.

"Mr. Murray!" he gasped. "Your cousin is dead in there! She's been murdered—strangled! Please come in and help me decide what's to be done."

CHAPTER VII

A few weeks ago I read in the Boston *News-Letter* that the old Pride home on Hanover Street was to be razed. It was an old copy of the newspaper; perhaps it has already happened. Upon the site was to be built shops, or a countinghouse, or perhaps a warehouse, but not another home, so said the writer, because the house was unlucky, its penalty never to remain in the possession of one owner for very long. It had finally sunk into a derelict state and was an eyesore to all who passed that way. It was an enthusiastic piece of sensational journalism: the writer even bringing up the specter of poor, mad Anne Putnam, whose unquiet spirit was said to roam the premises at night. Personally, I do not believe in Anne's ghost. She sounds like a figment of journalistic imagination, for she never made an appearance while I inhabited the house. But I would have no difficulty in believing in Silence Southwick's more robust shade. She would not have yielded her place without a struggle, and I could easily imagine her stalking through the dark little rooms, full of wrath to discover that she shared them only with the mice nibbling the walls.

After reading about the house, my thoughts dwelled on it until it became an obsession as it never did in other days: an obsession that I was unable to overcome until he suggested that I put my story on paper—all of it. Then, and then only, he tells me, I can begin to forget it. Heretofore my pen has raced steadily across the growing pile of manuscript, until I arrive at this point in my tale —Silence's murder—and I feel a growing reluctance to pierce the veil that cloaks the remaining days I spent at the house on Hanover Street. It is ever thus when I try to probe that part of the past. I think the mind is responsible, seeking to shield itself from pain. Undoubtedly there is much that is hurtful to me about those days, but I find it increasingly impossible to pander to that pain at the expense of clarity. It is an indulgence that I cannot allow myself any longer. I must, I will, tell it all. Only then, perhaps, can I exorcise my own particular ghost of regret and blame for what followed, the memory of a failure that has continued to haunt me in spite of the fruitful, satisfying years between.

If I close my eyes I can see us as we were that morning, assembled around the dining table, awaiting the judge's questions. A pale, watery sun struggled pallidly to relieve the gloom of the dark corners, for after a month of golden days, autumn had fled, leaving winter in its wake. There was a crisp bite to the air beyond the circle of warmth dispensed by a glowing basket of coals in the fireplace, and I shivered as I wondered if the aura of suspicion surrounding the judge and his attendant constable of the Watch might not be contributing to the cold atmosphere of the room.

Those assembled for questions included the family, which had dwindled to Honor and Edward, the Eatons, Marcus, Piper, and myself. Patience was not present. The night before, Usher, arriving on the heels of the Watch, had begged emotionally that she be spared the knowledge of her mother's death as long as possible, and Piper and I had been wearily glad to agree. So today she played at the pottery under Jacob's watchful eye.

I have wondered since about the judge's thoughts that morning, but at the time my own emotions were too bludgeoned by shock to do more than dimly perceive his chilly hostility. Like all weak men, he was unable to forgive that failure in others, and he was already finding his connection with the family an embarrassment. Only the powerful reputation of Edward Murray prevented him from treating us all as a pack of criminals. Later, applying a wry wisdom to my knowledge of him, I found myself unsurprised by his antagonism, for his vanity was enormous and he had always been alert to any ridicule of his dignity. Last night he had sensed his fellow jurists' unspoken criticism of his connection with an unsavory crime: the presence of the constable, implying as it did that his investigation required supervision, was mortifying to his pride. How resentful he must have felt; how strong the belief that he had been duped! He had given Silence Southwick his loyalty

ving her the indignities of a murder investigation, only to
e his kindness repaid by a second murder, this time embroiling
n as a witness.

For me, therefore, he reserved his most rigid disapproval, no less
because of his one-time courtship, the memory of which he had
shed with insulting ease. I had been the one to write the note
summoning him into this uncomfortable and embarrassing
episode and in lieu of my mistress, who was unfortunately no
longer available for censure, I should be made to feel the weight
of his displeasure. As his narrowed eyes swept the table and centered upon me with cold dislike, I realized that I had finally rid
myself of the suitor whose importunities had been so unwelcome,
although at what cost to myself I was yet to discover.

"Two murders in less than a week cannot be dismissed as a co-
incidence. We realize now that we were too hasty in dismissing
Obediah Watson's death as merely a quarrel between two potters.
All of you are under grave suspicion until proven innocent."

It was a numbing pronouncement. Last night, shocked into
silence as the others discussed the crime, I had assumed Thomas's
ponderous summing-up to be the correct one. "She was known to
be a miser and to keep large sums of money in her office. It looks
as though a thief gained entrance by the outside door and was
surprised by her. He had to have come in from outside, because
the carpet was, and still is, soaking wet."

But then, last night, no one was in the mood to question such
an expedient motive. We had just been subjected to the awful
sight of four stern-faced men in loud, pounding boots storming
through the house, searching for a hidden killer. They had not
been deterred by Joanna's hysterics as she was roused from her
bed, where she had been lying with a tisane for her headache, nor
by Katie's outraged scolding as she familiarly called each of them
by name.

The judge addressed his remarks to Edward, and I learned for
the first time that Silence had been strangled with the window
cord, which seemed to prove the impromptu nature of the crime.
I found myself reluctantly admiring the little jurist's skill as he
guided us smoothly through the events of our day so that, as he
ended, he had a timetable of everyone's activities. Proceeding on

the basis of the examination he and Edward had made of Silence's body within minutes of death, he was able to eliminate those who could not have committed the crime by virtue of having an alibi. For instance, Honor, Edward, and Marcus were together for at least thirty minutes before the judge arrived, and Patience had been sent by me to the kitchen fire to dry herself about fifteen minutes earlier. Piper, awakened by the sound of my voice, had joined her, and remained with Mrs. Margate and Katie until word was brought to them of the murder.

I listened admiringly to the judge as he readily assembled his facts and briskly disposed of his suspects. I was amused to realize that the Eatons and I, the three with nothing to gain by Silence's death, were the only ones left without an alibi. Beyond a dry statement to that effect, the judge made no other comment, but went on with further business.

One could not miss the change in the judge's manner and the easing of tension within the room, for even the law could not argue with the presentation of such unshakable alibis. Now the judge could return to the theory of an unknown murderer with a clear conscience and wonder comfortably about how he had gained entrance, for "Piper tells me that her mistress, expecting me as she was, had no intention of conducting business that day, so the alley door was locked."

We looked at Piper. Her eyes were swollen and puffed with weeping and it was obvious that she was suffering. To know that she had sat on, uncaring, yesterday, while her mistress fought alone and finally gasped out her life by way of a strangler's cord, would be a matter of bitter self-reproach to the anguished little creature. Piper's reason for living may have disappeared with Silence Southwick, but I knew she would have her own code of behavior, her private knowledge of her mistress's wishes, and nothing would swerve her from following that course. I found myself watching her cautiously, wondering if she was preparing to transfer that total loyalty to Patience, and wondering, too, what it would mean to the murder investigation. I knew Piper would not be swayed by the truth if she thought Silence would be better served by a lie.

replied rustily to the judge, "I did say that, sir, but I have thinking about it since, and I may have been mistaken."

he judge looked annoyed. He did not like to see a favorite theory go whistling down the wind. "In what way?" he asked stiffly.

"She did have me lock the outside door to discourage callers, but she also asked me to get down her legal box from the shelf. That is the box containing her bonds and mortgages. I have wondered if she could have been expecting someone who owed her money, and intended opening the door to him herself."

"It is possible," the judge replied testily. "Make a note of that, Constable. We will look into the matter, of course."

"I hope you will," Edward said smoothly. "We don't want another miscarriage of justice."

I looked at him wonderingly, curious about the purpose of his sardonic baiting. It seemed an ill sort of time to antagonize such a powerful opponent. If his purpose was to disconcert the judge, he failed, but the constable wore a thoughtful look.

"I suppose robbery was the motive?" Marcus asked.

The judge was hesitant. "Must be. Ordinarily I would not think so, for there was a sum of money left untouched in her desk, but it looks as if there was an attempt to steal her jewelry and the murderer was interrupted. By my arrival, I assume."

"Jewelry?" Edward asked slowly. In the dim dining room his face was unreadable, but I could feel his tension and the collective holding of breaths.

"Yes, there was a broken string of beads hidden under her skirts, evidently fallen from her neck. She was still carrying her pocket watch, but— I have some of the beads here for identification." He fumbled in his waistcoat pocket for his folded handkerchief, which he withdrew carefully.

"Mama never wore jewelry, Judge," Honor said.

"No?" the judge looked surprised, then gratified. "Possibly, then, we have something belonging to the murderer!"

"A string of beads?" Edward asked, startled. "Could it have been a woman, then?"

The judge shrugged. "A strong young woman, yes, indeed. But here, see for yourself." He unknotted the handkerchief and opened it, to disclose a handful of blue oriental beads. "Pretty things. Eastern in design, I would say, from that carving. If they were bought in Boston, we can trace them. Now, Piper, cast your eyes on these and tell me if they belonged to your mistress."

Fearing to see the diamonds and relieved that they were not, I leaned forward curiously to peer at the handful of beads in the judge's handkerchief. My beads. I had not thought of them again, nor seen them, since I put them away in my trunk after returning from Cambridge with Edward. My gasp went unheard, however, as Piper gave a strangled moan and slid gently to the floor in a faint.

"Why? Why would Piper swoon at the sight of your beads?" Edward asked slowly.

Piper had been revived and order restored. To the judge's questions, she had turned on him a sightless stare, so tormented that the words had frozen on his lips, and he had had no choice but to send her to her bed, pale and trembling, and temporarily abandon the investigation. I was ordered brusquely by Edward Murray to attend him in the office, and waited nervously as he took his leave of the judge before joining me there. As he paced the floor restlessly, his big, looming presence filling the small room, I wondered, watching him, if he did not find the confinement of his life chafing; if, having followed the sea for so many years, he did not long for the freedom it represented away from a desk and the city's financial houses.

He paused and looked at me questioningly. I was occupying the chair reserved for Silence's customers when paying off their usurious loans, and I felt something of their emotions, an inward quaking and dumb bewilderment for the unexplained twist provided by Fate.

"Well?" he asked impatiently. "What do you have to say about it?"

I shook my head, pleating the folds of my brown skirt with trembling fingers. "I don't know why she swooned. I could swear she was not in the kitchen when I returned from Cambridge, so how could she know they were my beads? And why would that

her swoon, anyway?" My face must have reflected my con-
~~~n.

He gave a wordless grunt of irritation, then turned to the
fireplace and kicked viciously at the smoldering log with a booted
foot, in much the same manner that another type of man might
kick a dog that lay in his path.

"Damn!" he swore beneath his breath, then yanked open the
door and let forth a bellow that could be heard as far as the
kitchen. "Jacob!"

But it was not for Jacob that he stood aside to allow entrance,
but the judge, grim of face yet faintly triumphant, followed by
Thomas, and lastly, a weeping Joanna.

"Oh, Emma, my darling, what have I done?" Joanna flung herself upon me as I stood up hesitantly. "Forgive me, forgive me."

"What have you done to her?" I asked fiercely, enfolding her in
my arms.

"Nothing more than question her—and the house servants—
since none of them were present at this morning's interview,"
Judge Dashwood replied. "They have all identified your beads,
Miss Ashton. They noticed them when you returned from a shop-
ping trip the other morning. And I might add, in view of the new
will, I find it most suggestive!"

"The will?" I faltered.

"Precisely. I have thought all along that Mrs. Southwick was
influenced to change her will as she did, and now I wonder if I
was not justified—"

"I think you had better explain what you mean, Judge," Edward drawled. "I know you were here yesterday to draw up a new
will for my cousin, but what has Emma Ashton to do with that?
Although she was fond of Honor, I don't see how you can charge
her with murdering cousin Silence, merely to prevent her from
cutting Honor out of her will—"

"I'll explain gladly!" The judge flushed indignantly. "I would
not make a charge on such flimsy grounds as those, Mr. Murray!
Honor, indeed! If Miss Ashton mur—did this terrible thing," he
added reluctantly, "she did it to profit herself, not Miss Honor."
He fumbled in his wooden legal box and drew forth a sheaf of

bound foolscap, which he slapped down upon the desk before Edward Murray.

Frowning, Edward picked it up and began to read. As he read, the frown smoothed out, and his face grew more impassive with each passing minute. At the end, he looked up, and with a kind of nervous horror I saw how he avoided my eyes.

"This is—most peculiar," he said in an odd voice. "Patience disinherited if she marries. And constrained, a prisoner, one might say, with Piper and Emma Ashton her jailers! And Emma Ashton—" He stopped abruptly.

"Yes," the judge agreed evenly. "Emma Ashton inheriting Patience's share of a fortune, upon her death."

Someone, Joanna, I believe, gave a hiss of dismay. I do not think I uttered a sound, for I had listened to him with dull inevitability. All along I had known that the judge suspected me of manipulating Silence to make a new and unwelcome will, but how could he, or anyone, recognize the bitter truth: that once again she had proven herself the master by ruthlessly outmaneuvering me?

The first will had been a just one, "the sort," so said the judge, "that any lawyer prefers to draw up for his client," providing, after a small annuity for Jane Piper, for an equal division of her fortune between her two daughters, with Edward Murray, their closest male relative, put in control of their guardianship and fortune. Upon the marriage of either daughter, his duties were to be relinquished outright to her husband.

Apparently, sometime during that fateful night before her death, or in the early hours of the morn, Silence Southwick had decided against marriage for her daughter, driven, no doubt, by Patience's behavior that night toward Honor, "although we know Miss Patience is a sweet, biddable girl, however deficient she might be. Indeed, my brother, the doctor, had assured Mrs. Southwick many times that marriage will have a calming effect on her.

"I received the impression," the judge added carefully, "that the questionable clause in the will had been inserted to bribe Miss Ashton into remaining with Miss Patience, since Jane Piper was elderly and likely to predecease her." By now the judge had seated

f behind the desk and was wearily polishing his quizzing
an unfailing sign that he was saddened and confused, since
h.. vanity did not ordinarily allow him to admit to failing
eyesight. "I could not budge her. She flew into a rage when I tried,
and insisted that she, Jane Piper, and Miss Ashton, the three who
knew Miss Patience best, had discussed the matter and agreed
upon its wisdom. Miss Ashton, she said, knew of her wishes, of
the new will, and had agreed to act as nurse. It was a convincing
argument and I had to give way, but under the circumstances I
cannot ignore it as a motive."

"I don't suppose you would believe me if I tell you that is the
first time I have heard any of this?" I asked steadily, although I
could see from his skeptical face that he not only disbelieved me
but scorned my lie as a cowardly evasion.

Joanna had been standing beside me, her arm lightly around my
waist, but she could not miss the judge's curling lip. She darted
forward and leaned across the desk.

"You are a prosy old fool," she cried indignantly, "just as I
suspected from the start! I may be a silly female, but even I can
see the lack of common sense in your deductions! The will was
never signed! How can it be a motive for Emma?

"Ah," the judge smiled foxily. "It would seem not, wouldn't it,
ma'am? But Mrs. Southwick, in her impatience to draw up a new
will, had already written it out by hand and had it witnessed. I
found it in her desk after her death. She showed it to me,
flourished it under my nose, so to speak, when I remonstrated
with her for changing her will. She told me that if I refused to do
as she said, she still had a legal, binding document. It is, of course,
if properly witnessed. In this case, however, ma'am," the judge
added sarcastically, the memory of being called a fool obviously
still rankling, "Emma Ashton cannot profit, for the will was
witnessed by her and Jane Piper, both of whom are beneficiaries.
Under the law, they cannot be allowed as witnesses, a fact that I
am sure Miss Ashton was unaware of."

Joanna burst into a passionate defense of me, an infinitely sweet
and touching tribute which left the judge unmoved. It was Edward, breaking in with an indifferent drawl, to whom he listened.

"Taking a more rational view, and without Mrs. Eaton's impetuosity, may I ask, Judge, why Miss Ashton would depend upon a chancy, handwritten will, when you were soon to arrive with a legal, binding document?"

"Ah, but there was the probability that I would persuade Mrs. Southwick to change her mind," the judge replied stonily. "I made no secret that such was my intention."

"And her motive for murdering Obediah? You have said the two crimes were connected."

"That was merely a possibility, sir. Coincidences do exist, and this may be one of them. Frankly, however, Obediah stood in her way—Mrs. Southwick's plans were to marry him to Miss Patience," the judge said doggedly. "Remove him, and she became dependent upon Emma Ashton."

"Remove him, and she turned immediately to Usher Tournais as a second choice," Edward said crisply.

"It's only a theory so far," the judge backed off sulkily. "We have to probe further, and who knows what we might uncover—"

"Your theory is still too thin, Judge," Edward interrupted. He seemed bored with all of us as he strolled over to the fireplace and began punishing the log again with his boot. "You are wasting your time with such speculations, and I am sure you want to solve this thing quickly, without wandering off into unprofitable side issues. If you have a logical theory, let us hear it, by all means, but there are too many holes in this one. Apart from all else, Emma Ashton did not benefit unless Patience died; and remember, she had the good Jane Piper and myself to crawl over before she could do away with a strong, healthy young woman no older, in years, than herself!

"Apparently you are loath to give up this version of her as a homicidal maniac, but bring reason to bear on Miss Ashton's character, sir!" He eyed the judge amusedly from his lounging position against the mantel. "She is incapable of the swift, daring judgment called for in this murder. Although she would be easily stupid enough to consider the handwritten will valid, you cannot have it both ways, Judge. She is giddy, foolish, and, like most females of her type, doesn't see six inches beyond her nose. She would no more consider taking on the task of Patience for life than she would fly, and why should she? Who should know better

/ou, Judge, that she had no reason to murder for the risky
ject of becoming an heiress, and then only if she murdered a
second time? She had marriage prospects, in spite of her flighty
predilection for playing off one suitor against another, and she
had refuge with the Eatons anytime she cared to return to them.
Why should she commit the act of a desperate woman? No, as
Mrs. Eaton advises, look elsewhere for your killer, Judge. Preferably, investigate the implications of that water stain."

His bored words and laconic manner, while successfully reducing my importance as a murder suspect, nevertheless placed me in
a more galling role of foolish irresponsibility, and invited the
judge to share with him his amusement at the picture he had
drawn. However, his words were also effective in chastening the
judge by recalling to his mind that I had been, until yesterday, his
choice for a wife, with, therefore, no desperate economic reason to
commit murder. Since the judge held himself dear, he was not
prone to disregard the value of such a recommendation as the
favor of his suit. Abruptly, with a start, he came to his senses, and
had the grace to eye me apologetically.

"Yes, of course. Of course. You are right. It is weak, very weak.
But there seemed to be opportunity, as well as motive, and—
However, we have other clues that we must investigate. We found
wig hairs twisted in the buttons of Mrs. Southwick's dress, and we
certainly can't blame Miss Ashton for those!" He chuckled forgiv-
ingly. "Piper mentioned the deed box: we will look into those
mortgages. We have already found a matter of interest there, as a
matter of fact. I am sure you know what I refer to, Mr. Eaton?
Mrs. Eaton?"

Joanna gasped, and if the judge received a malicious satisfaction
from her discomfort, he could be forgiven his small triumph, after
having been publicly called a fool.

"I expected you to bring that up, Judge. You could not fail to
discover it," Thomas said stolidly. "Yes, I admit that Mrs. Southwick had the power to disgrace my wife's family, breaking her
spirit and her mother's heart! Joanna's father stole from Mrs.
Southwick in order to pay off a debt she claimed. He wrote to us
about it—he was too old and infirm to play her particular game of
power. We pleaded with her to hold off making the disgrace

public, which, since his untimely death, would accomplish nothing but shame for the family. I was out yesterday and last week, trying to borrow the money to repay her. I assure you, sir, I did not kill her, however."

"What did she say when you asked for time?" the judge queried.

"She agreed—for a price," Joanna whispered when Thomas hesitated. "She wanted Emma. She must have always wanted Emma, if not in her home, then under her control. I thought it was because of Honor, but now I see that she wanted her available to remain forever with Patience. Jane Piper was growing old and Emma was young and strong. She needed her. She knew Emma wanted to come home with us, and we were told that we must discourage her, ruthlessly. Even refuse her sanctuary. If we did, she would forget about my father's debt."

"And did you do what she asked?"

"Not yet. I couldn't. I didn't know what to do—I was frantic." Joanna looked at me pleadingly. "I avoided Emma, avoided making any decision, as I always do when faced with one!" she added in bitter self-contempt. "I did ask Emma to appeal to Mr. Murray, hoping he would be able to do something. We needed time— Thomas is confident he can borrow the money, if he has time."

"And did you come downstairs yesterday to plead with Mrs. Southwick again, Mrs. Eaton?"

"No!" I cried before Joanna could speak. "She couldn't have gone to the office. I would have seen her!"

"But you weren't there all the time, Miss Ashton," the judge reminded me.

"You said the crucial time was the quarter hour before the body was discovered! That means after I sent Patience to the kitchen, doesn't it? No one, no one at all, went into her office then, or I would have seen him, for I had the office door in view all that time!"

Edward stirred restively.

"No?" the judge murmured, looking at me with hooded eyes. "I wonder if you realize just what you have confessed to, Miss Ashton."

CHAPTER VIII

By craning my neck cautiously over the hump of quilts, I could see the door: I watched it ease open gently. Long minutes passed as the shadows gathered, while I waited for one shadow, darker than the rest, to separate itself and move menacingly toward me. I was trembling with the release from strain before I acknowledged to myself that my imagination had been at work again, leading me to see danger in shadows and hear footsteps in what was no more than the settling of the old inn floors against the icy drafts that swept the corridors. The presence of a chambermaid, ordered to prevent just such intrusions, real or imagined, was not reassuring, nor was the sound of her peaceful slumber, which had continued without interruption from the rocker by the fire.

As for me, having been accustomed to one bed for seven years, almost a third of my lifetime, I was finding it impossible to accommodate myself to the rustling of the shuck mattress or the cold loneliness without Mrs. Margate's warm, comforting bulk beside me.

On an impulse, I sat up and swung my feet out of bed. I was wearing all of my petticoats, but the icy air struck chill to my bare feet and quivering flesh. However, the fire had been made up recently and I would be warmer there, securely wrapped in a quilt, than shivering in bed. I eyed my companion disgruntledly, remembering the size of the coin that had been bestowed upon her to keep watch over me tonight; remembering too the "Lawks a-mercy, I'm that feared we'll both be murdered durin' th' night!" an artless statement that had further increased the size of her largess.

Now she slept on, the deep, dreamless sleep of the innocent, while I wryly envied her serenity as I reviewed the mad impulse that had brought me to this inn, to keep an appointment that had resulted, so far as I could see, in nothing more than a further complication of an already precarious position. I reflected pessimistically that the incident would merely increase the probability of my guilt in the judge's mind, when brought to his attention, as it must inevitably be. The lump I carried on my head, I had already begun to regard as just punishment for one with my talent for stupidity, as Edward Murray acidly referred to it, and I shuddered to think of the garbled story of this night's exploits Marcus would tell at home, knowing that even at its censored best, the tale would hardly reflect to my credit. Added to these miseries, the slight, stuffy cold which I had contracted tonight had now developed into a sore throat. I reflect austerely that the blighting lecture that I had endured earlier from Edward Murray, while humiliating, might have its basis in fact, and therefore do me a great deal of good.

It had begun with Jacob, who had found me alone after my painful interview with the judge, and had conspiratorially produced a note he had been given by a pretty little woman in a noticeable state of pregnancy, a fact that had added to her fragility in Jacob's eyes. It had, apparently, been as easy this time to prevail upon him to be her messenger as it had been to wheedle her way into Silence's office yesterday. She had asked that the note be delivered to the lady who was the chaperon to the daughters.

Badly misspelled and poorly written, it had requested the honor of "spech wit yor ladie," but "bes to enform non," because of the confidentiality of the writer's information. A meeting place was suggested, the Green Goose Inn, at eight o'clock tonight. "I wil luk for yu," the writer added, and the shocking thought of a pregnant woman waiting alone in such a place, while I stayed away, forced my decision to go.

The Green Goose Inn was a respectable hostelry with excellent accommodations, located near the wharf, and it was frequently used by decent folk traveling by water but, because of its location, rough seamen patronized its taproom after the travelers had taken themselves off to an early bed.

There was a mizzling rain when the hackney carriage I had

hired for the occasion put me down at the inn door, and the smell of the sea was strong in my nostrils. The fog was thicker here: it had already enshrouded the tall-masted sailing ships riding anchor in the harbor, and the nearby buildings were swallowed in a shifting mist. In the way of fogs, it confused the ear as well as blinded the eyes, and the lapping waves and the clanging warning buoy set adrift in the bay could have reached me from any direction, had I not gained my bearings from the inn, which was a lively beacon amid the muffling darkness. The din and the smoky atmosphere had reached such proportions that the door to the outside passageway stood open, sending a stream of light into the street. In its beam, the fog eddied and swirled, then separated into little curls of vapor, and seeing it, the driver looked at me doubtfully. With a briskness I was far from feeling, however, I sent him on his way.

In the doorway, I wavered, then took heart from the fact that no one seemed to notice me. The room was full of loud-talking men, and the air foul with the smell of unwashed bodies and the stronger odors of cider and tobacco. I saw that most of the men present were users, in one form or another; I infinitely preferred the habit of puffing on a pipe, noxious though it may be, to the other, commoner use of the weed. Nothing was more distressful to my nerves than the frequent twang of the spittoon, or, in case of its inaccessibility, the river of tobacco juice that could be found running across the floor of any public house in this country. If a permanently stained floor was a measure of its popularity, this taproom enjoyed a brisk trade.

I lifted my skirts gingerly and stepped across the threshold, pleasantly relieved to be almost totally ignored. And then I saw why.

The lady whom I sought was seated inconspicuously in the back of the room, at a table, and it was obvious immediately that the eye of every man in the room was upon her. She was distractingly pretty, and dressed in the latest mode of fashion by one who, without doubt, could only be a French modiste. Her garment was made in the new post-Revolution style, hugging the bosom and falling in soft folds to her dainty little slippered feet, and it enhanced the full, rounded lines of her pregnancy to the point of voluptuousness, adding a touch of the tart to a sweetly innocent vision of motherhood.

I was no more immune to her charm than were the men around us as she stood up at my approach and smiled a greeting at me. Molly Haley had good reasons for sending for me, needing me for both bait and insurance. Later, working it out for myself, I believed that curiosity played a large part in it for her, too. She had been told about us, of course, but I had become a figure of much interest to her, probably because I was nearer her own age and, despite my menial position, possessed the respectability she longed for. Therefore, when she thought to use one of us, I came to mind.

Her first words to me, however, led me astray, although they certainly indicated the wide range of her knowledge about me. "Yer th' one, ain't ye? Th' one who'st marryin' th' jedge?"

I blinked and fumbled for a chair. Her face and figure would have done credit to the governor's table, but the words issuing forth from those beautiful lips were in the illiterate patois of a London slum.

Nevertheless, I was conscious of a vast relief. I had been bridling a strong curiosity to know why I'd been sent for, and more than a little uneasy because I was being summoned as the "girls' chaperon." As always, my motherly protectiveness toward Honor had been strongly to the fore, but now I thought I understood: her words, referring to the judge, alerted me. Apparently she wished to lodge information against someone and needed a go-between.

"No, no, you're mistaken," I stammered, in an attempt to clear up her misapprehension.

She smiled. "Gawn. Dun tell me thet! Yer th' right un, all ri'! Yer got th' pox, jus' like he sez. Yer th' one th' ole lidy tells me ter see. Emma. Spik ter Emma, she sez. Emma'll do it; Emma'll take care o' it."

"Take care of—it?"

"Aye, it! Sittin' right in me lap, it is, an' no name in sight!" she added savagely. "A bastard! I knows wot bein' a bastard means—I wuz one meself! It's th' streets fer 'im, if 'e's a boy, an' whorin' fer 'er. I swore I'd never bring a bastard inter th' world, an' I won't, but it'll take money ter set meself up, an' find a 'usband. I kin do it—wid money!"

I blinked. "Is that what you want, then, money? But you said in your note, you had information. Do you wish to sell it—to the judge, perhaps? Is it about Mrs. Southwick's murder?"

Her face paled. "No, no, not th' jedge! Never th' law! My infermation is ter be sold to th' Southwick family, an' you! No one else—"

"Why are you so frightened?" I asked gently. "You don't have to keep your baby, you know. You can still be respectable. There are institutions—"

"Aye, I knows! Grudgin' Christian charity!" she added ironically. "I wuz raised in a Lunnon workhouse, mum, an' I wants none o' that! Thet wuz all she—Miz Southwick—could say. Th' workhouse! Go ter Emma; she'll 'tend ter it!" Her eyes strayed to the open doorway behind me, then again sought my face. She leaned forward and raised her mug of cider in a sort of salute. I noticed that her hands, in spite of their dainty size, were horny with calluses. "I likes ye, dearie, an' I think yer got a good 'eart, in spite 'o wot I wuz tole about yer! A sour-faced ole maid, ugly wid th' pox, but it ain't so, an' I knowed it all th' time! I ain't a wicked gurl, dearie," she added earnestly, "in spite o' wot I seems. If I'd wanted th' streets, I'd stayed in Lunnon, but I transported, 'opin' fer somethin' better. An' first thing, I gets fooled by a smooth-talkin' dandy gen'lemun! I need th' money ter set meself up as a widder. Now, wot d'ye think o' thet?" She sat back triumphantly, and her eyes strayed again to the doorway, as though inviting others to share in her triumphant plan. They widened, and a smug look of gratification flashed over her face.

I glanced over my shoulder but the doorway was empty. "Do you see someone you know?"

She didn't reply. "Lookie, dearie, I ain't through talkin', see, but I gotta go right now." She rose abruptly. "If yer uneasy sittin' 'ere alone, ast th' innkeeper ter put yer in 'is private parlor, an' wait fer me there. 'Ear?"

"Oh, please," I cried, but she was already gone with a flick of her skirts.

I sat on alone at the table, growing more self-conscious as I saw the interest I was creating. A scuffle broke out among two or three of the men, and I saw that its purpose had been to draw my attention. Both the innkeeper and the waiter had disappeared and there was no one to ask about a private parlor, or to summon a hack. Any minute now, one of the men would accost me, and I lacked the tact to repel his advances without creating a scene. I fidgeted and angrily reflected that whatever information Molly Haley had, it would have to be worth more than merely the money to make up for the discomfort I was feeling. I thought of her undeniable beauty, the modish simplicity of her gown, and suddenly, thunderstruck, I perceived a flaw in the ingenuous little tale she had spun for me. How could she expect money from me to provide her with a new life, when the cost of her exquisite little French frock would have paid my salary for a year! Surely she, as a woman, had recognized for herself that my gown and cloak had seen years of serviceable wear, and therefore my position could not be a remunerative one. Unless the man who had so described me as a sour-faced old maid, with the pox, had misled her as to my circumstances? But why would he? Could it be that I was being led down the garden path by a scheming little adventuress?

I stood up abruptly and, heedless of the eyes on me, made my determined way toward the outside door. It opened onto a flagged passageway. An enclosed staircase led up to the bedrooms, and there were other closed doors at the end of the passageway, presumably to the private parlor and the kitchen, where I might hope to find the innkeeper.

I followed the tantalizing odor of freshly ground coffee to the kitchen. It was a big room, warm and steamy and smelling deliciously of buttery gruel. Hanging from the dark rafters were rashers of bacon and strings of onions and dried apples, giving off their own distinctive odors. The outside door stood open and was occupied by two small, grinning ostlers, shock-haired and barefoot, lounging across the sill. The only other occupant of the room, the cook, was bent over the pot of smacking, bubbling gruel, as she gave someone the rough side of her tongue in a loud, complaining voice.

"Drat thet no-good Jack! He heared me tellin' th' master I was puttin' on th' joint tonight, an' when I went ter look fer him, he'd gone missin'! I ain't even hed time ter make up th' fire yit! An' I know well, come breakfust time, he'll be back, hangdog, draggin' his tail in th' dirt, hopin' I ain't rememberin' how he ran off an' left me turnin' th' spit all night!"

"What's the trouble?" I glanced outside, where I could just make out, two or three feet from the door, a rough shed sheltering a dug-out pit blackened with the ashes of countless fires. An enormous joint of meat had been skewered onto a rod over the pit. I could guess the difficulty, for I had seen the same scene played out in other inn yards on my trip to Boston, and had pitied the small animals driven to such a task in the excessive heat. The heavy joint of meat, suspended over the glowing bed of coals, and the little bandy-legged spit dog, tied to the skewer and forced to go around and around for hours on end, rotating the joint of meat. Remembering how often I had baked like a well-turned roast myself, with my back to an open fire, I could sympathize with Jack, who apparently was wise enough to the ways of the cook to escape before she started to look for him.

I caught the eye of a grinning little ostler and knew that here was someone who could locate the missing Jack if he had chosen to. Taking a chance that he might have also seen my missing hostess, I inquired, and almost before I finished, his eyes lit up with the sparkle that that lady seemed to bring to any male's eyes, regardless of age. She had passed through the yard some time ago, going toward the stables, he informed me, and she had not yet returned.

The wind had freshened outside, blowing apart portions of the fog, and I stepped out confidently, rounding the corner of the house toward the stables. Immediately, out of sight of the lighted doorway, I was in a black pocket. I stumbled about blindly, stepping carefully to avoid potholes where I might break an ankle or foot, and with outstretched arms to protect my face and eyes from possible injury. Minutes passed before my groping hands touched the walls of what I thought was the inn; until a snort and the sound of shifting straw made me aware that I had found the stables. Comforted by the reassuring presence of the animals, I called out for Molly.

Afterward, I was never able to recall beyond that moment, so I never knew if the blow descended without warning and missed its target in the darkness, or if I, instinctively alerted to the presence of danger, shifted my position and so diverted a fatal blow. Either way, I dropped like a stone to the ground. When I awakened I assumed that I had been crying in my sleep, for my face was wet. By lantern light, I recognized Edward Murray, who was lavishly dripping water over me from the stable bucket, and Marcus, standing over me, holding the lantern aloft.

"What happened to you, Emma?" Edward demanded as soon as he saw that my eyes were open. "Why did you swoon? Did something frighten you?"

I muttered an incoherent protest at being sloshed with water, and he smiled slightly and slid an arm under my shoulders, raising me to a sitting position. Dazedly I put a shaking hand to my head, which was swimming unpleasantly, and Edward's fingers followed, probing. When he touched the tender spot I slid into unconsciousness again. I came to myself this time, lying on the settle in the private parlor, Edward's cape folded under my head. If I could have swooned again, I would have willingly done so, for the room was full of people, all talking at once, and a doctor had been summoned to see to my injury. His searching fingers had brought on waves of pain, shockingly intense, and I was humiliatingly sick into the basin held by a chambermaid. Afterward, Edward insisted on brandy rather than laudanum and had me propped against a pillow, where I sat, smiling muzzily, and listened to Marcus explain that he and Edward had been sent after me by Joanna, who, while searching for me in another passionate orgy of self-reproach, found instead the note, carelessly dropped in the office.

They had arrived to find me unaccountably missing, and learned from the little ostler that I had gone toward the stables, in pursuit of Molly. They had become separated while groping in the dark, until Edward had had the good sense to return to the inn for a lantern, picking up Marcus on his way back to the stables. A search had been made for Molly, but she and her baggage were gone from the room she had occupied for only two days. Since she had fled without paying her lodging bill, the innkeeper's wife felt fully justified in the prophecy she had darkly made at the time, that her new lodger was too pretty not to be troublesome.

A confused explanation from me that she had asked for money, and the mystery was solved to the satisfaction of the Watch, who had been called in by the innkeeper, unhappily alert to the reputation of his establishment. Mark his words, he said, she caught sight of a downier bird than a mere housekeeper, no matter how wealthy the household she hailed from, and I had become excess baggage to both her and the man she had, doubtless, newly acquired, and must therefore be discouraged. "An' almost killed in th' bargain, mum." He ran a sapient eye over my crumpled appearance. "You hadn't ort to be mixin' wit her sort, mum, an' th' sooner you take th' advice o' these gen'lemun an' go home, th' better."

That was the signal for all those who had no business in the room to depart. Obviously I was in no condition to return home tonight, and Edward had already arranged for a bedchamber, with a maid to keep me company, and another for himself nearby, so that he could escort me home in the morning. Marcus was sent away with a message to reassure the family.

"And now," Edward said silkily, turning back from the door, "you will explain to me, Emma, what led you into this harebrained escapade."

I had known I wouldn't escape his wrath. Thankfully for me, before I must reply, the door burst open and Usher Tournais made an impetuous entrance. He was dressed, as always, in the peak of fashion, and a slight disarrangement of the waterfall of lace and silk at his throat was so rare as to be immediately noticeable.

"What are you doing here?" I asked in blank astonishment.

"I live here," he replied simply. Edward's eyes narrowed, but Usher seemed unaware of our suspicion. "I have lived here for two years," he went on. "I noticed unusual activity from the window of my room, and came down to find out the trouble. My landlord has been telling me about your accident, Miss Ashton. I have noticed the girl, of course—who would not?—but I didn't know her."

Usher's concern about me was purely perfunctory. I think he

forgot my presence as soon as he turned to Edward Murray. He was pale and desperately anxious to clear up a matter that was apparently troubling his mind. It is said that all the world loves a lover; I saw for myself that even Edward Murray was not immune to the truth of the adage. He listened to Usher's passionate declaration of his love for Patience with a dawning smile upon his lips, and I watched indignantly as he changed from the flinty position he had taken with me to a state of jellied pliancy.

"I have no intention of withholding my consent to your marriage," he finally managed to say soothingly.

Usher blinked. "Thank you," he stammered. "I—I—was afraid you might feel it necessary to follow the dictates of the new will."

"No," Edward replied slowly. "It was never signed, so it isn't legal. But I am surprised that you knew the terms, in view of the fact that I just learned of them myself today."

"Of course I knew them!" Usher said. "I was told by Mrs. Southwick—that—day, about her new, handwritten will, and warned that if I intended to have Patience, I must marry her out of hand and forgo her fortune. Which I will do, if necessary," he added dangerously.

Edward laughed. "I had no idea that you were such an eager bridegroom, sir. You will be happy to know that the handwritten will is not legal, and Patience is yours. As her guardian, I have the power to allow the banns. As soon as this murder is cleared up, you have my permission to marry her. You were, after all, her mother's choice, and, therefore, mine." With difficulty, Edward compelled him to the door, damping his effusions of gratitude. He was laughing as he strolled back to the settle, where he eyed me wryly, correctly reading my expression. "How is your head?"

I sniffed. "You're wrong, you know. It isn't what Mrs. Southwick wanted for Patience. You heard the will. She didn't think it was wise for Patience to marry, which is an opinion I've held all along."

He looked at me in exasperation. "Frankly, Emma, I suggest you forget that other will, if you can. It has already caused you enough trouble, and you'll be lucky if that's the end of it. It is my opinion that cousin Silence was out of her head most of yesterday, and that will alone proves it. From what I can gather, her actions were those of a very ill woman. She didn't ask you if you wished to be yoked to Patience for a lifetime; she merely consigned her to your care as casually as one would a bale of goods. No, Emma, cousin Silence had the right idea originally about Patience; marriage to a sensible man, who is well aware of her shortcomings yet prepared to take her on in spite of them, with the added inducement of her fortune. Usher Tournais is such a man, for he has no delusions about her, and seems fond enough of her."

"Fond?" I cried indignantly. "Is that enough? For a man to endure Patience, he must be in love!"

"Love? Nonsense! Love is not necessary! He will care for her—to do otherwise would be to kill the golden goose. And Patience will not know the difference, I assure you. Yes, I think he and I understand each other. It must be left to such as you and Honor to speak of love!" He smiled.

In spite of my throbbing head, I leaped to my feet, casting aside his coat which had been covering my knees. I had just been fooled by a pretty face, knocked senseless and swilled with brandy, and I was in no mood now to be soothed with platitudes and set aside, with Honor, into a category reserved for love-stricken eighteen-year-old misses.

"And after you've married Patience off so conveniently, what then of Honor?" I challenged. "Do you intend to dispose of her in a like manner?"

"Apparently a blow on the head has not disturbed the talent you have for irritating me." He grimaced, pressing me back onto the settle. "And if I do expect Honor to marry in a like manner, what of it? Isn't it what you yourself would want for her? A home, a husband? Not so hastily, perhaps, and Honor, I admit, does present a problem I have not solved yet. That is, I have not solved the details. But she will live in New York, where I can be her guardian in fact. I intend to set her up in her own establishment, with a respectable lady as a chaperon, a lady of middle years," he added meaningly. "I anticipate that she will soon fall in love, as a girl of her beauty and fortune undoubtedly will find it easy to do, and marry."

"You speak as though all the details were settled," I snapped resentfully.

"They are, so far as you are concerned," he replied coolly. "Until this murder is solved, nothing can be done, however. But some order has to be brought back into this family of females. I did not ask for this guardianship, but I cannot in conscience refuse it now. However, I have no intention of devoting my future life to the problems of Honor and Patience! Once their respective positions are established, I expect each to become her husband's responsibility."

"Indeed? And what about the man Honor loves?" I asked dryly.

"I will deal with him if he shows up," he replied shortly. "I assure you, Emma, I am capable of doing so, and of putting Honor under restrictions so that she will never set eyes on him again, if it becomes necessary. She will find it harder to dupe me than she has you. You may rest easy on that score! However, I have my own thoughts about that gentleman, which only time will prove correct."

"And so you're going to take her away from me, just like that!" I panted. "Never allow me to see her again—"

"Dear me, did I say that? I have no objection to you seeing Honor as often as you like; I merely refuse to allow you the control of her guidance and care. The sooner you understand that, the better. I think you know that I blame you, in part, for this messy business of the diamonds, although I never once doubted your good intentions, nor your love for Honor. It is merely your good sense that I doubt, which tonight's episode has strengthened. Cousin Silence seemed to have had an inordinate respect for it, but then, she never understood you half as well as I do."

"Then you are punishing Honor because of my mistakes—"

"Confound it, Emma! I am not punishing Honor at all!" He ran his hand through his hair and glared at me. "I am offering her what any other eighteen-year-old girl would leap with joy to accept! Unlimited parties, pretty clothes, pin money, a doting guardian, and a kind, motherly, but not indulgent, chaperon! I tell you frankly that you are not fit to be that chaperon! Were I to clap the two of you together and give you your head, you would run away like a team of wild horses before I could stop you! You'd have Marcus Goddard in, given the run of the house—"

"I knew," I said furiously, "I *knew* you'd drag his name into it before you were through!"

"That last thing you blurted out to the judge this afternoon gave me a good idea of your common sense," he went on, as though I had not spoken. "It just proves you have no more notion of self-preservation than a five-year-old child! After I'd so carefully shamed him into giving you up as a suspect, you had to go and destroy your alibi!" He paused in his restless pacing to stand before the settle and and glare at me angrily.

"Alibi! What alibi?" I cried indignantly. "I had none! I accepted that from the beginning. The beads were mine, and that placed me on the spot, so far as the judge cared. How can you talk of alibis?"

"You had a way out, if you had kept your mouth shut," he replied coldly. "But instead of giving a thought to yourself, you were too anxious to clinch the safety of your friend, Joanna Eaton. So you declared that no one could possibly have gone into the office through the passageway without you seeing them! And what does that mean, you silly little idiot? It means that the murderer had to come in by way of the outside door, the alley door. And with Piper declaring that her mistress wouldn't open it to anyone but the judge, where does that leave you? You would hardly expect the judge to offer himself as a murder suspect, would you? Or perhaps that is just the sort of romantic noble gesture you might expect, after all? In truth, Emma," he added disgustedly, "how could you think I would allow you to live with Honor? A hotheaded romantic like you? Never! *That* possibility I would never allow!"

CHAPTER IX

"She is goin' to have to be told soon, Emma. You can't keep the poor creature in ign'rance much longer."

It had been two days since Silence's funeral, and, against my better judgment, Patience had not yet been told of her mother's death. Edward had allowed himself to be persuaded by Usher, unconsciously abetted by Piper, who was too sunk in apathy to voice an opinion. In the meanwhile, Marcus painted feverishly in an attempt to finish my portrait, and Thomas, with more time at his disposal, had made the loan he needed. Edward spent long hours in the office with Usher, briskly making plans to dispose of the house and pottery.

Now that all misunderstandings had been cleared, Joanna clung to me every waking hour, following me like a pale ghost, looking over her shoulder and searching the shadows. She was frightened of this house, of our future, for me and what the judge might discover to implicate me. She was also frightened of Patience, avoiding her whenever possible, and watching with round eyes Patience's restless, hungry search for her mother.

From the kitchen window I watched her progress as she prowled through the garden, stooping to peer under the hedges. I reminded Mrs. Margate that she was, thankfully, the concern of her guardian and her future husband, neither one of whom had asked my advice. I did not need the problem of Patience to complicate my future, for it was looking particularly hopeless to me just now, faced with the restrictions Edward was prepared to place on my friendship with Honor and the bleakness evidenced by Joanna's daily-growing loss of control.

And this morning the judge was back, prepared to ask more questions, which I felt singularly unable to answer. The servants had been excused from today's questioning, but Usher, as Patience's betrothed, was there in her stead.

To my relief, however, the judge ignored me in favor of a more likely suspect, one offered to him by the inquiry agency hired to find the diamonds. Needing the goodwill of the legal law enforcers, they had been prompt to come to him with their story. It hadn't taken him long to put together the missing pieces of the puzzle, particularly since he had been in the admirable position of having been granted Silence's confidence weeks earlier, when she told him of the missing gems and her suspicions of Honor. At that time it had been the judge who had suggested asking the help of her cousin, but, now, when he demanded of Honor the name of the man who accompanied her, she obstinately refused.

"No, Judge, he isn't involved in this at all. He's innocent, I assure you, and I won't name him, nor allow you to accuse him." Honor, white-faced, leaned across the table to face her tormentor. Her proud beauty and defiance touched the spirits of everyone present. Even the judge was moved.

"My dear child," he said compassionately. "Your loyalty does you credit, but you can't possibly be sure he isn't involved, and you may be shielding a murderer! What would your own life be worth then? I can always learn the truth from the minister in Marblehead—"

"It's all right, sweetheart," Marcus said softly. "I don't think anything can be gained by denying our love any longer. I am the man, Judge."

Joanna gasped and there was a small grunt of surprise from Usher and the judge. Edward straightened slowly from his lounging position against the door, but he did not seem particularly surprised.

"This is a shock, Mr. Goddard," the judge's voice came to me from a great, roaring distance, "and if true, removes you from suspicion, but—may I ask why you two deliberately set out to deceive Mrs. Southwick?"

"Nat Southwick was my foster brother," Marcus explained. "While I was in London, I learned six years too late of his death. News travels slowly, and I had believed he was angry with me for all of those six years; hence, his silence. When I learned that he had been murdered, I felt guilty and ashamed that I had allowed so much time to elapse without getting in touch with his widow. I didn't know if she even knew of my existence: Nat had never been communicative about me to his family. I realized it was too late to write, she might have remarried by now, but I thought of his daughter, and came home with the intention of doing something about her, and learning more about his murder. At first there was no wish to deceive, but upon making discreet inquiries, I learned much that was appalling.

"I deliberately arranged to meet Honor under an assumed name, and see for myself how she was treated by her mother. Honor knew me as soon as I identified myself, but said her mother would not. Her father had not talked about me to anyone but his daughter."

I blinked. By now my brain was working, creakily to be sure, but nevertheless it had returned to functioning order. By way of a few experimental deep breaths, I discovered that the temporary paralysis affecting me was nothing more than mingled shock and a deep chagrin that I had allowed myself to drift into believing that I had Marcus's love, when he had spoken only of friendship and respect. Nothing but a strong capacity for self-delusion could have led me to think it, and what a hardy plant it had been to thrive so well on such pale nourishment!

"Honor and I did not intend to fall in love," he added apologetically. "It came about as I grew to realize how lonely and vulnerable she was. Honor told me of the only person who cared about her, her good friend, Emma Ashton." He smiled at me and, God help me, I found the courage to smile back. "We did not want to deceive Emma, but we knew if we involved her, her position would become impossible when Mrs. Southwick learned the truth. We didn't want her to have to lie for us."

Edward threw me a look of pity, but I did not heed its meaning —it was foreign to the surge of blithe happiness I felt. Like a miracle, my world had righted itself, the sun had come out and lit the room with a blinding sparkle, and I knew an overwhelming relief. They had not wanted to hurt or cheat me, or lump me into Silence's category as someone unworthy of their confidence.

"As for the diamonds, I wanted Honor to wear them herself in a necklace. I even went so far as to design one for her. It is what her father intended, but—"

"But I stole them without him knowing anything about it!" Honor flashed. "And I told Marcus I would go alone to that horrid place if he didn't go with me! I don't want a diamond necklace; I intended to use the money for my bride clothes, when he and I eloped! He had nothing to do with any of it, and I will go to jail for stealing them, if necessary!"

"There is no question of going to jail," the judge replied testily. "Murder is the issue here, not the diamonds, and they were legally yours. I was counting on—that is, I believed we would find your accomplice to be the murderer."

"Your alternative, that Mistress Ashton is, is equally unacceptable," Edward said crisply.

"I am as loath as you are, sir, to accept Mistress Ashton's guilt," the judge replied stiffly, "although by her own words, she is the only one in the house that day to have the opportunity. As a law enforcer, I cannot dismiss that piece of evidence as lightly as you do."

The words were hardly out before Edward Murray sat down upon them with all the pugnaciousness of a terrier worrying a rat.

"I don't want to dismiss it lightly," he spoke between his teeth, "for by the very candor of her statement she has demonstrated her innocence, in my opinion. But if in making your case you are relying upon the examination you and I gave the body, then I must tell you that I will have to dispute you in a court of law. We are neither one medical men, and I have had only a limited experience with the dead aboard ship. When there is a hot fire in the room, as there was that day—"

If Edward was a terrier, the judge was a fox, with all of a fox's cunning, as he silkily introduced the names of the two witnesses upon whom rested the proof of his case against me. They were of excellent repute, he told us, a local small merchant and his wife with a business in mortgage to Silence, and on the afternoon of her death they had kept an appointment to make a payment on their loan. They had left her, alone but alive, at twenty minutes after five, ten minutes before the judge's arrival. Hearing of the murder and eager to cooperate, they had come forward with their story, thereby making their innocence more pronounced in the eyes of the law. The merchant bore a duly witnessed receipt, his payment was found in Silence's desk, and there was no reason to disbelieve his testimony, the judge added, particularly since Silence herself had asked the hour, then verified it by her own pocket watch.

"Which I have kept with me," the judge tapped his waistcoat pocket, "in order to vouch for its accuracy, if necessary. Already it keeps excellent time by my own timepiece." He threw me a triumphant glance.

I had been listening absorbedly, but now I came to earth with a bump. I could no longer hide from myself the knowledge of the web of circumstantial evidence tightly binding me, from which there would soon be no escape, nor the fact that it was being contrived from a maddening series of inconsequential, trivial events. First, the beads—how—why had Silence been wearing them?; then the will; and lastly, the words—my own—that had locked me, a prisoner of time and place, directly into the murder scene as the only person who could be guilty. No wonder Edward Murray had contemptuously called me a foolish romantic!

If he was dismayed by the judge's story, he gave no indication of it but smiled sardonically as he said, "Let's have no misunderstanding about this, Judge. I do not intend to allow you to pin this crime on that girl's shoulders. If an attempt is made to use her as a scapegoat, I will resist you with every weapon of power at my disposal."

"And I, too," Thomas added firmly. "I have conferred with Mr. Murray about this, and he speaks for the rest of us. Do not be misled into thinking that because Emma Ashton is poor and works in an inferior position, she is also friendless and without protectors!"

The judge's eyes flickered slightly but they did not waver from Edward, the only antagonist worthy of his mettle. Then he looked at me thoughtfully, and I knew he was giving careful weight to the strength of his case against me, judging its resilience in the face of the objections it was now expected to weather. The constable cleared his throat, as though to remind him of his duty, but it was Honor who provided a distraction that the judge, no less than I, welcomed with relief.

"Judge Dashwood," she said timidly, "you mentioned Mama's watch the other day, and again today. That is twice you have said the same thing, and I wondered if you really meant—*Mama's* watch?"

Piper's head swiveled slowly, as though on rusty hinges, and she stared steadily at Honor.

The judge was amused. "Yes, my dear, I really meant just what I said! You may keep it until the trial, if you like." He pulled it carefully from his pocket as he spoke, and I saw that it was a beautifully chased gold watch, obviously London-made. The judge commented on its quality: "A fine timepiece, as you can see. It chimes the hour, too."

Honor leaned forward and wonderingly touched it. "Judge, I told you Mama didn't wear jewelry. This is not her watch, but it looks very much like my father's!"

It *was* Captain Southwick's watch: not only Honor, but Piper, identified it, and when opened his name was found engraved on an inner lid. It was the watch he was winding as he strolled into the kitchen garden, minutes before his death. A half-dozen servants, watching from the kitchen window, swore to that afterward. It was also the watch, missing from his body, that had supported the theory that he had been killed by a casual tramp for its value. Piper, all of us, could swear with creditable confidence that it had not been in Silence's possession until now, and the judge, turning and twisting as he sought to plausibly explain its reappearance, found that he could not explain it, any more than he could ignore it. For the time being, at least, I could breathe easily, as I was granted yet another reprieve.

Marcus was wild with excitement now that his brother's murder was receiving a closer look, but the judge could tell him nothing new. He had not been in charge of the investigation but, as a friend of Silence's, he had given it more than cursory attention. In spite of the many rumors to the contrary, it was a cut-and-dried fact that there had been only one way of entrance into the garden that day: by way of the alley past the office door, while Silence's attention was momentarily diverted. She herself had admitted the possibility later, after vehemently denying it earlier. The other two entrances had been under the eyes of too many people. The outside gate near the pottery shed was in view of the kitchen, and the other entrance was through the shop and out the back passage door. Piper had been having a brisk trade that afternoon; nevertheless, no one could have slipped past her, and she herself could not have left the shop long enough to commit the crime.

Here the judge paused and eyed her speculatively, and I wondered if Piper had been a major suspect at the time of that long-ago investigation. "The very nature of the crime seemed to argue a casual, unplanned thing," the judge added.

"I was with her when she chose it," Piper murmured, lost in a private dream. She was pale, but she wore a purposeful air. She was holding the watch in one hand while her thumb caressed the engraved lettering on the lid. "It was just in from a London jeweler, and it cost her a sizable sum, but nothing was too good for him. Aye, he was a bonny lad, right enough, and had a roving eye until it fell on her! And she was more than a match for him—a real beauty, she was, until her accident! But how she loved him!"

"Yes, so I always thought," the judge agreed dryly. "I assumed she was honest when she changed her story."

"What are you trying to say?" Piper asked suspiciously.

The judge shrugged. "No one can ever know what motive might exist between a man and his wife, particularly now that both of them are dead. I think it's obvious what happened, and she had the watch, didn't she?"

Piper glared at him. "I've taken care of her, her clothes, her room, every day of the eight years since he died," she declared passionately, "and she couldn't have had the watch without me knowing, I tell you! I haven't seen it from that day until this!"

In the end, the Law retreated, slightly shaken by the violence of Piper's rejection and no nearer to the truth than before. As Edward was seeing him to the door, the judge paused to impart a last bit of philosophy: "We may never know the truth about any of this, Mr. Murray. These crimes may be connected, they may be isolated, but I can state one thing with confidence: some families attract tragedy. Look at the history of this one."

Edward returned briskly, looking less harried. Piper had

departed, but Honor, unwilling to admit her mother's involvement, was cautiously discussing the possibility of her guilt.

"Cousin Edward," she asked in a subdued voice, "do you think Piper killed my father?"

"I don't know, Honor," he replied absently. "She knows something, certainly. A talk with her seems indicated, since her fears are directly connected with those blue beads of Emma's. If you remember, she fainted when she saw them."

"What do you mean?" Usher asked blankly.

Edward explained, but his thoughts were elsewhere. At the first opportunity he asked, "May I see you in the office, Emma?"

He began forcibly, as though holding in check a strong inclination to speak violently. "It seems to me, Emma, you are beginning to acquire some sort of record for barely averting arrest! Are you ready to awaken to the danger you are in, and start thinking of, and for, yourself?"

I eyed him resentfully. Mercifully, he had not referred to my blighted hopes, but I did not pretend to misunderstand his meaning. "If you mean—my head has been filled, until now, with vain hopes—" I began.

"I mean that your head has been filled with moonshine," he interrupted irritably, "put there in part by myself, for which I beg your pardon!"

"But I am still alive to my own danger," I went on steadily. "All along I have been feeling as though a dark, malign Fate is drawing me into a sticky web." Tears were near the surface; I blinked vigorously.

To my surprise, he agreed. "Yes, I think you are being used. The presence of the blue beads was not an accidental thing. I want to talk to Piper about that."

I sniffed and blew my nose just as a timid knock on the door announced Piper's appearance.

"Mr. Edward, sir, please help me," she gasped.

"I hope to, Piper," he said kindly. "Come in and tell me about it." He hooked a chair with his foot and, drawing it to the fire, pressed the frightened little creature into it. As she faced us, her hands agitatedly working in her lap, I noticed how much change had been made in her by Silence's death. Never a large woman, she seemed to have shrunk in size to birdlike dimensions, which a nervous, bobbing, pecking motion of her head served to emphasize. She gazed at me in dumb entreaty. Piper! who had resented my coming and fought every step of my progress with all the strength of a naturally choleric disposition. All of the opposition had fled now: she seemed to have collapsed within herself. I had a sudden, vivid memory of Mrs. Margate's words when told of her mistress's death: "I knew she'd never make old bones. . . ."

She raised her eyes and gazed about wonderingly, and I knew she was seeing the strangeness of the room. Familiar and dear to her in all ways, a reminder of Silence, it had changed now in a subtle and, to Piper, hurting fashion, after only a week of male occupancy. Mud scrapings on the fender; the cold, dead fireplace, where, for most of the year, a blaze was kept stoked; the littered desk; high on a shelf, beyond the reach of either woman, the carelessly scattered sheets of foolscap. The windows were open, the shutters flung back, to allow light and air, and there was a constant passage of footsteps, shadowed forms, and sometimes an oath or snatches of words from the street activity. To a woman of Silence's physical infirmities, such public exposure would have been abhorrent; Edward Murray found it always stimulating, and occasionally amusing, but never disconcerting to rub shoulders so intimately with the unending parade that passed by.

Piper tore her convulsive gaze away from the silent wheelchair in the corner and turned to Edward. "I think Judge Dashwood intends to accuse my mistress of the captain's death," she began. "Please stop him, sir. You are her cousin. You can't want that, either! It isn't true, sir. No one here remembers that day as I do, but she couldn't have walked to the garden and she was just learning to use her wheelchair."

"We must see if we can come up with another explanation to satisfy the judge," Edward replied soothingly. "But I must know everything, Piper. You do understand that, don't you?"

"Yes, sir, and that's all right, sir. I just want to be sure my mistress isn't accused of his murder, when she loved him so."

I had wondered the other day to whom Piper's new loyalty

would go: I, who had heard her story, should have known it would never swerve from Silence. Piper was a draggle-tailed little gutter rat, half dead and permanently stunted from malnutrition, when she was dredged up from a scurvy-riddled ship to be sold, at thirteen, as an indentured servant. She had just survived a crossing of the Atlantic that would have made a strong man blench; seen her mother succumb to the bad food and water and buried at sea; she had endured the fetid air of the hold and fought off the advances of the ship's crew, who seemed to think any female over the age of puberty was fair game and theirs by right. Pretty Silence Mullins, only fourteen and looking for a personable maid, had chosen her from right off the Boston dockside, much to her father's disgust. A couple of years later, when Silence became a child bride to an adoring middle-aged husband, Piper had gone with her, already in thrall to her beautiful, spoiled mistress.

"When the captain was killed and she changed her story—you know about that, sir?—I thought she knew the truth and meant me to be quiet about what I knew," she began ramblingly. "I thought she approved of what I did. Not that words ever passed between us, sir. Lately, since the new will, I have wondered if I did the right thing, for apparently, sir, she hadn't known the truth after all."

"What are you trying to say?" Edward asked slowly.

"About Patience, sir. Patience and the captain. I never spoke of it to my mistress, for I thought to spare her the pain. She knew, as I did, that Patience hated him, particularly after he came home from sea the last time. He saw how jealous she was of his own little girl, and he wasn't going to have that, sir! He feared for his child's life, and rightly so, if you ask me. He saw the dolls she destroyed, the pets she killed, merely because Honor loved them. Sometimes, even—savagely—"

How did he die? I remembered blindingly, then, *You are lucky it was merciful.*

"But she was worse after he came home, truly, sir. The mistress tried to tell him she could be docile if handled properly, but he must give in to her in all things and not pet Honor in her presence. He was so angry! He said no, they must sell out and move to Tremount Street, where Patience could be confined as her grandmother was, and Honor have more room to play. The mistress, of course, could deny him nothing, so she agreed to do as he asked. Patience became so angry upon learning what was planned, she broke Honor's arm and threw her mother down the stairs. It injured her back, but the mistress knew she had goaded her into it, so she forgave her. She knew she lost her head with jealousy, but later Patience forgot what she had done, and clung to me and begged me so prettily!"

"Dear God," Edward whispered. "Do you mean you killed him for her?"

"I? Oh, no, sir!" Piper was shocked. "That would be a sin! I would not kill anyone! But when they questioned me if anyone went *through* the shop that day, I told the truth. That was all. Merely the truth. *They* were at fault, for not thinking of the daughter upstairs, sir! You see, she was only sixteen, and I guess they never thought it possible for her to . . ." Her voice trailed to a stop at the expression on his face and she gazed at us dumbly.

I gulped as my eyes met his, our faces wearing identical looks of whitened shock. Sixteen, and already a murderess!

"She walked down the steps and out the back door right after he did, and no one thought to question her. God!" Edward's voice was awed as he called once more upon the Deity. "Did she steal the captain's watch, Piper?"

"She must have, sir. She loved pretty jewelry, and when it was missing I knew she must have taken it. That first year, I searched for it through her things, knowing it must be somewhere, but she was clever, sir, she had hidden it well. My mistress must have found it, but the question is, how? And when? She never went upstairs to Patience's room, for she couldn't manage the steps."

"Until the night her clothes were destroyed." Edward's eyes met mine again. We both remembered that strangled moan and Silence's revulsion afterward, as she refused to remain in her daughter's room.

"And when Obediah made his threats, and she didn't comment on what he said, I was sure she knew then," Piper went on, still trying to justify the years of withholding a secret from her mistress.

"What did Obediah threaten?"

"To tell what he'd seen, or rather not seen, sir. He had been sent on an errand by the mistress and instead of returning immediately, he lingered in the alley with the hussy from the butcher's shop next door. And *no one* entered that way at all, in spite of Miss Silence's testimony! Obediah was the one to find the body, and he guessed Miss Patience was guilty. He kept quiet all these years, hoping to blackmail the mistress someday. But when he tried, she wouldn't listen, but raved at him!"

"Perhaps she willfully blinded herself to what she heard," Edward mused. "But why, Piper, knowing what she did, did my cousin punish Honor?"

"Punish?" Blankly. "She didn't regard it as punishment, sir, but discipline. Honor was strong and Patience weak; it was that simple. Too, she was afraid to show Honor too much love, for her own safety. As to why, sir," Piper added simply, "I don't know. A doctor would have to tell you that, sir, I can't."

I shivered.

"But with the new will, it is clear what she wants for Patience. From me and you too, Miss Emma." She looked at me pleadingly. "She wants Patience confined, as the captain once told her she must do. She decided her child's punishment herself, for when she found the watch, she knew. You and I are to be her jailers. She always liked you, you know," Piper added gravely. "That first day you came, so frightened and so nervous, she said to me after you left the room, 'She'll do, Piper. Someday when you and I are too old, she'll do for Patience.' She was happy to see that your face was scarred, for it meant you'd stay and Patience would not be jealous of you. How she laughed at the judge and the reverend, and enjoyed playing one against the other! 'Let them propose all they like, they won't tempt Emma! I know her too well!' A bit of mischief she had with them, you might say, Miss Emma," she added apologetically.

And a bit of mischief she had had with me, too, I added to myself when I thought of the miserable evenings I had endured in the parlor, fending off one or the other of my suitors.

Edward growled softly under his breath, then, with a strong effort, he centered his thoughts back on Piper. "Mistress Ashton can't help you with Patience if she is in jail," he said sternly. "Because of the blue beads, the judge suspects her of murdering your mistress!"

"The blue beads?" Piper's brow wrinkled with astonishment. "But why, sir? Miss Emma had nothing to do with them! Patience herself wore them out in the rain, and somewhere, outside, lost them. I saw them on her before she left the house. That's why I swooned, fearing at first that she had something to do with her mother's death. She must have found the beads in your trunk while plundering for your bracelet, Miss Emma."

"Ah—" Edward hissed, but shook his head warningly at me. Piper had no notion of the importance of what she had told. "We must talk to her at once then."

"Yes, sir, and do you think, sir," Piper added eagerly, "that the judge will be satisfied to drop inquiries into the captain's death? Miss Silence wouldn't want Patience accused publicly."

Edward nodded judiciously. "I think so, Piper. But let's find Patience first."

But Patience was nowhere to be found. Jacob, busy at the pottery wheel, had allowed her to leave when he saw the judge's carriage roll away from the door, shortly before noon. But now she was not to be found, and an exhaustive search of the house and grounds failed to turn up any sign of her. It was I who thought of the church, and more particularly of the new grave in the churchyard, as I sought to follow Patience's reasoning. Edward, deploying the searchers with the tactics of a General Washington, did not think much of the idea but he was willing for me to explore it.

"I rather believe she watched Usher leave, then attempted to follow him home," he said. "She may now be wandering the streets of Boston, lost, so I intend to alert the Watch on my way to the Green Goose Inn."

Piper, listening gloomily, was inclined to agree with him. "She doesn't like the church, Miss Emma, thinking it cold and dark. But she would have gone there or anywhere else if she overheard something to make her think her mother was there."

And that could have happened, I thought as I hurried toward the church. A passing conversation, floating back over the wall: a chance word or two dropped by one of us, and Patience could have easily seized upon an impression and followed it wherever it led. And once there, once having seen the new grave between the other two, what then? What would she think? If she guessed the truth, what hysterical outburst, what insane violence would follow? By now I was frankly running.

Within sight of the church, I slowed, gasping from the pain of the stitch in my side, deflated by the knowledge that I had, apparently, been wrong. The throng of curious, whom I had halfway expected to find gathered, was not there. Even from here I could see the mound of brown earth, but the churchyard was empty and all seemed as usual. Serene in its whitewashed simplicity, its wooden spire pointing heavenward, the church stood firmly planted in its own small green plot of Boston town.

I hesitated, dithering on the path, not sure what I should do next, when I glimpsed a tantalizing streak of scarlet disappearing around the back corner of the church, as brief and flashing as the flight of the tanager. I hesitated no longer, not questioning the providential glimpse I had been granted, but swerved that way, propelled by no more than instinct and the knowledge that Patience's cloak, like mine, bore a scarlet lining.

A mighty chestnut tree benignly shaded the windows at the back of the church, its spreading roots and branches preventing the street from encroaching too closely. An outside flight of stairs—in fact, the only stairs to the gallery and belfry—was attached to the back wall of the church, and it was toward those that my attention was directed. The door at the top was closing with a gentle hiss as I arrived, panting, to find that my quarry was still slightly ahead of me. As if to underline that fact, a crushed, damp leaf, kicked free from a shoe that had, as recently as seconds ago, ascended those steps, floated softly earthward, swirling and spiraling, to come to a delicate, gentle halt on the outstretched palm of my hand.

I started up the steps.

In the doorway I faltered and strained to make the adjustment from the noon sunlight to near-darkness. The gallery ran three parts of the way around the church and was divided in front by the chancel. Always dusty, gloomy, and cold, it lacked the windows to provide necessary light, and therefore seemed to serve no useful purpose of its own. It had been designed originally for the spiritual use of black slaves, but had never been thus occupied: fortunately so, since the mood of the congregation was, on the whole, abolitionist, and they had therefore never been called upon to compromise their principles.

My attention was drawn in an unmistakable way to the belfry trapdoor, which was reached by a ladder directly above the front door. Since this was the only means of escape from the gallery, other than the door behind me, I was not surprised to see Patience mounting it, her gray cloak bunched demurely around her slim ankles. As I watched, her head and body disappeared with a jerk, as though yanked up into the aperture, and the trapdoor clanged shut with a bang, but not before a teasing "Emma!" thrown roguishly over her shoulder, had begun its whispered echo through the empty chamber.

What could the minx be up to? It was a laughing, conspiratorial whisper; obviously, she had not learned of her mother's death, but I thought little of her chances to continue in that ignorance, once she stood upright and surveyed the churchyard from the vantage of the belfry floor.

The church was filled with that forlorn yet expectant solemnity that all churches assume when empty. I looked upon the pews below, their dark wooden railings polished smooth by the hands of devout Sunday worshippers, the whitewashed walls reflecting back the sun from the dazzling prismatic light, caught and held, like a leprechaun's rainbow, in the tiny panes of mullion glass. Their glitter only served to intensify the gloom of the upper floor, making it easy for me to imagine myself watched by unseen eyes, easy to see faces in the shifting shadows.

I willed myself to follow Patience. She could not be left to find her way down alone: she was capable of any sort of foolish action if she saw her mother's grave and recognized it as such. I thought of the small, boxy belfry, with its waist-high wooden wall and the dangling bell rope overhead. Here the sexton had stood when he rang of Silence's death, six strokes for a woman, then the series of short, quick strokes giving her age. From here, two days later, as she was carried from the church and lowered into the grave, the mournful, tolling bell had signaled her passing.

I shivered, touched by an uneasy premonition, and with a last wary look over my shoulder, mounted the ladder.

The trapdoor was locked.

"Patience!" I called angrily, rapping on it smartly with my knuckles. "Open this door! It's Emma! Let me come up!"

I pushed again, and with an ease that mocked the anger behind my thrust, the trapdoor swung upward, revealing a pocket-sized view of the brilliant blue sky. Patience apparently was hidden behind the door. Cautiously I mounted a second and third step of the ladder. Then, with a silken rustle and flashing streak of scarlet, I was enveloped from behind in the folds of Patience's cloak, lifted bodily up the remaining two steps, and thrown to the floor, where I lay blinded in the soft, smothering thickness as my hands were ruthlessly tied to my sides.

Dimly I heard the slam of the trapdoor.

"Patience!" I shrieked, outraged. "Come back! Don't you dare—"

I stopped abruptly. Although blindfolded, and with my senses muffled, I knew that I was alone. She was gone. Sputtering with anger, floundering about on the floor like a headless chicken, I swarmed out of the cloak to find myself alone, as I expected. Overhead, the sky tilted, then righted itself, and I sat up cautiously, spitting out the stuffy taste of thick wool.

A portion of the bell rope had been used to tie me, and not very adequately at that, since I had been able to break free in less than a minute. Yet it had given Patience the precious time she needed to get away. Altogether, I thought grimly, it was the sort of miserable little trick I might expect from her, and I could be thankful that her sense of humor had not extended to a more serious prank.

I rose unsteadily and shook out my skirts, then bent to pick up her cloak. She deserved to have it left behind, I thought viciously. As I straightened up again, a cry attracted my attention, and I leaned over the enclosure to peer below. I saw first the faces, staring up at me, and all wearing similar masks of stupidity. Then I saw the figure lying at their feet, sprawled like a limp, broken doll. I didn't need anyone to tell me who it was. Patience. And it was obvious that she was dead.

CHAPTER X

"Why didn't I hear her jump?" my mind worried tenaciously at the puzzle. I was huddled in a corner of my little box, shaking with vertigo and unable to move. A minute or two had passed, and, hearing the sounds of running and shouts, I supposed dimly that someone would eventually help me down. People usually helped one, I thought idly. It was a problem that did not greatly interest me: I even found myself yawning repeatedly, as though to demonstrate to myself my indifference.

I sternly repressed the last yawn and took myself firmly in hand. I couldn't remain where I was, too dizzy to stand up, too frightened to climb down. At this rate, I might dawdle all night, while my fears increased and I was forgotten by the crowd below. I had to make an effort to help myself. I began to crawl forward, fighting down waves of cramping sickness, until I reached the trapdoor, and then found I could lift it only a foot or two before I had to rest, gasping, and wait for my churning stomach to settle.

"You can't get away with it, you know." It was Edward's voice, beneath me, and so casually unconcerned that I assumed he didn't know of Patience's death or of my own predicament.

I widened the gaping hole slightly.

But I could not see Edward. The man standing directly beneath me, hanging on to the ladder with a crooked elbow, was not he. I could see from his dark, clipped hair that he was in the habit of wearing a wig. The small slice of vision I was granted was inadequate for much else, beyond one booted foot outstretched and poised as though ready to clamber farther up the ladder, and frighteningly, a slim brown hand, clad in lace ruffles and gripping a big, exceedingly dangerous-looking pistol. The menace that tautened the slim figure and whitened the trigger finger of that hand was unmistakable.

Then Edward moved into my line of vision, large and solidly reassuring. From his face, he did not seem unduly disturbed to be facing an armed man, until one noticed his clenched fists and slightly quickened breathing.

"Stay where you are!" The warning was sharp. "If you move another pace forward, I shall have to kill you, then do something very unpleasant to Miss Ashton, who is perched right above me. Remember, I can move up the ladder before you can reach me!"

I gasped. Edward started and glanced up quickly, taking me in where I crouched, framed by the open door. I saw that my presence had proved a distraction to him, but before I could move, Usher, with the suddenness of a snake, retreated a step or two up the ladder, until he was directly beneath me. "Don't close that door, Miss Ashton," he called urgently. "If you do, I'll kill Mr. Murray instantly and take my chances on getting away!"

I froze, stopped in my tracks as effectively as though a noose had dropped around my neck.

"Close it, Emma. Lock it and call for help," Edward said calmly. "He won't dare shoot me, for the yard is full of men who will be coming upstairs in just a moment."

I swiveled like a limp doll swaying in the wind, but Usher's next words halted any notion I might have had of following Edward's instructions.

"Not so quickly as all that, I think," he said smoothly. "I heard you telling Marcus Goddard to keep the crowd back while you went in to get Miss Ashton alone. I think he'll do just as he was told, for he is an admirable fellow in all respects! It was then that I returned back up the stairs, seeing my way of escape cut off, and decided to use Miss Ashton as a hostage."

"Do you think I'll let you take her?" Edward asked as though amused.

"I think you'll do anything to avoid getting her killed!" Usher agreed cordially. "But rush me if you like. Although this pistol discharges only one bullet, at this range I can be sure of a direct hit!"

"No!" I screamed, scrambling to the edge of the yawning hole. "Stop! I'll be your hostage!"

Usher laughed maliciously. "I thought so. Really, this is a most amusing situation. I wonder if I am the first one to suspect. And even I might still be ignorant if I hadn't listened to my beloved Patience," his voice was rich with irony, "who was as clever as a monkey when it came to ferreting out secrets! She told me of the tender feelings she suspected and was full of glee at the thought of Honor's discomfiture."

I was too frantic for embarrassment, and Edward's face merely expressed his contempt. "Did you think I did not suspect you too?" he asked cuttingly. "Why do you think I was so close on Emma's heels when I learned you had been seen coming this way?"

"You didn't!" Usher cried, outraged, his arrogance pricked. "I fooled you from the beginning! When I ranted of my love for Patience that night, I saw you convinced! I didn't make a single mistake, unless you count the blow that didn't quite kill Emma Ashton—"

"From which she survived," Edward agreed icily. "What about Molly? You've killed her, I presume?"

"Not at all," Usher replied sharply. "I wouldn't kill a pleasing little armful like Molly! Oh, I whipped her well for her indiscretions, but then I forgave her! She had only hoped to jostle me into marriage or, failing that, sell her information to Patience's guardian. She's waiting for me, and, when the time is right, she'll swear that I was with her during all—all the murders. She wants respectability, you see, and I've promised her marriage. I wager the judge himself won't be able to shake her story, once I finish with her."

I listened to this artless confession with a sinking heart, for I knew it wouldn't have been made if Usher intended allowing either of us to leave the church alive. I now saw that his purpose in demanding that I come down the ladder was not to use me as a hostage, but to kill me, after first killing Edward. Doubtless he had already planned the arrangement of our bodies so that one would be a murder, the other a suicide.

Apparently, Usher realized, equally as soon as we did, that he had given himself away, for he risked a quick look upward. "Come down here at once, Miss Ashton, or I use this pistol on him right now!"

"Stay where you are, Emma!" Edward cried sharply. "He can't possibly get away with another murder! He is doomed, as soon as the judge hears about the beads—"

Usher laughed shortly. "Yes, those beads! They were a mistake, weren't they? The one mistake I will allow you to say I made. I thought to use a trinket of Emma Ashton's, to involve her by using the will, which I saw at once was worthless, but I depended upon a broken reed when I asked Patience to bring me something from her trunk. Little did I know the simpleton would wear it herself, and I had another stroke of bad luck when Piper saw her! So, soon as I heard about it today, I knew what had happened. I knew I would have to kill her to keep her mouth shut. All for nothing!" he added despairingly. "But once again my luck held, when Emma Ashton came along as a convenient scapegoat to take the blame for Patience's murder!"

"Nonsense! There is no talk of murder outside," Edward said soothingly. "Everyone believes it was suicide. On a fast horse, even now you could—"

"Until they find the bell rope around her neck," Usher interrupted ironically. "I couldn't depend on the fall killing her." He grinned sourly. "Don't think to fob me off by stampeding me into flight, Mr. Murray, for I prefer to remain here and take my chances with the law, rather than with the Indians."

"If I were fanciful, I would almost think you had a grudge against Emma," Edward said stonily.

"Now that the rapiers have been unsheathed, I don't mind admitting that I dislike her intensely," Usher replied viciously. "As a matter of fact, she makes me sick! Any physical impairment, any —ugliness—always has, since I was a boy! Yet, in that house, I was surrounded by cripples of one kind or another. Silence in her wheelchair, Patience was an idiot, and Piper a stunted hunchback! It has been a penance for me, to be forced to sit across the table from Emma Ashton at dinner and gaze upon that blemished face. . . ."

Edward's lips drew back into a snarl. He shifted but did not complete the movement before Usher raised his pistol. When Usher spoke again, his voice was shrill and breathless with excitement, and I saw that he had been given an additional weapon by Edward's reaction to his crudity. Now he saw how he could madden him with words. "Her interference didn't end with spoiling my meals! I was kicked out like a cringing dog, and Emma Ashton given a chance at the money that should have been mine! It wasn't merely that Silence found the watch; Molly had been at work, and she was too straitlaced to have a womanizer in the house. So I imitated the judge's voice at the door, wore a peruke like his, and Silence was fooled for the few moments it took to get inside. I confess to you, Mr. Murray, I shall also enjoy the next few minutes. Miss Ashton," he called roughly, "this time I mean what I say! If you don't come immediately, I'll shoot and take my chances later on convincing the judge you're guilty. In fact," he added reflectively, "it might be more pleasurable that way."

Despair washed over Edward's face. From where I sat, I could see Usher's finger begin to tighten slowly, and I knew that he had finished posturing and boasting before his audience. So I did the only thing left to be done: I dropped, like a stone, straight down upon his head.

"I want to know if he tried to wriggle out of his confession," I demanded imperiously.

It was much later. I broke my ankle in the fall, and viewed what came afterward through a jumble of pain. Succumbing to the torment of a rough jolting during the carriage trip home, and later to the exquisite agony of Dr. Dashwood's ministrations with splint and bandages, I was not much use to any of the persons who crowded around and asked questions of me. From the sound of muffled cries, hushed voices, and the bustling figures that passed through the kitchen, I dimly perceived that a great deal must be happening, but under the influence of a generous dose of laudanum, I found it inconsequential and of no interest to myself. Now, wide awake and wound securely in Mrs. Margate's flannel wrapper, I was receiving guests in the kitchen, sitting like a duchess in the middle of my feather bed while the littered remains of a meal on a tray rested in my lap.

Edward laughed heartily at my pert question. "He would have wriggled like a worm, if that luck he boasted of had shown any sign of continuing," he said. "After I had seen you to the carriage, I went back to find him, by that time conscious and trying to sit up and pretend that he was an innocent victim of circumstances. However, someone had brought in a torch, for it was near dark, and in the light, traces of sparkling mineral clay could be plainly seen smeared down his ruffled shirt front, where Patience had marked him in the fight for her life. These men, remember, had just seen her body and had noticed her hands, and try as he would, he couldn't deny such plain evidence! My good friend Jesse Lee," he added, smiling, "would call that evidence the handprints of God."

"He is still trying to pretend that he is innocent," the judge said heavily, "and beyond cursing you and Miss Ashton, which he has continued to do in a steady, unending stream since we jailed him, he won't say another word. He demands that we send for Molly Haley, who he says can swear to his presence with her during the times of the murders."

"He may be surprised there," I said unexpectedly. "I talked to her and I don't think she is as eager to perjure herself as he seems to think."

"Why did he kill Mrs. Southwick?" Marcus asked.

"I think you all know the answer to that," Edward said quietly. "She learned the truth about Patience the night before her death, and the next day, from Molly Haley, about him. She had already rewritten her will, but now he was out of favor as her lawyer. His hatred turned on Emma, for he more than half suspected that she had coerced her into making the will. He decided then to implicate her, anticipating that the judge would think, as he did, that since Silence was wishy-washy about her wills, Emma would expect her to change it once again."

"Harumph." The judge shifted nervously. He had already sent more than one apologetic glance my way, and I knew that, given encouragement, I would have my old suitor back on my hands. "He was, unfortunately, right. I have a great deal to answer for.

But he was lucky with his timing, for how could he know that Miss Ashton wouldn't have an alibi?"

"He couldn't," Edward agreed. "He was more concerned that Patience would, for it was no part of his plan that she be accused of her mother's murder. He was lucky, yes, but remember that he knew the habits of the household, and he watched from the street, after sending Patience inside, and saw Emma lead her away, probably to the kitchen. He couldn't know that Emma, through her own impetuous tongue, would entrap herself." He gave me an ironic bow.

"Yes, he was lucky and clever, but he was not particularly wise about people," Edward added. "He seriously misread Emma's character, as well as Obediah's. He assumed, like Silence, who dangled her moneybags before Emma's nose, that she would be dazzled by the lure of a fortune, and would need no other motive. And he simply could not comprehend Obediah's indifference to that same fortune, when he himself was preparing to barter his soul for it in spite of his revulsion toward Patience."

"Why did he kill Obediah?" Honor asked in a low voice.

"Your mother, being the lovable skinflint she was, was prepared to strike the best bargain possible with Obediah. She was in his debt, but so long as there was a chance she could bully or cajole him into marrying Patience, she would never have accepted Usher as a son-in-law. It wasn't until Obediah, fighting for you, Honor, with his back to the wall, threatened to expose Patience that Usher saw he couldn't allow his golden girl to be destroyed before he had her fortune secure."

"And will Mog be released from jail?" I asked wistfully.

"Oh yes." The judge glanced at me, bright-eyed, inviting me to share his magnanimity. "It was the first thing I did when I brought Usher in. We don't lag when we discover an injustice, Miss Ashton."

I was glad, for of late I had been dreaming of Mog, spurred on, no doubt, by my own close brush with prison. So recently had the horrifying aspects of the Bastille been freely publicized in the press, with the stories of its condemned men left to languish for years and descriptions of their sufferings, while America, a loyal friend of France, sought a reasonable explanation for the excesses of the Revolution. Such a picture of my own future, cast into prison for years on end, forgotten by the world, had begun to haunt my dreams, with Mog's despairing face frequently superimposed upon my own. I had known myself to be without family, as he was, and wondered how staunch my friends would be if they became convinced of my guilt.

I did not answer the judge and, sighing wistfully, he arose, while Edward watched him amusedly.

"I can't help but feel that I have made a poor showing in this case, Mr. Murray," he said in a woebegone manner. "I feel responsible for Mrs. Southwick's death, for if I had not notified him that she was about to change her will, Usher would never have hurried over here and made his plans to kill her."

"Nonsense!" Edward said briskly. "You're not to blame yourself for what was no more than a humane impulse, sir! You were thinking of Patience's happiness. I might argue the same thing— that by meddling in the pottery that afternoon, I caused the quarrel that resulted in Obediah's death."

I wondered dismally where I would find my own absolution. Murderess though she was, Patience had been, at times, curiously endearing. I had known, when I silently acquiesced in the decision to withhold from her the knowledge of her mother's death, that we were also denying her the right to grieve. I had abandoned her, ignoring her wild, growing apprehension and thereby making it easy for Usher to entice her to the church; even, perhaps, making her death necessary because I did not question her.

Yes, my guilt was as great as theirs, and I unwillingly foretold that it would remain with me long after the memory of Patience had faded from my mind.

The telling of my story cannot be complete without the narration of two more events that took place soon after the arrest of Usher Tournais for the murder of Patience Pride, and others. Molly Haley, contrary to his expectations, quietly left town on the arm of a peddler before she was required to perjure herself by providing him with an alibi. It is noteworthy, too, that Mog O'Shaughnessy, with a recommendation from Edward Murray in his pocket, left Boston the day after his release from prison, headed for the state of New Jersey and the pottery works there. For the rest—well, the rest is personal and, except for the following, does not concern the reader.

The first was the receipt of a letter by Marcus, offering him an opportunity to work in London under his old master. He was wildly eager to leave at once, and rightly so, for to a young artist London was the hub of the world. Here, he could sit at the feet of Sir Thomas Lawrence or the Americans, John Copley and Benjamin West; here, he could study the magnificent portraits of Gainsborough. There was much, yet, for Marcus to learn.

So, I saw Honor married after all. In a simple ceremony attended by the Eatons and Edward Murray, I stood beside her and watched her given into Marcus's keeping. I wept, and afterward our usual roles were reversed, and Honor comforted me, allowing me my tears as proper and fitting to the occasion. The wedding had been performed by the kindly Jesse Lee, since the Reverend Wilford had professed himself outraged by the unbecoming haste, and refused to lend his countenance to the marriage. Even then, however, the ship that was to take the couple to England lay in the harbor, awaiting the tide, and they could not afford to delay.

From the dock, we waved them off until a few unseasonable snow flurries obscured our vision and drove us back to our carriage. Marcus and Honor stood together on deck, their arms closely entwined, while slightly to their rear, her stance fiercely protective, stood a small, indomitable figure. Piper. She had not argued with Honor when told that she could not accompany her, that she was to remain behind in America: she had simply packed her trunk and announced her intention to go. "Miss Silence would want it that way," she replied, which closed the argument with a finality that could not be brooked, since for Piper it was the only acceptable standard of loyalty. So, Honor had reluctantly given in for now—and for how many future years? I wondered—while she continued to bear the yoke of Piper's gentle tyranny.

The night before, Honor and I had stayed awake, exchanging confidences and memories, while the Watch called every hour until the midnight one. Briefly, for a little while, she had been mine again, the old Honor, with her dark head on my shoulder, our hands clinging, and it had been Emma whom she had wanted with her. But that was last night. Today, I waved good-by and watched her turn to Marcus while the ship slipped away on the turn of the tide.

In the end, the portrait came to me. I carried it to my marriage as my only dowry, a wedding present from Marcus. He did not name it so, but I knew what he meant. He brought it to me the last afternoon, knocking gently at my door and, when I opened it, tentatively offering the big, cumbersomely wrapped package.

His eyes were shamefaced as they met mine, and something else, too: tender and a trifle regretful.

"It's yours, Emma. It should belong to you, not to me, and certainly not to anyone else. I want to apologize for not seeing before this what should have been obvious to any portrait painter worth his talent. I was blind. Will you forgive me, Emma, for not understanding that you once did me the very great honor of loving me?

"When I realized what the portrait meant, and remembered how I'd boasted of it being my best work to date, and that it must be exhibited, I was ashamed. I have not signed it, and someday, when you can be proud that your portrait is an early effort by Marcus Goddard," he smiled in whimsical self-mockery, "then I shall be happy to put my signature to it." His smile took on a mischievous glint. "I have told Mr. Murray that the portrait is not for sale, and he seems most disappointed. I can't give myself much credit for sharpness there, either, but if he wants it, he must get it some other way. You may tell him for me that he can't have one without the other."

But apparently Marcus told him himself. We returned from the Long Wharf to find that our trunks had been brought downstairs, awaiting tomorrow's journey home, and the Eatons comfortably settled before the fire in the parlor. Edward had been very gentle with Joanna since learning that she had been the one to knot Patience's clothes that night. Very real terror is easy to understand, and he could see for himself the difference Patience's passing had made in calming her frenzied fears.

As for me, I could trace from those sad days the happiness that filled me with an almost unbearable joy. Even a woman laboring under the crushing burden of my diffidence could not fail to misunderstand the meaning of the way Edward Murray had fought to prove my innocence. Nothing had been said: I merely waited quietly for the inevitable outcome, and judging by what followed, he apparently assumed that words were unnecessary when he had already made his intentions clear.

I mentioned the portrait as soon as we were alone, but he seemed indifferent to learn that I had it. Finally I faltered to a stop in my telling, confused by the warm, laughing look in his eyes. When he reached for me I was ready.

However, I consider his last words on the subject a masterly statement of self-confidence, particularly in view of the fact that he had just released me from a tumbled, breathless embrace, and nothing, absolutely nothing, articulate had been spoken for the past five minutes.

"You may have it and welcome," he drawled, as he reached for me again. "I don't mind," he added generously. "I have the original."

Boastful man! He *was* right.